CW00421835

Thank you, Jacob – for your tireless work and commitment to the success of The Apprentice. I'm forever grateful for your kindness, patience, and support.

For Mum and Dad

For my darling Izabella.

The Apprentice: Redemption

Olusegun Akande

"Redemption can be found in hell itself if that's where you happen to be."

Lin Jensen

1

Awaken

A tall oak tree stands alone in the middle of an ashen-coloured field. Its gaunt, beaten bark was bereft of life or soul, as though bled dry by the leech-like grass around it. Fading away like a hapless patient at the hands of a cruel terminal disease, its withered branches yearned for life to end, ghostly pale green leaves suspended between life and death. A pathetic state of meaningless existence.

A cruel sun tortures the once magnificent tree with its merciless, scorching heat, its unyielding rays focused only on its powerless subject. Blood-like beads of dew unfold from bark and branches. Pain. Agony. Sorrow. Despair.

Behind the dismal and forsaken scene lies a grove of trees, plants, and bushes, beautifully adorned and studiously aligned in the picture-perfect pattern of a winding maze. The alluring array of tulips, daffodils and trees is a wonder to behold, drawing a young girl towards its clandestine clutches, like a spider's web entrapping an ignorant fly. As Liza nears the grove's enchanting domain, she recognises the peculiar and ruthless determination with which the sun sought to torture the sullen oak tree. Was there a reason for this cruel mockery? Did the tree's existence insult the sun, or had it perhaps even angered this celestial being? Was it deserving of its sunstruck scorn?

Suddenly, the young girl finds herself in the middle of a labyrinth of trees, arranged in pristine formation to ensnare those naïve enough to be fooled by their radiance and beauty. Lost, confused, and alone, her heart beats faster as her unenviable situation becomes clearer. Where is she? Why is she here? How will she ever get out? Will she ever get out? She turns to her left and begins to run, hoping to somehow find a way out of her situation. A tiny glimmering light reveals itself; a faint spark of hope. But no matter how fast she runs, the light neither grows brighter nor draws nearer. After running frantically for several minutes, she stops, gasping for breath as she bends over to place her hands on her knees. The light continues to glimmer in the distance – no closer, no brighter.

A malicious tease. A forlorn hope. What now? She looks to her right. Nothing. An endless hallway of trees, malevolent in their false beauty. She glances left, then right, then left again.

A faint giggle emanates through the trees, serenading the air like an endearing sonnet. Familiar. Innocent. Kind. Gentle. Her heart begins to slow as the sweet nature of the giggle warms it. She has heard that laugh before. She recognises its purity and innocence. Is it coming from behind that thick nest of trees before her? Without a moment's hesitation, she pushes and squeezes her way through them, oblivious to her pain and discomfort.

"Anna, is that you?" she asks as hope and love – emotions now alien to her – soften her hardened and brittle heart, liberated from the padlocked metal she had once, not long ago, captivated such emotions within; a Pandora's box too dangerous to open. Here they are once more; faint and feeble, but strangely welcome, nonetheless.

The chubby young girl in front of her is oblivious to her presence. Blonde curly locks of hair dangle over the girl's face as she gazes longingly at a picture frame in her hands. She was full of innocence and compassion, unbroken by the cruelty of life's twists and turns, untarnished by its multitude of woes. Joy. Hope. Love. Peace. Kindness. Gentleness. All wrapped into one carefree soul, bereft of the torture of slight or anger.

Liza peers at the moving pictures in the picture frame. *Must be well over fifteen years ago.* The picture tells its own story: Liza and Anna are climbing a tree. Or, rather, Liza is climbing the tree, while Anna desecrates it with her feeble attempts to get a foothold to lift herself off the ground. Anna is not only comfortable with her physical ineptitude, but is so at peace with herself that she cannot help but laugh at her own expense. Liza is urging Anna to try one more time, but her friend is crippled by her incessant giggling at the base of the tree. Her final attempt results in another calamitous landing on her backside. Liza laughs so much that she almost falls off the branch she is standing on.

"Anna... is that...?"

The chubby young girl looks up. The radiance of joy fades as her smile melts into a sad and desperate frown, causing Liza to shudder. Almost as though she can hear her friend's thoughts, Liza finds herself overcome with guilt and shame. She knows all too well why: years of butchery and slaughter; heartless executions driven by hate and malice; five years of actions so driven by evil that she no longer knows any other way than violence and anger.

"What happened to you, Liza?"

"I... I don't know. I... I can't stop it. It's like it controls me," replies Liza, tears rolling down her face.

"But this isn't you. You have to find a way to stop this. You have to."

"I... I don't think I can. I think it's too late. It controls me now. There's nothing I can do to stop it."

"No, Liza, that isn't true. You just don't want to stop it. You're scared of the alternative. There's nothing to be scared of, Liza. I know you're still in there. You have to find your way back."

Liza stares at the ground, unable to look her friend in the eye. The terrible things she has done, the countless and brutal exterminations of so many lives, and the pleasure she derives from it. She doesn't dare try the alternative, nor does she have any desire to. The power she now has is too great to simply throw away. No; she wants *more* of it. Shame. Guilt. Pleasure. Remorse. Power. Delight.

"You have to try, Liza. I know you're still in there!"

Anna begins to fade away as the oak tree evaporates, leaving behind a scene of empty nothingness.

Distant beats of music can be heard from the room next door as Liza opens her eyes. Another dream about Anna; a further attempt to stifle her with guilt and shame. When will she learn? There is no guilt or shame anymore, only the thirst for power – a thirst driven by fear and hate. Never again will she allow herself to be at hope's mercy. Power was all that mattered. Without it, she would simply be another hapless mortal, forever lurking between wishful thinking and imminent disaster, false dawns of joy inevitably accompanied by ceaseless despair. Better to have the power to determine her own fate – and the fate of others – in the palm of her hand. Without power, she is nothing, little more than an unknowing, pathetic fool waiting for disaster to sneak up on her. No more. Screw Anna and her childish ideals of kindness.

A heated conversation was unfolding in the room next door; torrents of anger woven in rhythmic beats. They were arguing again. A woman was, once again, pleading with her boyfriend to care a little more – be a little kinder, show a little more respect... love her. When would she learn? When would she finally wake up to the reality of her foolish stupor? He was never going to love her. She would forever be what he always intended her to be – a convenience, a rush, an object. Nothing more. Why continue to put herself at his mercy? She had no self-respect – naïve, feeble, pathetic.

Liza could hear him clearly, his nonplussed voice bleeding through the paper-thin walls. It was unremorseful; cruelty lacking any care or concern. Part of her hated him for taking advantage of an innocent victim, but another part admired his ruthlessness. He knew what he wanted and refused to allow the mind-numbing ideals of a foolish young girl deter him from being who he was, from using whatever power he had over her to get his way.

The woman next door sounded more desperate than ever before. Anger, pleading, emotional blackmail – she was using whatever means possible to make him feel guilty. Still, his voice remained stone-cold, remorseless, and bereft of any semblance of emotion.

"Why are you like this?" the woman through the walls said. "Is it so difficult to be nice to me just once? Just once, that's all! Just one time! Can't you pretend – at least pretend – that you love me? That you care about me? I... I can't take this anymore,

Will. I can't. It's tearing me apart. I'd rather die than continue like this!"

And there it is, the suicide threat. This was a tactic used so often that it now resulted in no reaction at all. Whatever feelings of fear or guilt such a suggestion could stir in him had dissipated long ago; her cries of 'wolf!' no longer worked. Not that they ever did. There was one occasion, the very first time she insinuated such a desire, when he momentarily darted a look of shock and concern in her direction. Nonetheless, such momentary weakness was fleeting, fading the minute he realised she was simply attempting to manipulate him with emotional blackmail. Yet here she was, trying it again. When would she learn?

Liza closed her eyes and tried to picture the two arguing. A mishmash of eyeliner and mascara trickled down the woman's face, interlinked, as though dancing in sync to the beat of the music. Her teary blue-grey eyes caught his once more – a moment of hope promptly doused as he looked away, finding solace in the adjacent window. Her attempts to incite some sense of pity annoyed him immensely. She repeatedly attempted to make him feel bad. Bad? Feel bad about what? She should know better by now. It was always just about instant gratification for him. Nothing more. Nothing less. It was time to leave; he had heard her threats of ending it all too many times to deem them worthy of response. He told the woman that he was leaving, that she needed to calm down, that he would return in a few days, maybe a week – just enough time for her to get her act together.

Liza knew such returning was nothing to do with any emotional attachment. He was not 'coming home' – he was coming back for more: more fun, more sex, more arguing… then he would leave.

The whole cycle would repeat again.

And again.

And again.

Liza could hear every word, sense the tension of their silence. She could feel the ice of the man's cold heart as a surge of anger began to take hold of her; a violent fury founded on her disgust for the woman's pathetic nature, another imbecile experiencing the cruelty of love and hope. She was angry at her, not him; her stupidity, her weakness, her very nature.

Liza's body shook a little as her rage increased. Slightly concerned, she closed her eyes to calm herself down, conscious of the sheer destructive power that she possessed. But the more she resisted, the more her body shook, yielding to a state of near convulsion.

The half empty glass of water on her bedside table trembled, moved by some invisible force to the table's edge. Struggling to contain whatever had seized her, Liza opened her now blood-red eyes, straining to regain control of herself. The water in the glass was piping hot, with a steady procession of steam rising from it, as though some sinister, hellish force was trying to crawl out of its liquid tomb.

A blazing sensation began to consume her body as her rage intensified, bursting outwards in the form of a smouldering fire, covering the surface of her skin. It was an insatiable fury; unquench-able, uncontrollable, and yet somehow liberating. She closed her eyes again as her state of panic sub-sided, surrendering to whatever dark presence was at play. The more she gave in to it, the greater was her sense of release, as though enabling a previ-ously unknown form of herself to surface.

An opening. A welcoming. An awakening.

The flames of fire on the surface of her body increased in intensity, causing the window cur-tains to catch fire as the room was consumed by the scorching heat. Now at one with her fiery rage, she opened her eyes once more, delighted with her newfound destructive capabilities. Never in her wildest dreams could she have imagined she could possess the same ability to decimate with fire as the dragons did.

Whatever this was, she liked it. It was pure, unrefined power, a greater ability to cause havoc. She relished the thought of striking deep, merciless fear in the hearts of others, the sense of power and control that such fear brought with it – perhaps now she could show Zoldon that *she* was the one to be reckoned with, not Justina.

Liza closed her eyes once more, connecting further with her newfound power. Thirsty flames coursed through her veins, growing increasingly violent as she removed all barriers of restraint, carefree of whatever consequences might ensue. Before long, her room was a cauldron of fire, curtains fully ablaze in her fiery glory. Violence. Fury. Destruction. Liberty.

Unknown to her, a group of students had gathered outside her room. Some were screaming for help, whilst others were helplessly banging on her locked room in panic, unable to touch the scolding-hot door handle, let alone clasp their hands on it. The feverish smoke from the flames surged through the cracks of the door as though released from centuries of torture, viciously filling the hallway with consummate ease, setting off the fire alarm.

"Where's Liza?" shouted Justina as she ran towards Liza's bedroom. The handful of students had abandoned their rescue and were scuttering towards the fire exit, spluttering and wheezing as they used whatever means available to cover their mouths and noses.

"Where's Liza?" shouted Justina again. She grabbed one of the students. "Where is she?"

"I... I don't..." the student coughed, barely able to speak. The smoke-filled hallway made seeing, let alone breathing, a near-impossibility.

Justina could see the girl was struggling to reply, covering her mouth and nose with her right arm as the suffocating fumes enveloped her. "Get out of here, quickly. Quickly!" she shouted, stirring the panic-stricken girl to life. Upon reaching Liza's door, she banged on it as hard as she could, but there was no reply.

Justina looked leftwards, down the corridor, to see whether anyone was close by. She could hear students spluttering in the distance as they scrambled their way down the fire exit, but the opacity of the dense smoke and avalanches of water raining down from the sprinklers made visibility unfeasible. She glanced right, then left again, before deciding she could wait no longer – nobody would be able to see anything anyway. She took a step back before raising her right hand, blasting the door open with ferocious force.

Liza was elevated above the bed – horizontal. Tongues of flames encircled her like a fusion of violent energy. Her eyes were closed as if she was at one with the festering fire around her.

Unaffected by the smoke or the fire, Justina grabbed Liza, violently shaking her into consciousness. "Liza! Liza, wake up! Liza, open your eyes," she said, careful not to shout too loudly.

Liza opened her eyes, unsurprised by the destruction around her; their unremorseful, fiery redness at peace with the scene she had conjured. Her lips curled slightly as she embraced the reality of yet another stage in her unrepentant journey. The more she surrendered to the lure of hate and rage, the more her power grew. Her hazel eyes fixed on Justina in the knowledge that she was growing increasingly stronger and more dangerous than her accomplice. Though on the same side, she would always view her as her rival. There was a time she was jealous of her, envious and resentful of Justina's ability to control her powers with such consummate ease. But why thirst for control when she possessed something far greater and more destructive? Rage… fury… unbridled hatred.

"What the fuck's going on, Liza?" asked Justina sternly, unable to hide her disapproval. Her accent still bore traces of an American upbringing; the twang could never desert her. Nor would she ever want it to. It was something she carried with great pride. However, the years in an English boarding school and university had taken their toll, for she was more British than American now. Any semblance of an American mindset had since been vanquished and replaced by middle-class England.

"Not entirely sure what you mean," replied Liza, taking pleasure in Justina's discomfort. Her voice was cold and callous, emanating a disdainful arrogance, accentuated by her public-school accent.

"What do I mean? What… Look around you, Liza! Your room's on fire and the entire building has been evacuated. What the hell is this?"

"Well, let's see now. I was lying on my bed, minding my own business, when suddenly, this happened. Fire. From inside me. All around me. Quite cool, isn't it?" Liza's voice dripped sarcasm.

"Cool? Cool, Liza? What the fuck's wrong with you? People could have died!"

"Did they?" asked Liza, half hoping her new ability had already proved fatal.

"You just don't get it, do you?"

14

"Get what?"

"The bigger picture! You need to stay focused on the bigger picture. We can't afford to have incidents like this. They only bring unnecessary attention. What do you think is going to happen now?"

"We order a pizza?"

"A fire, Liza; you set a building on fire. You think there'll be no questions asked? No consequences? Use your head."

Liza's rage-driven eyes widened, blazing like a festering inferno waiting to explode as Justina's words shredded her already tetchy nerves. To be scolded by her accomplice was one thing, but to be made to feel like an idiot was a step too far.

For a brief moment, she considered unleashing her tempestuous furore, burning Justina to cinder with volcanic fury. Not that she knew how to; her new ability was an unknown quantity. She had no idea how to summon it at will. It was, no doubt, an accidental discovery that would tip the balance of power in her favour, but one she had no understanding or grasp of, for now. The burning rage in her eyes dissipated, giving way to a cloudy white of normalcy as she accepted her reality – or what would, at least, be her reality until she could control this new power. Justina was right, of course, though that only served to make her remarks even more aggravating.

"You're right, Jus. But I honestly don't know how it happened or where it came from. It just... happened. Wasn't intentional."

"We'll get to the bottom of it soon, I promise. But for now, we need to figure out how to get out of this. Where are the electrical sockets?" asked Justina, scanning the room with determined eyes.

"Huh?"

"Your electrical sockets, Liza. Where are they?"

"Here." Liza pointed at two sockets behind her bedside table. "Why?"

"Yes, of course, makes sense, same as all the other rooms," said Justina, pulling the table towards her and pointing her hands towards the sockets before blasting a small hole in the wall. "There, now we can say the fire came from the sockets. You were asleep; unconscious because of the carbon monoxide, okay?"

"Err, yeah, but..."

"No buts, Liza. That's the story. Stick to it."

Liza hated being bossed around by Justina. It reminded her of their school days, a time during which Liza's desperation to be liked and accepted meant total subservience to Justina. To make matters worse, Justina was usually right; she always saw the bigger picture, was always in control of her emotions. Justina was nothing to Liza but a thorn in her side. Liza yearned for the day when she would be the one in charge, when she would be the one calling the shots, admired and feared by those once her masters. Her jealousy of her wiser accomplice grew with each passing day, twisting her entrails tighter and tighter, like a wrench squeezing the few remaining breaths of a screw, never to be unfastened. But on this occasion, her angst was faintly soothed by thoughts of what she could do with her new powers. She would have to learn how to use them, of course, how to unleash them at will, but once she learnt how to control them… The thought was far too exciting for her to get lost in her feelings towards Justina.

"So, what do we do now? Join the others outside?" asked Liza, yielding once more to Justina's authority.

"Yes, but stick to the story, Liza. Then we have to go see Ms. Carlisle," replied Justina.

"Any idea where she is?" asked Liza, scrambling around for her trainers.

"Probably in her office."

"I still find it odd that she's the Dean of our College, don't you?"

"Yeah, I guess. But I'm sure stranger things have happened. Guess she fancied a new challenge or something. Hopefully this will be one of those times when we'll be grateful for having her here," replied Justina.

Ms. Carlisle was appointed the Dean of Berkley College, Oxford, a few months after Liza and Justina resumed there. She had been instrumental to their admission, ensuring they both attended the same college at the university, as though vicariously living her life through theirs. For whatever reason, she not only felt Justina and Liza's lives were interlinked but believed their best chance of thriving rested in their being together, as though one without the other would lead to catastrophic failure. Despite her lofty position, she never failed to make time for both young ladies, overseeing their development like an overbearing parent. In many ways, she continued to watch over them in the same manner she had at Marsden Girls', grooming the two young ladies to always avert pitfalls and distractions with a ruthless precision. She served as a diligent guardian, nurturing her stewards to always see the bigger picture, no matter the costs or sacrifice. "Focus on the objectives," she would say. "Focus on the objectives; be determined, persevere, and you can achieve anything. There is no reason why you cannot achieve whatever you want to; there are no excuses."

Ms. Carlisle did not fail to notice how Justina had comforted Liza after Annabel's tragic and mysterious death. She had effortlessly slipped into the shoes of Liza's dead friend, as though she had always been destined to do so, born to heal a heart shredded by the loss of a dear friend. Watching the two teenagers develop such a friendship and dependence on each other gave her great joy, not that she ever showed it. Outwardly she never veered from her nature – a quiet satisfaction when things were good and a stern word whenever necessary. To display joy was weakness, tantamount to encouraging complacency and inevitable shortcomings. She would always push them, drive them to dizzying heights of excellence. So much so that the two girls were somewhat relieved to get away from her watchful eye when university beckoned; college life provided a much needed respite from the high expectations of their former house mistress.

Liza and Justina were grateful for Ms. Carlisle's determination to ensure they attended the same university, especially during those first few weeks. In whatever shape, form, or guise, at least they had each other, two lives forever intertwined by the inevitability of their fate. Any anxiety that the mystery of their future brought was comforted by a shared and honourable pursuit. Such mystery defined the norm of university life; friends came and went, as did relationships and one-night stands. Some of it was fun, some awkward and some outright painful. But at least whatever lay in the future lay waiting for the both of them.

Both young ladies had been summoned to a meeting with Ms. Carlisle a few days after she resumed office. Much to their misfortune, they had arrived some minutes late, wrongly presuming their former house mistress would be less strict than she had been at school; they were undergraduate students now after all.

Ms. Carlisle had dismissively waved her left hand as Liza and Justina entered her office, pointing her left index finger in the direction of the two chairs in front of her desk. There was not even a glance given in their direction, let alone any form of verbal recognition. Instead, she had simply huffed and puffed in visible irritation as she scoured through a heavily marked-up document lying before her.

The large standing clock behind her tortured the girls for several minutes, increasing their anxiety with each vicious tick. It was as though they were back at boarding school. Nothing had changed; they were still the same little girls that lived in constant fear of their house mistress, dreading whatever reprimand or punishment that may be coming their way.

Liza had noticed how Ms. Carlisle looked exactly the same as before. Her face was utterly alien to the wrinkles that typically accompanied old age; her hair immaculately brushed and rigidly kept in place; her piercing, stern eyes sat perched behind the same silver-rimmed glasses, ready to pounce at the slightest hint of inefficiency or weakness.

Five minutes had passed, then ten, fifteen, and even twenty. Not one word, not even a glance. Liza began to feel a little indignant; they were no longer at boarding school, so why be treated like kids? But although it angered her, she still feared her new dean, still desperately wanted to be in her good books.

Justina, as cool as ever, as though ice ran through her veins, fixed her eyes on the mantelpiece behind Ms. Carlisle. Sitting on top of it was a picture with a quote, which read: 'The Freedom To Do As You Please May Be Your Greatest Enemy'. Something about the quote intrigued her, as though she had heard or seen it somewhere before. It resonated with her, stirred her senses. The more she studied the quote, the more at ease she felt. Ms. Carlisle's resumption at Berkley College was the best thing that could have happened to Justina – to their mission; the stern lady sitting in front of her would unknowingly keep her and Liza on track, ensure they remained focused on their mission. Her eyes glistened, invigorated by a renewed zest to remove free will once and for all. Granted, she had not seen Zoldon for some months; not that she had been avoiding him. He had instructed the girls to keep their heads down, practice using their powers whenever they could, and remain focused on the task at hand, in preparation for the next and final phase. But this was a wake-up call. Why the long wait? No more waiting; she decided there and then that she would visit Zoldon's lair that weekend.

"Is that what university life has done to you?" came the voice they had been so painstakingly waiting for.

They dared not reply. How could they? What could they possibly say to pacify the already irritated lady in front of them? They had not been apart from her so long as to forget about the futility of making excuses; better to ride out whatever storm was approaching.

"Have you nothing to say for yourselves? I asked you a question. Well? Do not just stare at me like a pair of mummified lollipops; explain yourselves."

"Our lecture finished late, Miss. We got here as soon as we could," said Liza.

"Poppycock, Liza! Your lecture finished on time as it always does. You simply did not make haste. Need I remind you two that your attitude to timeliness inevitably mirrors your attitude to life? You're here to be the very best you can be. Seize each day with both hands; do not idly wait for things to happen." No excuse would suffice; it was far wiser for them to remain silent and take the rollocking on the chin. They motioned their heads to convey their understanding.

"Did you learn nothing from your time with me? It is abundantly clear to me that both of you need a refresher course on the importance of getting things done; some whipping into shape, so to speak. Be warned, young ladies; you may be a few years older, but do not for one second think that I will be, in any way, easier on you. Expectations and results; nothing has changed. I will be just as vigorous with the both of you as I ever was. You would do well to remember that."

The blood that had been steadily boiling within Liza cooled a little as she accepted her reality.

Like it or not – and Liza did not – Ms. Carlisle would continue to have a major influence in her education; there was no escaping it, not for now. at least.

A faint smile caressed Justina's face, her zeal re-ignited as though awoken from a long sleep.

2

A Corner of Paradise

On the edge of the outer realm lay a serene oasis, a haven of greenery with trees of all shapes and sizes, their shimmering leaves perched on verdant branches. Tulips, gazanias, rose petals, and purple freesia serenaded one another in blissful harmony as the gentle rush of a waterfall hummed a gentle melody, sprinkling wildlife with its soothing vapours.

Surrounding this small patch of heaven was a sea of undulating hills, where gentle slopes of lush green grass stretched over a horizon of perfect tranquillity. It was a peaceful place, a safe place – a forgotten piece of Eden amid an ocean of wasteland, conveying a tiny glimpse of the Outer Realm's former splendour. There was a time when such radiance adorned every inch of this once glo-rious terrain; a time long since forgotten, when beauty was the norm.

Encamped in one of the many sumptuous valleys was an assortment of baby dragons, run-ning up slopes with reckless abandon and inevi-tably sliding down as their weak limbs lost foot-ing. Untroubled by the civil war that had ravaged the greater part of the realm, they were playing fire tag, chasing each other with great zeal and deter-mination to smear their nearest victim with their feeble flames, wheezing and spluttering as they clumsily mastered their natural ability.

One in particular seemed altogether unable to grasp the game. Straining both head and body to blow, it could manage little more than to burst into a coughing fit, though its determination knew no bounds. Over and over again it tried, at first chas-ing its prey up the hill, before losing its footing and sliding down like a limbless morsel as it un-successfully clutched at the ground beneath him, in a vain and desperate attempt to prevent the im-minent splat that left it spread-eagled on its stom-ach, with its nose buried in the grass.

Undeterred, it rose to its feet and again com-menced its shaky climb, sprinting up the hill with the force of a ravenous predator, only to once more fall prey to its clueless limbs. Another attempt, another splat. Again, it got up.

Unaffected by the laughing and teasing of the others, it summoned whatever strength and pride remained and scrambled up the hill, each perilous step drawing him closer to another inevitable fall. Somehow, and to the great amusement of the others, it managed to climb to the top, paused for several seconds to catch its breath, before finally being able to attempt to do what really mattered. It breathed in, chest expanding like a proud soldier at a parade, before letting out a calamitous puff of black smoke, resulting in a coughing fit so frenzied that it once again lost its footing and slid down the slope before landing in a tumultuous heap at the bottom. By now, all the dragons were in hysterics, including three grandiose adult dragons who were keeping a watchful eye on their subjects from a distance.

"Oh dear, that little lad of yours is a bit of an odd one, isn't he?"

"Mind your own business! And leave my boy alone," replied Mordrid, forever proud of her baby.

"Yes, but... Look, he can't even blow a flame. Not even a little one. What's the matter with him?" asked Percival, perplexed by the baby dragon's incompetence.

"I said, mind your own business, Percy! Anyway, you know as well as I do that he came several weeks early, and we all know how that can affect the little ones. It will just take a little more time for him to get the hang of it, that's all. He'll come right in the end; you'll see."

"Yeah, whatever you say, Mord. Maybe in a few trillion years he might just be able to blow a tiny flame," said Percy, laughing loudly at his own joke. "Oh look, there he goes again, scrambling up the hill, like a delirious rodent on stilts. Oh... go on, son, go on... oh... oh... oooooooh... and there he goes again, rolling down the hill in all his glory."

"Hey! Leave him alone. I'm warning you, Percy. I won't tell you again," said Mordrid, glaring at Percy, who by now was flat on his back, laughing uncontrollably.

"Okay, okay, I'm sorry," replied Percy, still gripped with laughter. "I... I'll stop, promise. I'll stop. Just need... just need to...." Unable to withstand the image of the baby dragon blowing a puff of black smoke, Percy surrendered himself to another torrent of boundless laughter.

Mordrid, still glaring at her friend, remained silent, unable to say any more – after all, what was the point?

"I know it offends you, and quite rightly so; after all, he is your son. But he does have a point, Mordrid," said Tarson – a much older and graceful dragon – with a smile.

"Yes, I know, Tarson. It's just..."

"Just what?" asked Tarson, "Percy, enough. Stop that."

"Well... I just... don't know how to," Mordrid continued.

"You don't know how to?" asked Tarson, getting to his feet and glowering down at Mordrid in fierce indignation.

"I mean, of course I know how to; of course, I know how to teach him. It's just that..."

"It's just that what? Speak up, Mordrid," said Tarson, growing more impatient, his stern eyes bulging as fumes of aggravation welled up within his muscular torso. A pent-up anger forever grew inside him as the frustration of his fellow dragons' idle existence increased with each passing day. He had been one of the great ones – courageous, fierce, respected, and much revered for his fortitude and no-nonsense manner. He was always relied upon to fight the good fight, defend the innocent against wrongdoing or tyranny. Resolute in his ideal of right and wrong, he was one of the first to back Raphael against his scheming sibling. Ready and all too willing to lay down his life for the greater good, he not only supported Raphael with rank vigour but made clear his intention to destroy all that dared stand in his way. Unafraid to ruffle feathers, he spoke his mind, and left no one in any doubt about what he was willing to do in support of his master.

But that was the problem: what he was willing to do. Fight? Kill? Destroy? Die? He knew he would gladly sacrifice his life for what was right – peace, unity, or love. But was his master willing to make such sacrifices? What price was he willing to pay to preserve all that was good? Did Raphael have what it takes to bring down his brother? To do what was necessary?

The thought was a chink in Tarson's sense of trust in Raphael; a suspicion of weakness that gnawed at his subconscious, like a febrile sickness gnawing away at bone as the body grew more frail with each passing day, a wasting disease with an inevitable conclusion. Why continue to back an impending disaster? Why die for a leader in whom one increasingly lacked faith? One without the spine to do what needed to be done.

Zoldon and his cohort were greater in number, though Tarson still did not doubt his side would win the day. Nothing could defeat them; they had a greater cause. With that, combined with a bottomless reserve of courage and a ferocious tide of determination, how could they not win? In time, their fortitude would either win over the minds of others or intimidate them into submission – but their leader was weak, naïve, lacking in ambition.

Tarson's faith in love and hope was just as great as Raphael's, but why fight for a leader who was clueless as to how to preserve it?

His mind drifted to that fateful morning, and a decision that would forever fuel his growing frustration...

"So that's it, then? You're really going?"
Avmar had struggled to understand why her older sibling was so determined to lead them to certain death. "Zoldon can't be trusted, Tarson. What makes you think he really wants peace? You know what he's like."

"This isn't about us, Avmar. The future of our kind is at stake – who we will be, where our hearts lie, the kind of world we want the little ones to live in. You must look at the bigger picture. I do this not for us but for our kind, our very existence. Can't you see that?"

"No, no I can't, Tarson. Our 'kind', as you so put it, will always be around, no matter what you do or whose side you take. Why—"

31

"Enough, Avmar!" Tarson had yelled, taking an aggressive step towards his sibling, with wings outstretched, deep black eyes bulging, and nostrils flaring. "There will be no more talk of this matter. I've made my decision. I – we – are attending the meeting. That is the end of it."

A solitary tear had trickled down Avmar's face, searching her coarse, jagged skin for solace.

Lost in the agonising labyrinth of his thoughts, Tarson stared into the abyss of the surreal terrain surrounding them. Though peaceful and far more aesthetically pleasing, it seemed meaningless, devoid of relevance – a futile existence. The longer he stared into the endless horizon of nature's tranquillity, the more pathetic he felt, his head gradually stooping towards the grass beneath him, as though being slowly put to sleep by lethal injection, unaware of his defeated demeanour.

"You miss her, don't you?" said Mordrid.

No reply. Why should he? Nothing really mattered anymore. His sister was dead, her life cruelly decimated by the flames of Abaddon and Zoldon, tricked into death like so many others. Tarson blamed himself; after all, he was the one foolish enough to trust Zoldon. His stubborn arrogance prevented him from listening to reason.

"You mustn't blame yourself. Raphael made the decision to attend that meeting, not you... Well, I guess you..."

"You're not helping," said Tarson forlornly, his crestfallen voice no longer self-assured. "It was my fault. I told her, I ordered her to attend. There's nothing you can say that can change that."

"I guess what I'm trying to say is that you simply can't continue like this. You'll die of a broken heart if you're not careful. Life goes on, Tarson. Think of these little ones; they need us – they need *you*, Tarson," said Mordrid, conscious of the possibility of touching one too many nerves.

The baby dragons had abandoned their playful climbs up the slope in favour of a game of tag, revelling in their newfound ability to fly, albeit just a few feet high at a time, flapping their fragile wings with all vigour, determined to stay in the air for as long as possible, coughing and spluttering as they repeatedly tried to breathe fire. One day, they would cause hearts to shudder in dread with their majestic wings painting the skies in deathly shadows; maybe one day they would restore some balance and heal the wounds of a kingdom torn by malevolent violence. They were the reason he decided not to go. Why he changed his mind at the last minute; he chose to give hope a chance by preserving the lives of the young ones instead of attending that fateful meeting.

*

"Always knew there were more of them. As far as I'm concerned, every dragon that chose not to attend that meeting is our enemy," said Liza, assessing the scene of the horizon below, her cold, dark eyes masking the hate and resentment oozing freely through her veins.

"Not sure I know what you mean, Liza. They could just as easily have avoided the meeting because they didn't side with anyone," Justina countered, determined to stay focused on their mission.

"That's crap, Jus. Sitting on the fence can lead to eventually turning against us. They're either for or against."

"Don't agree. Not everything is black or white. What matters is that they don't get in the way. Anything else is an unnecessary distraction. Don't let your anger get in the way of the big picture."

Liza made no further comment; her mind was already made up. If anything, her accomplice's comments simply strengthened her resolve to surrender to her desire.

"Our mission is just to capture them, Liza. They're not our enemies, so there's no need to kill them. We capture them and imprison them to make sure they can never get in our way, that's all, nothing more. Understood?"

Growing increasingly irritated by each and every word Justina uttered, Liza somehow managed to remain silent. What she found particularly irritating was Justina's manner – she spoke as if she was intent on making an enemy of Liza. Liza felt as if she was still perceived to be the weaker partner after all these years. She was the one with 'no self-control', who 'lacked the ability' to see the bigger picture – a novice, without wisdom, careless and unreliable. One day she would cut herself loose, tear away from her shadow with such violent force that nobody would question her again. Why not now?

"Liza, I said..." Justina continued.

"Sure," replied Liza, cutting in so as not to have to listen to any more drivel.

"Right, so we're agreed, then?" asked Justina.

"Sure."

Rising from their hiding spots in their hooded cloaks, like an evil mist ascending from the ground, the two ladies commenced their slow descent.

Justina led the way, while Liza trailed a few steps behind, eyes a dark blood-red of venomous hate, eager to unleash the torrent of evil coiled around her. The hairs on the back of her neck were already standing on end in anticipation of an imminent act of cruelty. The closer they got to the happy scene, the greater her thirst for destruction grew.

"Right, this will do. No need for us to go any further. We can do it from here," said Justina. "Remember, we're not to harm them in any way. Just use our powers to create a wall around them. Once they're surrounded by our wall, we put them in chains and take them back."

"Sure," replied Liza, raising her right arm in unison with Justina's in the direction of the dragons below them. The trees began to shake as Justina and Liza released a powerful surge of energy, causing everything in its path to surrender to its brutal force.

As the ground began to shake, the baby dragons feverishly flapped their wings, unsure of what was happening. They flapped and clutched their way towards their elders, hoping to find solace for fear-ridden hearts, but the more they tried, the greater the force was against them.

The older dragons responded in the only way they could, breathing out their flames to defend their territory, but the more fire they breathed out, the more they endangered themselves, as the flames simply rebounded off the transparent shield that had encircled them and returned to them with even greater force.

"Stop! Stop it! The more we breathe our fire, the more we put the little ones at risk. Stop, Tarson!" pleaded Mordrid.

Recognising the harsh reality of their situation, Tarson grudgingly stopped, once again falling prey to Zoldon's plans. Was this the end? After all this time – not fighting, not attending the meeting, choosing to flee for safety – just to die without so much as a whimper, trapped in a cage like a feeble bird of prey: hopeless, weak, and pathetic.

The others were still, now. Even the baby dragons had ceased their futile scramble to safety, panting for breath, with hearts beating their final ensemble. An eerie silence engulfed the terrain as they awaited their gruesome end. They had seen it before, on that fateful, cursed day – a horrifying scene they could never forget. They had watched from afar as pungent vapours of bitter flames scarred their minds – comrades singed to ashes, innocent lives destroyed, hearts forever broken by Zoldon's cruelty.

"Be still; we mean you no harm," shouted Justina, her voice now tempered with reason. "This is not your end... but try to resist and you *will* go the way of all the others."

A part of Tarson wanted to resist with all his might, but the sight of the others around him caused him to pause. To resist would result in certain death – he could fathom his own surmise in such a futile struggle, but not that of the others, not the little ones. Once more, he had to surrender his instinct for the sake of others.

A dark silhouette of wings careered across the skies, gliding towards them in a grim shadowy silence as time stood still once more.

"They're here," said Justina, looking up to the skies as their masters approached.

But the imminent arrival of Zoldon and Abbadon was an irrelevance to Liza. They had no part in this; what would happen next was down to Liza and Liza alone – they were all in her hands now. She would determine their fate; or her powers would, at least, whatever course the fury welling up inside her decided to take. Her blood-red eyes darkened as her heart beat faster and harder, releasing the festering bile within.

Once more, the ground began to shake as a new and more potent force emerged. A violent fury coursed through her body, burning red veins bubbling beneath her now-darkened skin like an erupting volcano. As she surrendered to the raging fury of fire inside her, she felt liberated, as though finally accepting who and what she had always been. A wry smile etched across her face as she closed her eyes and unleashed her putrid flames.

"Close your eyes," said Tarson, fully aware of their imminent death.

"Tarson... I'm scared," said Mordrid. Tears welled in her eyes as she felt the gruesome pain of the flames on behalf of the babies around her.

"Just... close your eyes," said Tarson, looking into Mordrid's eyes with a faint and gentle smile.

"Liza, no!" shouted Justina. "No, Liza!"

But it was too late. Stretching out her hands towards the hapless dragons, Liza unleashed a torrent of vicious flames, piercing through the transparent wall and engulfing all within it with bloodthirsty violence.

"Shall I stop...?" Abaddon started, slightly unnerved by Liza's evident rage.

"No, Abbadon. Let her be. This is precisely what I've been waiting for. There's no turning back for her now."

"But, Zoldon, surely…"

"Look at her. The fire. The anger. The hate. Priceless! Nothing can stop that."

A raging fire blazed for several minutes, smothering the screams of its hapless victims as it turned them to a smouldering, flaky, black dust. A sinister smile ensconced Liza's face as her fertile fury subsided once more. She was the real power now and that was all that mattered. That was all that had ever mattered.

3

Liza

"What the hell were you thinking, Liza? How could you do that? What the fuck's wrong with you?" shouted Justina as she alighted Zoldon's back.

Justina had been silent throughout the journey back, utilising every ounce of her self-control to breach the fury inside her, but upon arriving, she could no longer hold back. To make matters worse, neither Zoldon nor Abbadon had said a word. Nothing. Not even a 'learn to control your anger, Liza'. Their voluntary silence was just as disturbing as Liza's actions.

"Hey! Don't turn your back at me, I'm talking to you," said Justina, shoving Liza in the back with both hands. It was a momentary burst of anger that shocked all, especially Justina herself.

Liza continued to walk away, the smirk on her face conveying her pleasure. Justina was ruffled, angry, maybe even out of control... finally. Once again, Justina stepped towards Liza and shoved her in the back.

Liza stopped in her tracks, closed her eyes, and breathed in slowly before exhaling again, revelling in the knowledge that hundreds of brooding dragon eyes had fixed their gaze on her, waiting for the inevitable hate-fuelled response. Her volcanic-like eruptions were a part of who she was, a necessary component of her DNA, a volatility so revered that many of those eyes believed she was the key to victory. But she wanted to be more than just a vessel of untrained explosives that everyone feared.

"I understand your anger, Jus," said Liza, exuding a sinister calm, "but I don't regret what I did. Anyone that isn't on our side is an obstacle that must be removed. And yes, permanently. They may not be a danger to us today, but they can be tomorrow. We can't afford to take risks. Surely you, of all people, understand that?"

Caught unawares by her new calm and mature accomplice, Justina felt numb, unable to respond to the wise words she had just heard.

Liza continued. "I feel your pain, Jus. Trust me, I really do. But we cannot take risks. We must do what needs to be done. Yes, I give in to my anger and violence sometimes, but it's always for the greater good. Maybe... maybe we're getting to a point where—"

"Where what?" asked Justina, interrupting Liza mid-sentence, all too suspicious of where she was intending to land.

"Well, I just think that maybe you should take a back seat for a little while. You and I both know there'll be a lot of unpleasantness in the coming months; probably something that I'm more suited to than you, don't you think?"

Liza's soul was clear to see as Justina peered into her eyes. It had been her quest all along: power, to be the one calling the shots. Justina had recruited her all those years ago, but it was her time now, and there was no denying or stopping it.

"And you're okay with this?" Justina said, turning to Zoldon, suddenly feeling both vulnerable and uncertain.

There had been a time when such a question would have been unthinkable, but times were changing; they had been for a while. The more violent and sinister Liza became, the more she gained Zoldon's respect; Justina's time had passed.

The closer they got to their goal, the more Justina's significance lessened, as though she was slowly being tossed aside to make room for the brutal force of nature that would end matters once and for all. They all yielded to Liza now, and Liza knew it as well as they did – it was only now that such truth was dawning upon Justina herself.

An uneasy silence seized the air as Zoldon's eyes reluctantly fixed on hers, like irreconcilable magnets surrendering to an inevitable collision. The usually piercing nature of his glare betrayed a sense of guilt; he had groomed her from so young and, despite his ulterior motives, he was the closest thing she had to a father. But a father must always keep his eyes on the bigger picture.

"We've come a long way, you and I," Zoldon said to Justina, his voice soft, yet lined with poisonous malice. "I nurtured you like my own child; nothing can take that away from us. But we have come to a point where the path ahead is even more violent and destructive than the path behind. As strong as you are, this is not your moment."

There, he had finally said it, finally aired the reality that had plagued his mind for so many months – a reality many believed he would be unable to accept. It was a father telling his firstborn she was no longer his heir. He cared for her, but nothing and nobody could outweigh his ultimate objective – and he had groomed Justina to understand that; she was the personification of it. It was the reason she was always so controlled and assured, why nothing swayed her attention from the overall objective. Yet, here they were – the moment had finally come, but still, something in her eyes told Zoldon that she was unprepared for this, unsure of what it all meant. Had she lost her focus? Had she become no longer able to see the big picture, instead allowing feelings and pride to cloud her judgement? She should know better. She must.

"It's time to unleash her, Justina," Zoldon continued. "You and I both know what she's capable of. Right now, she's our biggest asset. Think not of how you feel but of the overall picture."

He was right. Of course he was. Justina knew it as she had for several months. Ever since they fought all those years ago, she had suspected that Liza's powers would continue to grow and grow. It was a reality that had been staring her in the face ever since she almost killed her: the dragons had needed her, not the other way round.

But seeing them whispering in dark, ominous shadows during the past year, plotting schemes beyond Justina's understanding, was a little too much for her to take. How could Zoldon abandon their relationship and trust Liza so quickly? So easily? Had Justina just been a pawn all along? Something to be used and disposed of without a second's hesitation, without regret, without remorse? She was simply a means to an end. Whenever Justina saw Zoldon, Liza and Abaddon sketching out the future, like three auspicious masters of the universe, she felt alone and betrayed. For several months she had cut a forlorn figure, wrestling with the past and present, like an aging boxer looking in the mirror and seeing a younger, leaner, faster self as against the slow and cumbersome reality staring back.

Zoldon's mind drifted back in time to the moment he realised what he had – a ticking time bomb that had to be used to his advantage for fear of it turning against him. At the time, he had no choice but to embrace the gift in front of him; to do otherwise would have been futile.

"Justina told me something happened in your room, Liza. Tell me more."

Liza struggled for words. Although a little shaken by what happened, she felt strangely invigorated, as though nothing and nobody could prevent her from doing whatever she wanted. After all, she was just as powerful, if not more so, than the dragons. The only difference was that they could fly; but who was to say she would not be able to do that in the future? She felt invincible, but also anxious and in need of approval.

"I'm... not entirely sure how. It just kinda happened."

"What do you mean, it kind of happened? Had you sensed anything like that inside you before?" asked Zoldon, curious as to how a human could possess such power.

"I mean just that: I have no idea where it came from. Never sensed it before; it just happened. But I get the feeling that it's more likely to happen when I'm angry... really angry."

"Why do you think that?"

"I was in my bedroom, listening to one of the other students talking to her boyfriend. She's such an idiot; the guy's so obviously using her, and she can't see it... or she refuses to see it. Either way, she's a fool. So weak and pathetic. The more I listened, the more I realised how pathetic we humans are. We're our own worst enemies, always making choices that are bad for us, even when disaster is staring back at us. The longer it went on, the angrier I got."

"Angrier with the girl?"

"No. Well, kind of... but... angrier with her, as if it was happening to me, if that makes sense. As if it was happening to all of us – like I was listening to the boy talking to me. It made me so mad. And that's when I started to sense it."

"Sense what?" asked Zoldon, recognising what he had suspected about her from the very beginning.

"At first, it was just like a lukewarm feeling inside me. But the angrier I got, the warmer it got, until it was like a really hot sensation. And then..."

"And then what?"

"It felt like it was talking to me, pleading with me to set it free. I didn't want to do that at first because I didn't know what was going on, but it just kept pleading and pleading, telling me that 'we're one.' That it was the 'real me.' Then, I slowly began to relax, little by little, like in tiny spurts. And... and the..."

"Yes? Go on, Liza."

"Every time I let go slightly, I felt a little bit more alive... like I was feeling glimpses of my real self. And the more I felt it, the better I felt. I began to give in to it more and more. The more I surrendered, the greater the release. And then I saw it."

"Saw what?"

"I opened my eyes, and there it was... flames everywhere. Coming out of me as though we were one. Like each tongue represented a different part of me. It felt so good... liberating... Yes, that's how I felt: liberated. It was like I'd been a prisoner all my life and had suddenly been set free. I closed my eyes and surrendered completely. I had to; it was the only way."

"The only way? What do you mean by 'the only way'?"

"You really don't know? I'd have thought it was quite obvious. Power. I have so much inside me, hiding in the darkest crevices for fear of being shamed in some way. I no longer want to feel bad about being me, where my power comes from. No more shame; better to give in to my hate and anger, so that I can be true to who I am, who I've always been."

Now she had said it; uttered words she had dared not consider before. They had been wrong for so long, stifling her powers with ceaseless demands for self-control, each time squeezing a little more air out of her, like a long and agonisingly painful death. She yearned for his approval, now more than ever.

49

The blackness of their surroundings grew darker still as an eerie stillness gripped the air, leaving two sets of eyes to do the talking. Zoldon placed his eyes on Liza's, in the knowledge of the unease a glance from her own eyes could inflict on whomever was unlucky enough to fall victim to them. His gaze peered into hers, dissecting mind and soul with sadistic ease. But this time, her eyes were different. He sensed no fear, nor dread, just a desire for approval, for some recognition of all she had done… to let her know it was okay to be her. And yet, there was something else. Something far more sinister and dangerous, waiting to be unleashed, some dark, brutal force that even he could not manage or control.

It would either be unleashed or force its way out; that much was clear.

Nothing could stop it… but maybe it could be directed. Somehow steered to stay on their side.

"I'm glad you feel able to speak freely with me, Liza. That couldn't have been easy for you. Fear not, I understand your pain. One might even say that I can relate to it. My brother shackled me for most of my life. Prevented me from being my real self for so many years. It was… so painful, excruciatingly so at times. I felt like I was trapped under another dragon's skin. I can only ask you to accept my apology for putting you in similar shackles for so many years. I see now that it is not by chance that our paths crossed. You must be you, Liza, you must always be you. I see that now."

Liza closed her eyes, sighing deeply as though breathing for the very first time. Each breath peeled off another layer, enabling the person cocooned inside to breathe more easily before finally being birthed. She opened her eyes anew, her true self given life for the first time.

Now she was free.

"Do you see her, Justina?" Zoldon said, half in eager anticipation, half in pure wonder. "This is Liza's true self... this is who she was born to be. And when the world sees her as she truly is, they will fall to their knees in fear. A new day is dawning, Justina, and with it, a new power has been born. I think it is time to unleash it, don't you?"

4

Beyond

Over the next four months, Justina's role became more and more reduced to that of a spectator – an involuntary one at first, but in time she accepted her declining relevance with less reluctance, preferring to watch from afar or not at all. She could just about stomach the torching of adult dragons, convincing herself that their sitting on the fence was just as dangerous as opposing them, but burning innocent baby dragons was a step too far, no matter how the unholy trinity tried to justify it. "They are tomorrow's foes," they said – she disagreed; let them decide whether or not they will be tomorrow's foes when they're old and capable enough.

The unholy trinity – that is what she privately called them; an irony delicately placed within another. She had always believed her cause to be just and true, a pure and righteous crusade to save humanity. And, in her heart of hearts, she still believed destroying free will was the right thing to do. It was the never-ending violence and destruction that weighed on her, with each unnecessary slaughter breaking her heart that little bit more. They deemed it necessary – a 'deep cleansing' that would ensure a better and peaceful future, but they revelled in the gory expeditions.

Liza gleefully torched innocent victims, as though she was on a personal quest to find new levels of cruelty, whilst Zoldon and Abaddon admired their creation and encouraged her to sink further and further into her dark abyss.

How could such brutality be just? How could such violence and destruction forge a better world?

She had always envisaged a quick fix: defeat Raphael's army, take the conductor alive, and force him to erase free will – a simple and clean plan with far fewer innocent casualties. Yet, they had not even uttered the word 'conductor' for months. They knew it could have all been over quickly and far less painfully if they focused their attention and energy on capturing the conductor; they were just too engrossed in their mass killings.

Liza's hate-fuelled powers had given Zoldon an additional quest: destroy everyone and everything not on their side.

In time, she found ways of evading their missions – it was better for Liza to carry out her executions without unnecessary assistance. She enjoyed throwing their words back at them.

On one such occasion, she found herself in a café in a less fashionable part of town, slumped on an old brown leather sofa with her head arched back, staring at the ceiling, enjoying a brief, caffeine-fuelled afternoon respite from studies. It was an old-fashioned type of a café, with a chestnut brown wooden door welcoming its weird and wonderful visitors. The whole place was a throwback to the eighties; sets of leather sofas faced each other with low, rectangular, box-like coffee tables perched between them. A large golden chandelier dangled from the middle of the ceiling, suffocating uninvited energy with its dim, sombre light, like a leech draining its victim's blood. An old jukebox was playing live music in the background, performing to an audience of two, its music barely audible except for the distinct cackling in between songs, giving it the authenticity it demanded. Not that the two members of its audience were paying it much attention; one was crippled with doubts and the other seemingly lost in time.

How she got there or why was a mystery; she had never been there before. Everyone knew that part of town was the domain of pseudo punks and goths, two types of people that were alien to her. With the soles of her feet placed on the edge of the table, she drifted into myriad of thoughts and questions. It was as though this eerie café in an unfamiliar part of town enabled her to let go, allowing her mind to unravel.

She thought about her family. With her eyes closed, she could just about see them. It had been many years since she had allowed herself to remember them; to do so would have been a distraction, a weakness. They looked the same, of course they did; why would they not? It was her that looked different; she was the one who changed. Tom was still that sweet little boy that loved to wind up his younger sister, and Mum and Dad were… well, Mum and Dad.

A faint smile surfaced momentarily before being swiftly hounded away by overbearing shadows of guilt. What would they think of their daughter now? Would Tom be proud of his sister?

The heartbreak of losing them so suddenly was the reason she took this path. She did not want anyone else to experience such pain and anguish again. Nobody. Her heart was true. Surely it was.

Her mind went back to Liza's first kill – Justina was so proud of herself that day; not only had she recruited her but her apprentice had taken a momentous step. That particular mission was a very necessary one. Every single one of those dragons had been ready to fight and defend their cause – letting them live would have been a catastrophic error of judgement. It had to be done; but why throw Liza in the deep end so quickly? Was Justina to blame? Did she create the monster Liza had become?

Her personal inquisition was momentarily interrupted by the creaking sound of a door. Justina sat up, quickly burying her thoughts.

The one other member of the audience was leaving – a plump-looking black woman in her mid-fifties, with a Mohawk revealing an active and rebellious past. She seemed content, happy to be lost in thoughts of yesteryears, preferring for time to stand still.

Justina watched her amble slowly down the pebbled street in an old and faded pair of blue ripped jeans and a black baggy jumper, stopping a few times to read posters of upcoming concerts and exhibitions. Justina could just about see the woman's raised brows as one particular poster grabbed her attention. She stood there for several minutes, digesting the information of an upcoming live concert like a sponge with water, warmed by the memories it stirred and excited by the opportunity to once more go back in time. She imagined how exciting her life must have been when she was younger – concerts, riotous parties, travelling, a great group of friends. But where were they now? Why was she all alone, clinging to memories and dreams? After dissecting the poster over and over again, her excitement faded, and the glow that had varnished her face dissolved, leaving etchings of sadness and longing in its wake. The joy she felt reliving her past life was momentary; all that remained now was loneliness, despair, a life utterly devoid of hope.

"Fancy a wee drink, madam? Looks like you could do with a wee dram of the hard stuff."

"Huh?" said Justina, looking up to find a young man standing in front of her. The café had felt so lifeless that the fact that people actually went there to have a hot or cold beverage had slipped her mind. "Sorry, what did you say?"

"Just wondering whether you wanted a wee drink? No matter if you don't; not gonna kick you out or anything," replied the waiter with a weak and nervous laugh. Whatever confidence he had earlier possessed had been shredded with a simple question.

His nervous demeanour and gruff Scottish accent were somewhat endearing. Now, almost at attention and not knowing what to do with his hands, he swiftly turned around and made for the counter to grab a notepad and a pen, before turning once more and marching back to his customer in a business-like manner, eyes squarely focused on the pad in his right hand. She could see the whites of his knuckles as he held his pen tight, ready to scribble her order. He was nervous – she had made him nervous. She felt something she had not felt for another human for many years: pity – she felt sorry for him.

"Are you offering?" she asked, trying to make him feel more at ease.

"Offering?" he said slowly, his deep brown eyes searching for some kind of warmth as he glanced in her direction, desperately hoping for her to rescue him from his precarious state.

"You mentioned a dram of 'the hard stuff'," said Justina, adding light laughter to soothe his nerves. For some reason, she was touched by his nervous nature and felt a strong desire to ease his discomfort.

"Oh, ah yes, the wee dram. Well, as I'm sure you know, us Scots take the hard stuff very seriously. Like you lot and your tea. The solution to everything!" he replied, the strain on his knuckles easing as his heart pounded less frantically.

"Yes, yes I guess they do," replied Justina, laughing a little more naturally.

"They?" he enquired. "Ah wait, you're not English, are you? Is that a wee American accent I hear?"

"So, it's still there? Damn! I've been trying to iron it out for ages, but it just won't go."

"Aye, they never do. It's like they purposely stick around because they know they're no longer welcome. Loitering in the background as if they bloody own us. Mind you, I guess they probably do."

He kept talking. He talked of home, of coffee, of school. Justina simply listened, laughed, flirted… She liked his accent. She had always had a soft spot for the Scots, their warm friendly nature and blunt manner. She had only once been to Scotland, she told him. She had chosen to enjoy the final sprinkles of summer in a little town called

Stewarton, about six miles or so from Kilmarnock. She had worked throughout the holiday and was in desperate need of a break before commencing her university sojourn. Not that the weather was any good; she could only recall one afternoon of sunshine in four days. But, despite the dark grey skies and their incessant drivel, she loved the place. Thin, windy roads stretching through fields of resplendent flowers and overgrown grass, with field after field of cows lazily chomping their way through the day. True nature, beauty thriving freely in the wild. It was unencumbered, not manicured to perfection by human hands.

On one occasion – she explained – during a long morning walk, she challenged herself to get to the very top of a monstrous hill. The challenge seemed fair and reasonable at first, but she soon realised the climb was much further than she had thought. As the hill's slopes unfurled, revealing previously hidden stretches and mounds, she grew more determined to reach its peak, stopping every twenty metres or so to marvel at the view below.

She imagined experiencing such marvellous beauty on a daily basis. The tranquillity was a stillness that was alien to the rest of the world, a timeless peacefulness, unshaken and unbreakable.

Time had stood still that morning, opening previously padlocked doors.

For a fleeting moment she had allowed her heart to breathe, embracing the beauty around her in a stolen moment of serenity. How could such splendour exist in such a fallen world? She briefly considered a new and poignant question, knocking on her door of certainty like an uninvited guest, and temporarily shaking the surest of foundations. It was curious… intriguing, but not welcome.

Gathering herself and slamming the doors shut, she resumed her climb. Upon reaching the top, she witnessed a peculiar sight of two sheep grazing, with a lone small black fence for company. Something about them fascinated her, at peace in a world of their own. How had they got there? So far away from the others, and yet so comfortable in their surroundings. She had stood there, watching the two sheep for some minutes, envying their freedom to leisurely spend their days as they pleased, with the quality of greenery their only concern. After some time, she arched her head back, allowing the grey skies' darting arrows to caress her face. As the light drizzle made way for a heavy downpour, she stretched out her arms in surrender to mother nature.

The unwelcome guest knocked on her door once more, this time a little louder. She opened the door and looked her in the eye, daring her to speak. But the guest did not say a word. There was no need to; she was not a visitor. She had always been there, forever lurking in the shadows, mocking her subconscious in the knowledge that she could not be ignored forever. The bartender merely sat there, listening with intrigue to Justina getting carried away by memories of a simpler time.

"I so love you guys. The country and the people, I mean," added Justina, suddenly conscious of sounding like a deranged groupie, which, of course, she was not. She liked him. Not only did he make her laugh but he seemed to be a good person. She especially liked his slightly nervous demeanour; it suggested he did not quite realise how handsome he was. But she barely knew him, so how could she possibly love him? Love? Obviously a slip of the tongue. Surely, he knew that.

"Aye, nae worry, my friend. You'll love me soon enough," he replied.

Confidence as well as a quick wit, Justina thought. She laughed along, conscious of crossing over into flirtation territory. Or had she already started flirting with him several minutes ago?

"So, you're American, you like the hard stuff, and you love me, as well as Scotland and all Scots, but I don't even know your name."

She paused, taking a moment to consider her situation. Here she was, in a café with a man she barely knew, but one she wanted to get to know more. What would he think of her if he knew who she was, what she had done? Her heart began to beat a little faster as the tiny hairs on her arms rose to attention – adroit, miniature needles anticipating a momentous decision. She was about to open a door she might never be able to close, ceding control to an unknown quantity.

"Isn't it a little early for names? You haven't even served me my drink yet," she replied, hoping to direct the conversation to a different path.

"Aye, had a feeling that question may have come a little too early. Apologies. Please, don't feel you have to tell me your name. Not important... for now at least. Alex, by the way."

"Sorry?" said Justina, somewhat confused.

"That's my name, Alex. But don't feel you have to tell me yours. Please, feel free not to. In fact, don't tell me. Never tell me; I'm no longer interested – never was," he said, putting the back of his right hand on his forehead before closing his eyes and turning his head sharply to the right.

Justina laughed a very natural laugh. She felt happy, free of her worries and troubles. She had come to the café to figure things out but had found an escape. It was him. No matter how temporary it was, he had helped her escape. She was experiencing a version of herself she never knew existed, a version that was happy, funny, flirty even.

"Stop! You're making me laugh too much," she pleaded, grabbing her stomach as laughter morphed into a fit of giggles.

He laughed along with her. Such laughter had been alien to him for so long also; little did she know how much she had helped him. Something about her made him leap out of the dark, roar, and grab life once more, reacquaint with his former self... his real self, cocooned in solemnity for so long. She made him feel warm on the inside, like the sun had risen once more.

Her eyes seemed to glisten even more when she laughed. She was no longer the forlorn looking lady he had approached some minutes ago but so much brighter; she seemed so happy now, transformed.

They chatted and flirted for several hours, both forgetting their troubles and Justina still refusing to tell him her name.

Alex spoke of how his once joyful and love-filled existence had been shattered two years ago when the love of his life died from a brain haemorrhage without warning; she had never been sick, she simply passed away. His world came crashing down, destroying everything in its path – friends, family. He withdrew from all those close to him, choosing to immerse himself in the grim despair of his tragedy. It was the reason he had come to Oxford; not to study, but to get away from Glasgow. He had managed to successfully reapply from Glasgow University to Oxford on the merit of his grades and some particularly positive references from alumni who had since moved to Scotland to teach – he had to; he had no choice. As if being reminded about Jenny by every corner of the city was not enough, the manner in which close friends looked at him with such pity was too much to take. Everywhere he looked, wherever he went, had been a daily debilitating reminder of his loss.

The more they talked, the more Justina found herself not wanting to leave. She wanted to know more about Jenny, about *him*, his family, life in Glasgow. He made her feel safe… far away from the terrors of her everyday life.

Only when the sun drifted away did she accept the inevitability of having to return to her college digs.

"What did you like most about her?"

"Jenny? Now, that's a tough one. So much to love and admire about that gal…" His eyes drifted downwards as a gentle air of melancholy descended on him. "Her cheek… Aye, definitely that cheek of hers. You never quite knew what was coming. Thing is, she wasn't like that with anyone else; just me. She saved all her cheek for me." He laughed.

"She sounds like an amazing person. Do… do you..."

"Do I what?"

"Do you... I hope you don't mind me asking, and please feel free to tell me to get lost if you do..."

"Get on with it, woman! My stubble has already grown into a full beard whilst waiting for you to land."

"Sorry, it's just... Okay, you were in a really amazing relationship. Love, joy, fun, excitement; sounds like you had it all. But then, all of a sudden, it all gets taken away from you. That's painful… cruel, even. Do you… do you ever wish you had never fallen for her? That you'd never experienced being in love?"

He paused, contemplating how it would feel not to be haunted on a daily basis by memories of a happy yesterday. For a brief moment, he wished he had never known such love and joy. But what kind of life would that have been? It would have been a hollow existence, devoid of feeling or meaning.

"Not for one second. I experienced a love that many others can only dream of. Don't get me wrong, there are times when I wonder what it would be like to not feel such pain. It would certainly make my life a whole lot easier, a pain-free life. How great would that be! But despite the agony and grief, I'd do it all again. What's that saying? 'Better to have loved and lost than never loved at all'?"

She had considered that sentiment a few times before, but always deemed it to be nonsensical and foolish. It was the first time she had heard some-one actually say it. He meant it; she could tell. He really meant it.

"Justina."

"Sorry?" replied Alex as he opened the door for her.

"Justina; my name is Justina."

"Justina," he repeated slowly, sampling each syllable like a curious old wine. "Well, Justina, I hope this won't be the last time we speak."

"I sense it won't be."

"Good. Well, you know where I am. Don't wait too long before you come again."

"Aye, I won't," said Justina mockingly. "Besides, you still owe me a wee dram of the hard stuff."

For the first time in over a year, he felt alive again, curious about the future; maybe it would not be so desolate after all. He still missed Jenny, the anguish feeling just as bitter as it was when she died. He cried whenever he thought about her, a daily occurrence that had become a part of him, an addendum to his life. Songs, bookshops, rock bands, posters on the street, smells of certain cafés – they all possessed the power to stir memories, opening boxes of sorrow he had sealed and shelved. The pain had never left him; he had simply learned to cope with it better as the months passed. He watched Justina walk all the way down the street until she turned left at the end and was no longer in view. His lips curled upwards, mirroring the warm glow in his heart.

Justina sensed his eyes on her back as she walked down the street. She was tempted to look back, maybe give a wave or a smile, but she could not. To do so would be too keen, too open – weak.

She continued walking, eyes focused on the corner ahead, determined to resist all temptation to look back. If only she was sure he was not watching her; then she could allow her feet to skip in sync with the merriment of her heart and the butterflies in her stomach. She had never felt this way before, seized by a nervous excitement she could barely contain. *Is he still watching me? I just want to see his smile one more time. What's wrong with that? No, I mustn't. Focus; just keep walking. What the hell's going on? This isn't me; I don't do this. Focus. Don't let go now; you've come too far. Who am I kidding? I can't wait to see him again – no harm in that.*

Having the doors of her heart so forcefully pushed wide open was the last thing she expected or wanted when she entered that café several hours before. A place she had never been to, nor even knew existed. She had delved into a wretched corner of the city and found joy... life... hope.

She was relieved after turning the corner, as though a huge boulder had been lifted off her shoulders. As she began to breathe more freely, she suddenly remembered the poster that the woman was staring at. What could stir such powerful emotions? She turned around, briefly walking back towards the café before stopping in front of the poster. *From the Jam: Playing at Oxford Town Hall.* Although she had heard of them, she knew little about them. But the picture on the poster told her they were a classic rock kind of band, which made sense, bearing in mind the lady's appearance. The poster must have transported her to happy times of youthful exuberance – no cares or responsibilities, a time in which she must have felt as though she and her friends could never be separated. A time, perhaps, when they thought they were invincible, special, and that they would be forever.

She could still see the expression on the woman's face, as though she was staring back at her from inside the poster. The light in her eyes portraying a forlorn joy of memories from yester-year, hounded by despair of the present age.

Justina could feel her pain, as though she was experiencing it herself. She imagined having lived such a full and gregarious life, only for her light to be dimmed further and further by the ravenous tentacles of age and time, gleefully bleeding the air out of her, dying a little more each day.

She stood there for several minutes, staring at the poster, wondering whether it was worth it, opening oneself to happiness, only to have it taken away. By the time she turned to leave, she was not quite so exhilarated as she had been before. None-theless, she could not stop thinking about him, so much so that she giggled when she remembered his "wee dram" introduction.

Then, just as the smile that had etched itself on her face returned, she was hit by a deafening noise – a sound so high-pitched that her eardrums almost imploded, battering her senses and causing her to fall in tortuous agony. She covered her ears with her hands and hid her head between her knees.

The loud din tore at her jangled nerves for several minutes before fading away.

Now breathless, she turned around to see if anyone had seen her, but there was nobody there. Never had she experienced such a thing before. Was she the only person who had heard it?

Her ears rang for several minutes as she knelt on her hands and knees by the side of the road, eyes feeling as though they were about to explode, wondering what had happened.

Eventually, she summoned the strength and courage to get up, placing her left hand on the wall for balance. But no sooner had she got to her feet that the deafening screams returned, this time throwing her to the ground with violent force. In the midst of it, she could hear cries of anguish, but not cries of humans… dragons. They sounded like tortured souls, dying a slow and painful eternal death, burned alive.

71

She could feel the flames tearing and melting their bodies, the dense smoke suffocating their lungs. She squeezed her eyes, hoping for the pain to go away. It didn't. For what seemed like an eternity, she experienced the cruel and painful death of dragons she had slain, burning like rotting cattle. Hapless cries of desperate mothers attempting to shield their little ones from puerile flames. She could hear them – their screams, their groanings, their cries for help; every plea for the release of death to come take the pain away was excruciatingly etching itself into Justina's mind.

Only after she had died with every single dragon that she and Liza had torched to death did the despairing cries fade away. Glued to the ground, she was unable to move, for fear of it starting all over again. But deep down she knew it was over; at least for now. Little by little, her senses returned, shaken, unfiltered, bruised.

Her mind was racing, searching for meaning, but an overriding question demanded immediate attention: why were the souls of the dead reaching out to her? Was this her own personal torture for the pain she had inflicted on others, or was there more to it?

Eventually, she clawed her way to her feet and sauntered slowly down the street, swaying from side to side like a drunk person, unable to steady her feet and not in control of her limbs. On and on she went, staggering her way through the back streets so as to avoid the density of the city centre, all the while conscious of the reality that she would still have to navigate her way through the High Street at some point in order to get back to her digs. The hope was that her senses would be fully restored by then – though hope and reality were bitter enemies at best.

There was very little improvement by the time she reached the High Street; her ears were still ringing, eyes watering from putrid smoke, and feet and limbs doing as they pleased. She was worried about resembling a down and out miscreant, and it did not take too long for her concerns to be justified as those walking towards her either crossed to the other side or veered away, taking a wide berth for fear of catching whatever ailed her. The sight of them keeping their distance and changing direction heightened her worst fears – she had lost control; a door had been opened, and it was quite possible that she would not be able to close it again.

5

Ms. Carlisle

"So, have you always been her driver? Worked for her, I mean?" asked Justina, somewhat uncomfortable about labelling an individual she barely knew as a 'driver'; he could be a relative, a brother doing his sister a favour. But then, as far as she knew, Ms. Carlisle had no relatives; Justina had done her research.

Ms. Carlisle was an enigma, a lone reed standing tall in an oasis of mediocrity, barking orders and demands at all those in her vicinity, in a vain but heroic attempt to restore virtue and discipline. It confused Justina, somewhat, that Ms. Carlisle could afford such a home so far beyond Oxford's own boundaries, though she figured she must have had some place to return to after a term of work at the college – Oxford accommodation was fine for term time, though perhaps unusual living for the holiday periods.

Justina had always respected her, what she stood for, but her personal life was a mystery. No matter how deep Justina burrowed, she always came to a dead end; there were no relations, no friends. Ms. Carlisle was a lone existence; it was as though she was carefully crafted in another age and placed in the present to give the world some backbone.

Yet here they were, being driven to her house, an unknown destination that was taking forever to reach. They had already spent several hours on countless motorways, seamlessly passing signs and exits to various cities in a dreamlike fashion, with the never-ending acres of fields on either side of them their constant companion. Mind you, he was wearing one of those chauffeur cap thingies. She could not recall exactly what they were called, but as far as she was concerned, the cap said it all; a brother or a relative would not be wearing one of those chauffeur thingies – unless, of course, Ms. Carlisle's employees were her relatives, which surely even Ms. Carlisle would feel uncomfortable with.

The driver's light-grey eyes darted towards the rear-view mirror, gently placing themselves on hers as the faintest of smiles reluctantly announced itself before scuttling off again.

Justina was a little irritated; she had asked a simple enough question. Was that his answer? A vague smile? What the hell did that mean? A simple 'yes' or 'no' would suffice. After all, they had more-or-less placed their lives in his hands; the least he could do was answer a simple question – she needed answers and he was not helping. She thought about asking again, this time with a little more demand in her voice, but in all likelihood, he was Ms. Carlisle's driver, so why risk the possibility of him reporting her for being rude?

She briefly glanced at Liza, who was silent as usual. She had barely said a word to her for several months, preferring to remain in whatever world her mind had crafted for her. Justina could not really tell what was going on with her; she kept to herself, always in her room, probably playing with flames – she could do that now.

Zoldon had taught her to control them, to summon them at will and direct them with pinpoint accuracy. Liza had always been a fast learner, eager to get better and better at using her powers. It was what drove her, what she lived for.

Now, the only time she spoke animatedly was when she was with Abbadon or Zoldon; aside from that, there was a constant discomforting calmness about her. Nobody ever knew what she was thinking or how she was feeling. The old Liza had worn her heart on her sleeves; Justina had always known what was going on in her mind.

Slightly angled to the right, Liza's head was arched back, leaning on the headrest. She was awake, eyes firmly focused on something, but Justina could not tell what.

Justina recognised the futility of trying to guess what she was thinking; Liza had become a mystery of dark complexities. They passed a sign to their destination – mere miles remained. Justina wondered what he was up to… Alex… They had been out together many times since they first met at the café; they had even kissed. He often wanted them to spend a night together; so did she, but she could not take the risk. No matter how disillusioned she felt about her cause, she needed to remain focused; inviting love to roam freely in her heart was something she simply could not afford to do.

Besides, what was the point? Love, hope, and all manner of feeling and emotion would soon be switched off forever. Why fall in love, only for it to be permanently erased? But in truth, deep down she suspected she might already be in love. It wasn't something she knew or understood. Just a deep longing to be with him. An inability to keep him out of her mind. She felt a restless desire to experience different things with him, thoughts and feelings that made her feel hopelessly lacking in control, that made her feel vulnerable and weak.

"We'll get there when we get there, Jus; re-lax," said Liza calmly. She did not turn to face Justina but continued staring at whatever was monopolising her attention.

Nothing troubled her anymore. Her moments of confusion and unmitigated anger were a thing of the past. Now at one with the dark rage that fuelled her powers, life was straightforward. The light that once shimmered in her heart had been extinguished; she was finally at peace with herself. In her mind's eye was the day she learned to control her flames, the day she was pushed to the very edge of herself.

There was no doubt that Zoldon was pleased with her new ability, but he had made it very clear that it would destroy her should she not learn to use it properly; she must harness and control it before it overpowered her.

Deep down, she knew he was right, but a stubborn arrogance fuelled a suspicion that he merely wanted to keep her within his claws – still, there was no harm in learning what she could do with it.

On a dark stormy morning, they had flown to a desert in the middle of nowhere, pushing against terrifying gusts of wind. As bullets of torrential rain incessantly pelted her face, she could not help wondering why Zoldon persisted. Surely it was the wrong kind of weather for such training?

But he would not stop, trusting his strained, outstretched wings to navigate them through the tempest. The last time she had ridden on Zoldon, she had been a novice, entering his world of schemes for the first time, having reluctantly accepted it was better to feel nothing as against the inevitable grief that follows love and hope.

The violent obstruction of angry clouds had reduced their flight to a crawl. For many hours, they had meandered across the skies, as though getting as far away from the others as possible to protect some sacred treasure. They had long passed the endless sea of lifeless fields and dead water, which for many years was how she depicted much of the outer realm; only during the past few years had she seen its other, greener pastures. She glanced at the dense forest beneath, and wondered how many dragons it concealed – runaways who refused to take one side or the other. Liza took a mental note before looking ahead once again. Whether those dragons realised it or not, their decision to sit on the fence made little difference to their safety.

The mass of forest beneath them came to an abrupt end, giving way to a beach-like terrain of golden brown; Liza glanced all around but could see nothing else. Zoldon began to descend, pushing a little less as the winds eased. The closer they got to the ground, the more it became apparent to her that the golden brown below was sand. A desert in the outer realm was not something she could ever have imagined or thought possible. Yet here they were, about to land in the middle of one – a slightly cold, rainy, windy desert.

"Why here?" she asked as Zoldon's claws touched the sand.

Stretching his wings once more before closing them again, he waited for Liza to jump off in order to look her in the eye before answering her question. There was a cruel thrill of excitement in her eyes, eager to be released from the shroud of fear that had encircled it. He waited, the prolonged silence allowing fear to tighten its grip. But despite this, she stilled as her heart slowed its adrenaline-fuelled rush to a calm, sedate pulse.

"Fear and anger – that is where your power comes from. Used properly, they are unstoppable. Somewhat cruel, Liza – that is what you must be for us to fulfil our ultimate objective." He paused again, protruding eyes examining the depths of her soul, searching for hidden etchings of hesitation.

Happy to oblige, she gazed back, allowing his gaze to roam freely; she had nothing to hide.

Slow seconds and measured minutes passed by, screaming for a release from the tension he had carefully crafted. The last time he had entered her mind, he had encountered a soul tortured by the past and the present, a tug of war between hope and reason that was tearing her apart. The conflicting voices were a cause of concern that almost led to him rejecting her, but in her he had sensed an anger and fear that would ultimately lead her to the right path.

There were no such concerns on this occasion.

She was standing on top of a mass of ruins, surrounded by an avalanche of dead bodies; dragons – even baby dragons – humans, mothers, fathers, children… smoke rising from their charred remains.

As Zoldon surveyed the desecration around Liza, his eyes were drawn to one in particular;

a young woman with mousey-blonde hair covering much of her face. He peered closer, hoping the dread that had suddenly seized him was misguided. Blue-grey eyes; a well of emotion threatened to besiege him… He stepped back; nothing and nobody was going to deter him.

"A little cruelty can at times be the very best form of kindness," he said finally. "But I see that isn't something you need to concern yourself with."

A faint smirk, accompanying the twinkle in her eye, wormed its way across her face. "Show me how," Liza asked – or, rather, demanded.

The further they went, the narrower the roads became, brambles and thickets smothering time and space as they entered an unknown world. Rubbing the inside of her left palm with her right thumb, Justina noticed a faint trace of sweat. A little perturbed, she closed her eyes, slowly inhaling then exhaling, over and over again. Senses that had not dared to challenge her for well over a decade were bearing their ugly fangs once more, attempting to cause upheaval. But they were no match for her. Focusing only on her breathing, it did not take long for her to regain control.

When she opened her eyes some minutes later, the scene had drastically changed: the strangled, narrow road had given way to a wider and more civil one, with a beautiful array of symmetrically aligned trees on either side, escorting them towards what looked like a magnificent edifice on the horizon. Though unable to fully grasp the finer details of the sprawling building in the far distance, she was awestruck by its imposing nature, standing tall like a beacon of splendour amid an expanse of greenery. The closer they got to it, the more her spine tingled in wonder and awe. The guard of trees merged into gardens of splendour akin to Nebuchadnezzar's Babylon; rows of hedges manicured to perfection, resplendent lawns adorned with glistening green grass. As she gaped with incredulity at the extent of wonder before her, she spotted a peacock, idly strutting through its environment, as though waiting for its next adventure. She rested her eyes on the green, red and black creature for several seconds before a gigantic shadow diverted her attention.

She was fairly sure it was some kind of a large bird gliding above them, but when she looked up, there was nothing but a warm blanket of clouds. She craned her neck, straining to catch a glimpse of the mysteriously hidden creature, but whatever it was had gone.

The sound of a heavy gate scraping open across a gravel drive tore her from her thoughts. As she eased the strain on her neck, she noticed the chauffer looking at her through the rear-view mirror. Feeling a little embarrassed by her uncontained excitement, she quickly checked herself, regaining what little composure she had left. Just as she was beginning to take it all in with some semblance of calmness, her eyes growing accustomed to a radiance of beauty never seen nor imagined, the paved road dissolved into an immaculate stretch of gravel, a conveyer belt of black, grey and brown pebbles, carrying them to their destination.

Into view came a beige, L-shaped mansion, with big, symmetrically-aligned rectangular windows and dark wooden beams that gave it the authentic aura of a classic countryside estate; a wonderful merging of the old with the new. There was nobody waiting to welcome them, no one standing in front of the tall, black wooden door with its long, vertical, silver handle.

"I'm guessing she's in the back garden," said the chauffeur as he opened the door on Liza's side. His voice was not what Liza – nor even Justina – had imagined; she had expected it to be suave, like something out of Downton Abbey, but he sounded more street than country.

Justina waited a few seconds for him to come to her side, but quickly realised he was not going to and so shuffled across the back seats to alight the car. She was pleased to be able to finally stretch her legs – not that the car was in the least uncomfortable. The air seemed so much cleaner than the polluted urban one she had grown accustomed to. The pores of her lungs opened up, alive again. Glancing from left to right, then left again, she embraced the beauty and serenity of it all – the resplendent house in front of her, the backdrop of the countryside behind it, even the alluring nature of the pebbled stones beneath her feet.

"Incredible, isn't it?" she said, turning to Liza.

Liza was not interested in the array of splendour before them; her attention was fully focused on the fountain in the middle of the garden. It looked like most fountains do, shooting streams of water into the air before droplets danced in sync, diving down. There was an object standing in the middle of the fountain itself, drawing her attention.

She made her way to the fountain, drawn like a magnet towards the mysterious figure behind the waters. Upon reaching it, she was a little disappointed to glimpse an ordinary looking man in a tunic. Save for the thick nest of hair on his head, there was nothing about him that intrigued or inspired... except his eyes. Were there rivers of water behind those dull, beaten eyes?

"Bit odd that one, innit?" came a voice from behind her – the chauffeur. She was surprised to hear him speak again. For five hours he had not said a word, then he had spoken twice in the space of a few minutes.

"Who is he?" asked Liza, turning around to face her inquisitor.

"No idea, to be 'onest. Best ask the Gov; all I do is drive, Miss. Living the dream, me – living the dream," he said, bursting into faint laughter. "I best take you to 'er."

Liza followed him, turning her head a couple more times to catch a glimpse of the forlorn look-ing individual in the centre of the fountain. De-spite his plain features, she was drawn to him, as though they were somehow connected.

"Come this way, please, Miss," said the chauffeur as he passed Justina. "She's probably pottering in the back somewhere. She's always do-ing one thing or another back there. Never stops."

He was like a completely different person; five hours of driving and not a word, yet now he could not stop.

Justina wondered whether he had somehow been swapped with an identical twin, or even cloned. The thought made her chuckle, amazed by how different people can be in different environments. The three of them walked in silence for several minutes, accompanied by the crisp squelching of shoes on immaculately curated gravel. They passed a garage of classic cars on their way and Justina paused for a few seconds, impressed by the collection – she did not know much about cars, so had no idea what makes or models they were but was fascinated by their pristine condition. They were antique, dated, but irreplaceable – exquisite, pristine, and classy. She could never have imagined Ms. Carlisle to be so fond of cars; it seemed she had many layers, and the more they peeled off, the greater the mystery.

"Best come along, Miss, otherwise she'll 'ave mi guts for garters; we're late enough."

Justina resumed her walk, following the talkative chauffeur through a labyrinth of quads and paths. He slowed a little as they approached someone on all fours beside a flower bed. Wearing a green Barbour, the person was tugging away at something at the back of the bed.

"Ah, you're here. Whatever took you so long, Jeffrey?"

"Sorry, Miss, just that—"

"Never mind that; no time for explanations – you're late enough as it is. Are they with you?"

"Yes, Miss."

"Good. Thank you for coming, ladies. Now, I know you must be tired, but I thought it might do you some good to take a little fresh air after your long journey. Take them to the hilltop, Jeffrey; I'm sure they'll appreciate the view at the top. And you'll need some boots. I've left a few pairs by the door of the greenhouse. I'm sure you'll both find ones that fit you. Probably best to take an anorak as well. It's all there – everything you'll need."

Liza squinted her eyes to get a better view of whatever it was that was being grappled with in the flower bed. Only Ms. Carlisle could conduct a conversation with such authority without so much as a glance in their direction.

"Well, don't just stand there like rabbits in bright lights! I'll catch up with you at the top. What the devil is wrong with you? Why won't you come out?"

As they walked off, Liza turned her head back once more towards her dean, still grappling with something, head buried deep within the flowers. They had not even seen her face; she did not so much as pause in whatever she was doing. Dismissive, rude even, and sending them away like five-year-olds. Yet, for some reason, Liza did not resent her for it. Ms. Carlisle would always be Ms. Carlisle.

The greenhouse was more akin to a miniature woodland situated inside a huge glass building; glass gates against doors, inviting onlookers
to its own particular world of forestry and pathways. As they put on their perfectly fitting boots,
Justina marvelled at the intricate and vast nature
of the terrain behind the glass gates. It was the sort
of place one could happily spend days lost in, buried in an enchanted land of wonder and beauty.

"How long did it take, Jeffrey?" asked Justina.

"'Ow long did what take?"

"The greenhouse. It's like a mini city in there.
How long did it take to do it? For everything to
grow?"

"Oh, as long as anything else that grows, I
guess," replied the chauffeur, somewhat evasively.
"Come on, ladies, we'd better get goin'. Trust me,
she'll be there sooner than you think."

They walked across green meadows, up and
down gentle hills, across muddy farmland, and
even through streams, until they finally reached
an imposing climb, by which time the grey clouds
had revealed their hands; the rain itself was not
heavy, but sturdy and consistent enough to slowly
soak them all. For over an hour they walked up the
steep edifice, often clamouring for better footing
in the increasingly wet conditions – heads down,

the backs of the hoods of their anoraks taking a steady beating of rain.

Justina turned her head back to check on Liza, though she did not quite know why. Liza had been growing increasingly withdrawn and insular for several months. She reminded Justina of a cat – only remembering others when it is convenient for them, otherwise staying away. But a part of Justina wanted to make sure Liza was still there and not traipsing off in another direction, looking for something to kill. She was several metres behind, skulking up the steep climb inside her maroon anorak, in the company of her own moody cloud, but at least she was in view.

"How long is this climb?" shouted Justina, hoping someone who knew could hear her in the rain.

"Eh?" the chauffeur returned.

"The climb, how long is it?"

"Sorry, Miss – can't hear ya. Be better up top, we'll be there soon."

The rain and wind grew heavier as they staggered, heads bowed, up the final hundred metres. The hilltop arrived very suddenly, without warning or welcome. Everything came to a halt, and in the blink of an eye, both the rain and the wind ceased as though someone had flipped a switch.

Justina inched forward, assuming the ground beneath her feet would continue.

"Justina, wait," said Liza, grabbing and pulling her back. "Look."

Several hundreds of metres below them swarmed layer after layer of violent waves, crashing into an undaunted barrier of rocks and boulders. Justina's spine tingled as she took in the huge distance to the bottom. Liza had saved her; to have fallen would have meant certain death.

"Thanks, Liza," she said gratefully, wondering why the chauffeur had failed to warn her first. "You could have warned... Where is he?"

"Who?" replied Liza.

"Jeffrey. The chauffeur, where's he gone?"

"No idea. Haven't seen him since the rain started getting heavier."

"That's weird. You don't think…"

"Nah; if he had fallen, we'd see his blood splattered on the rocks. Besides, pretty sure he knows the terrain. Can't believe this view. Had no idea we were so close to the coast, sea, or whatever."

They stood there for several minutes, gazing into the mesh of water and rocks below, gripped by cold chills of their brush with death, astounded by the panorama enveloping them.

"It's magnificent, isn't it?" came a voice from behind them. "A beautiful view, and yet one that sends a vicious chill down your spine."

Surprised to hear the voice of their seemingly ever-present mentor, Justina and Liza turned to see Ms. Carlisle standing behind them, the light smidgen of dew on her Barbour a gross misrepresentation of the recent downpour. A noticeable glint in her eye conveyed her fondness for the peak on which they now stood.

Justina wondered whether she had been able to uproot whatever had been bothering her by the flower bed – a strange thought, bearing in mind the mystery with which she had caught up with them so quickly.

"It's known as Pelonious' Peak."

"Pelonious, Miss? Is that someone's name?" asked Justina.

"Indeed, it was, Justina; a great folklore in these parts. As the story goes, Pelonious was a great and, in many respects, cruel general in the Roman army, who emigrated to these shores in AD 43, after meeting his first true love. She was a slave girl, and as you know, in those days, a slave couldn't just up and leave. But because of the immense power and influence he wielded, it didn't take him long to secure her release. And as soon as he did so, he married her. Before long, she bore him a beautiful daughter, his second true love – he adored his little girl even more than he did his wife. In an ideal world, that would be the end of the story, living happily ever after, but as you both know, life doesn't work like that. After five years of a blissfully happy marriage, tragedy struck. His wife fell ill and died within days. It was a truly bitter pill to swallow. Furthermore, he blamed himself, believing he was being punished for the many atrocities he'd committed."

"What atrocities? You said he was cruel earlier, but you didn't elaborate," said Liza.

"Battle was a brutal thing in those days. They had to take the most drastic measures to ensure victory. And it wasn't just about victory in battle; even more important was the matter of ensuring your defeated enemies could never rise against you again."

"I think I know what you mean," said Justina. "Slaughtering entire villages and stuff?"

"Precisely. But for quite some time, ever since he met Penelope – that was her name – he hadn't seen it that way. After her death, he spent several years paying penance in various ways; self-imprisonment, self-beating, starvation – all manner of things. But nothing sufficed. Then he heard about a monastery on the British Isles that people went to in search of redemption, and without a moment's hesitation, he crossed the seas."

"What about his daughter?" asked Liza, eyes blazing.

"Some say he left her in the care of his sister, some his mother, others his mother-in-law. At first, he would go back to see her once a year, but over time, he just stopped, believing it to be better all-round if he let her go. You see, he became fascinated with the idea of vanquishing feelings and emotions. He spent many years researching the heart, mind, emotions, all in the aim of finding a solution to life's heartaches and grief. The more he dug, the more he realised there was but one solution."

"And what was that?" asked Justina, almost dreading the answer.

"What do you think? Cut out the source, of course. In a moment many deem as abject lunacy, he cut out his heart with a blunt knife. But oddly enough, he didn't die. For several days, he wandered around with his bloody heart clenched in his right hand like a prize trophy, bereft of thought or feeling – a triumph over creation."

"And he didn't..."

"Die? He was last seen climbing this hill on a clear sunny day, staggering towards the peak. Upon reaching this summit, where you now stand, he committed his final act of defiance, throwing his heart into the water below, like an unwanted piece of cloth. Now, here's the interesting part: as the story goes, his heart never reached the water but was caught by the jaws of a dragon before it landed, and carried away to an unknown destination. They say his heart lives on, fuelling the determination of those that want to see an end to suffering and grief."

"And what do you think, Miss? What's your opinion on suffering and grief?" asked Justina. She had always seen Ms. Carlisle as a matter-of-fact person, but never for one second imagined her to be someone who would sympathise with their own ideals.

"I suggest you both take another look at the water below. Tell me what you see," replied Ms. Carlisle.

They inched towards the edge, searching for an unknown answer.

"What do you see?" asked Ms. Carlisle, a little more forcefully.

"Nothing, just… nothing," replied Justina.

"Meaning?"

"He did it. Nothingness. He found his answer: without heart, there is no feeling. So, there are others like... Wait, you're with us as..."

"Yes, I am. More than you know," came a different voice, one even more familiar to them. Slowly turning their heads to face their inquisitor, hundreds of scenes of conversations they had sat through with Ms. Carlisle in the past flooded their minds. Suddenly it all made sense – the attention to detail, insistence on focusing on the bigger picture no matter what, the steely stares, strenuous discipline, disappearing during school exeats, getting to the hilltop so quickly…

Standing in front of them was their master. Liza staggered backwards with surprise and wonder. She had seen dragons shapeshift before – Raphael himself had once taken the form of an old man. But Liza had known Ms. Carlisle for years, been mentored by her, even. Theirs was a bond that was as usual to her as it was unique – to think that Ms. Carlisle was a mere figment – naught but a creation of her master – saddened her, somehow. Though she was equally angry that she had not managed to work it all out sooner.

"Zoldon… it's you… I didn't know it was you," Liza managed to blurt out.

"It would surely be a poor disguise if you did!"

"What happened to his daughter?" asked Liza, fascinated with the story she had just heard.

"Upon finding out about her father, she dedicated herself to his cause. Through her descendants, her… *their* spirits live on," replied Zoldon.

"The statue, that's him, isn't it?" said Liza.

"Indeed! Now, I summoned you both for a reason. We have reached a critical moment, and it is time for you to see the wider picture. I've arranged for you to meet with the Prime Minister; tomorrow, in fact. She's expecting you at two p.m."

"His daughter, what was her name?" pressed Justina.

A sad gentleness sullied Zoldon's usually cold eyes as he stared into the vast stretch of water below. With a laboured sigh, he looked up to the clouds, then unfurled his wings before slowly setting off.

"Jeffrey is waiting at the house to take you back. Make sure you're on time tomorrow."

6

Pelonious

Like swarms of bees chasing numerous pots of honey, an ocean of people busily go about their business at the Roman port of Osita, fifteen miles or so from Rome.

To the unknowing eye, it is a flurry of confusion – thousands of people amassed in one place for varying reasons. Traders on ships to-and-from different harbours carting goods: cattle, horses, wine, tin, timber, oil, perfumes, silk, leather, lead. Entire families are milling around waiting to emigrate to new shores as the Roman Empire stretches its tentacles across the world – Africa, Europe and the Middle East.

Much of the world belongs to Rome, and the port of Osita is its beginning.

A thick, pungent smell of wine, sweat and horse dung governs the air, daring newcomers to enter at their peril. Every so often, the crowd momentarily pauses at the sound of heavy marching feet and beating shields, and gives way, the din of noise briefly subdued as silence descends like a thief in the night. It is a brief and sudden moment of order in the midst of chaos, as legions travel to invade new territories, or prepare to be posted to serve in already conquered lands.

It is often possible to differentiate between those on invasive missions and those posted to already conquered territories; the eyes of those going to actual battle burn with excitement and pride. Still so young, after many months of rigorous and strenuous training, their restless souls groan, hungry for action, endeared to the glory that accompanies victory. This is their time, their opportunity to shine, their moment in the story of Rome's mighty empire.

Those posted to serve in already conquered lands hunger less; the experience of being on the road for months on end and the harsh realities of battle have made them wiser. Long gone is their thirst for glory and fame, and in its place is a simple desire to survive the mission unscathed; to return safely to their loved ones. Feared, respected, and revered, they pass, making their way towards their ships to embark on a new and uncertain journey. And in the blink of an eye, the busy mass resumes its organised madness, and the clamour is restored.

A little girl squeezes her father's hand as they weave in and out of a crowd of feet, legs and knees. Some are covered by garments and tunics, and others are not, revealing sweaty, dirty limbs. She keeps looking up to the sky for respite, to breathe a little easier, but it has been several minutes since she saw it; all she can see now is the back of bobbling heads and visibly strained faces.

The beat of her heart continues to gather pace as she slowly drowns in the noise and melee. She needs air, but there is none. She squeezes her father's hand tighter still, desperately hoping to be rescued. He looks down and, upon seeing her panic-stricken face, picks her up and holds her close. Now able to lay eyes on the clear blue sky, she rests her head on his shoulders and is once more able to breathe. Her fast, racing heart fills him with despair. There was a time when she had it all; joy, peace of mind, the security of two parents who cherished her.

Despite the chaos around them, his mind drifts to happier times; on the front porch of their grand mansion with his wife and daughter, idly allowing the day to drift by. With eyes closed, his head is resting on the lap of Penelope, who is busy knitting a garment for their daughter. Imara, barely three-years-old, is sat on the floor, surrounded by her dolls, gingerly combing their hair and dressing them in preparation for a lavish banquet.

"Papa see," she said, turning to her father with one of the dolls. *"Livia is ready."*

"Ready for what?" asked Pelonious, smiling with eyes still closed.

"Ready for the banquet, Papa. Get ready too, Papa."

"What time is this banquet, my darling daughter?"

"The banquet is soon, Papa. Get ready now."

"Alright, alright, I will. Just as soon as all your dolls are ready."

"They are ready now, Papa, look."

Pelonious opened his eyes to see his daughter's dolls sat in row, immaculately dressed in an array of brightly coloured tunics, with strings used as belts around their midriff. "Wow! Don't they look gorgeous, Imara. But I think that one's tunic is a little short. You should probably dress her again; she looks a little odd."

"Which one, papa?" asked Imara, as ever, believing her father's every word.

"That one," he replied, pointing to her left. *"And I believe the one next to her could do with a change too."*

"Oh, okay, Papa, I'll get them some new tunics." She promptly got up and sprinted into the main house, shouting the name of the servant girl.

"There was nothing wrong with those tunics, you just want a little more sleep. You're terrible!" laughed Penelope. *"Stop playing tricks on our little girl."*

"So, why didn't you intervene?"

"Because there was no point. She always does whatever you say. She is surely your daughter, Pelonious."

He smiled, knowing it to be true. A special bond existed between the two of them, right from the first moment they laid eyes on each other. Theirs was a relationship few could fathom or understand. Before long, Imara was back, with servant girl in tow.

"Papa, which one?" she asked, pointing to the five different doll tunics in the servant girl's hands. This time, he opened his eyes and sat up before getting to his feet and walking towards the servant girl.

102

Standing at attention and unaccustomed to being in such close proximity to her master, the servant girl held her breath, and stretched her rigid arms forward.

"Hmmm..." said Pelonious, leaning forward a little to peer at the tunics. "This one, and this one."

"But that's a red dress, Papa. Look," Imara said, pointing to one of the other dolls, also dressed in a red tunic.

"Ahh! In that case, this one."

"Yellow! I like yellow, Papa."

None of this is her fault; she did not request to enter this world. She does not deserve what is about to happen to her.

The crowd makes way as yet another company approaches, marching as one into an uncertain future. Pelonious is irritated by the improperly tied bootstraps of one of the soldiers. His eyes widen, gritted teeth behind his clenched jaws. For a brief moment, he wants to scold the reckless soldier for lowering standards. If they knew who it was they were passing, they would be more thorough about their appearance. But he is able to stop himself. He is like any other man now. Those heady days are long past; consigned to an abandoned previous life. He gathers himself and holds his little girl tight, comforted by the smell of her soft, wavy hair.

"Papa, where are they going?"

"To do battle, princess. To war."

"Why?"

He sighs. The same question had tormented him for months on end; endless sieges in the name of the empire's unabated thirst for conquests. Victories, glories, fame; for what, exactly? For a time, it had got the better of him; he enjoyed the power and prestige, and the fame that came with it. He became known across the land as the Ruthless General, feared by the enemies that Rome created for itself. He was revered far and wide, born to kill and destroy anything standing in the way of the empire's world domination. He revelled in it; each victory increased his wealth and power to unimaginable levels, and yet the more he gained, the less it mattered. One day he decided he had had enough and put down his sword for good, believing there was more to life than butchery, wealth and power. Although many in the corridors of power objected, there was nothing they could do to deter or stop him. Who could dare stand in his way?

"Who knows, my love? It just... never ends."

Once the soldiers pass, the chaos resumes, and they continue to squeeze their way through the mass of people around them.

"Are you sure about this, dear brother?" sounded a voice beside him. "Have you thought about...?"

"Enough, sister!" says Pelonious, in a hushed but firm tone. "How many more times must I explain? You have my orders; do exactly as I've asked. No more questions."

There is a steely glare in his eyes, one his sibling – Antarta – has not seen for many years. He was, for a moment, forceful, detached and unapproachable.

"Look! Over there," he says, looking towards a ship on the far left. There was nothing extraordinary about it, save for the emblem on the mast. His emblem. His ship. "Remember, you are not to say my name. I am nobody, just an ordinary traveller. Nobody is to know. Understand?"

There is no answer. Antarta heard him but is too lost in her thoughts to respond. The little girl in his arms will soon be in her care, and she fears she may not have the wherewithal. How will Imara respond when she realises her father is leaving her?

Everyone knows how close they are. What if she never recovers?

"Antarta, did you hear me? I said..."

"I heard you, brother. It's just... are you sure about this? Look at her. She's already lost her mother, and now..." Her words fade as the realisation of what is really troubling her becomes apparent. She places her tear-soaked eyes on Imara, who has fallen asleep in her father's arms, safe from the madness around them.

Pelonious gently places his hand on his sister's shoulder and lays his eyes on hers, affectionate and caring. "I have to do this. You know I do. For her sake, if anything else. I'm no good to her like this."

For a moment, his sullen eyes, usually so adept at concealing the sorrow that is slowly crushing his heart, paint the true picture. She can see his pain. She places her hand on his. She is drowning in sadness, but she must get herself together and do her duty. Without warning, his tenderness is gone. He withdraws his hand and takes a small step back, cradling his daughter one last time before handing her over.

"I will visit regularly, but she's yours now. Look after her like you would..."

"Do you really feel you need to say that?" she asks, surprised by his words.

"Thank you for this, dear sister."

"What will I tell her when she wakes?"

"Tell her the truth. I've travelled in search of fixing the world. We have spoken, she and I, she knows why." He places his right hand on his little girl's hair and his left arm around his sister's arm, drawing both of them close one final time, squeezing tight for several seconds before letting go. He turns around and makes his way to the ship, determined and unflinching, not looking back. Just as he is climbing, he hears the only voice that can stop him.

"Papa, no! No, Papa, don't go! Don't go, Papa; Papa, please!"

Every part of him yearns to turn around and run back to her, but what use would that be? He is no good to her as he is; she is better off without him.

"Turn around and go, sister," he whispers to himself, refusing to turn his head for fear of changing his mind. "Go, damn it!"

Again and again, Imara screams as her aunt bundles her away. Her world is tumbling down, ending before her very eyes. Despite his promises, she somehow senses she will never lay eyes on him again. The more she screams, the more life drains away, slowly morphing into a cold, silent haze. Her broken heart, pumping profusely some seconds ago, begins to fade, resembling a loose morsel, bereft of will or desire. She never recovers. The light goes out that morning.

"Where to?" asks the ship's captain.

"Saxony."

"And what is your business there?"

With eyes fixed on the mass of water on the horizon, Pelonious chuckles.

"I said, what is your..."

"Redemption," says Pelonious, this time looking the captain in his eye. Taken aback by the cold authority of his eyes, the captain retreats, making way for Pelonious to pass. Pelonious' answer surprises the captain, unaware of where it came from. Redemption – has that always been his reason for this sojourn? The guilt of his actions as both a soldier and a general has been simmering beneath the surface for some time. It is the reason he retired so abruptly all those years ago, letting go of something he knew to be wrong, and striving to be a better person, coming to terms with the notion that all men and women are equal.

His love for Penelope taught him that. Her death left him in no doubt that he was being punished for his often cruel and brutal actions. But seeking personal redemption at the cost of abandoning a five-year-old girl...?

For several days, Pelonious ponders the notion of redemption and what it means to him, why it is so important. He left the daughter he loves to protect her, believing that, by separating himself from her, she will be safe – far from whatever punishment the deity might inflict on him. But deep down, he knows there is more, a lurking mist prevailing over his actions.

The three-month journey was relatively peaceful and without incident, save for the death of a seven-year-old boy – one day he was happily playing with his sister and the next gravely ill, stricken by fever, and never to use his feet again. For several days, his parents attended him, desperately trying to nurse him back to health. But every person on the boat knew their attempts were futile. At first, Pelonious would sometimes sit with them. He never said anything, just sat with them, staring at the deck with his sullen eyes. He visited the family every day, at times sitting with them in silence for several hours. Then one day, as he was making his way to them, he heard the blood-curdling scream of a heartbroken mother. For several minutes she screamed as her life shattered into a million pieces, until eventually replaced by a deep and desperate cry as her energy dissipated. Pelonious stood there for some time, motionless, unable to decide what to do. Only when the crying ceased was he able to move, slowly making his way to the side of the boat.

As he stared at the reflection of the sun's gentle glow, he was strangely captivated by the rhythmic patterns of the water, gentle ripples kissing the boat, then gliding away again. He wondered how far back each would go before returning. Metres? Miles? It was impossible to tell. The water was as one – no telling where it began or ended. But it did end. Somehow it always ended – everything did. In that moment, he understood the reason for his journey.

Saxony, an island reputed to be a fortress of barbarians – a horde of bloodthirsty species in human form, with no fear of death. Despite their lack of numbers and the disorganised manner of war, time and time again they inflicted the most painful defeats on Rome's beleaguered army. But, despite marshes drenched in Roman blood, it was also an island adorned with regions of serenity and beauty. Villagers went about their daily lives in the countryside, surrounded by picturesque terrains – lush fields of dewy grass, the tranquillity of hills and valleys, streams and meandering rivers, plus an assortment of idyllic forests. Perfect for monasteries.

Pelonious had long heard about the monasteries hidden away in secluded parts of the island, havens of peace and solitude. One in particular, Nantaire, has caught his attention. Located halfway up a mountain, it is hidden from the naked eye. With rooms and temples etched deep into various crevices, it is an ideal location for what he needs to do, a place to pursue his findings without distraction or attention.

It does not take long for him to convert to Christianity; Rome's deities have never served him particularly well, and he is determined to get as far away from his previous life as possible. Christianity becomes a critical stage of his journey to redemption. With Christianity comes love and unending hope, but the more Pelonious tries to surrender his heart completely, the more he considers the pointlessness of life.

Love, hope, joy, sadness, anguish, grief – to what end? The biggest weakness of any man or woman is whatever he or she loves. At some point, the object of that love will no longer be there. Surely, there is a way to protect oneself from the inevitable misery that would always follow – to feel nothing, to be safe from harm, shielded from the perennial turmoil of life's journey.

For days on end, he analyses the nature of mankind, penning endless scrolls of thought as he dissects the reasoning of the mind. The more he thinks, the deeper he sinks into a dark abyss of confusion and despair. The faith he has converted to proves to be of little help. The redemption he so desperately craves taunts him like a hideous ghostly shadow.

Still, he keeps searching for his answers, refusing to accept there is no solution, until one day, Pelonious reaches the end of himself.

If there is a God, he or she has either grossly miscalculated, or perhaps revels in humankind's suffering. The only solution is to remove the very source of joy and sorrow.

The mind needs to function, no matter what, even if to simply do and not do. But the heart, what good is it? The vessel that powers the human body is surely the root of all grief and sorrow.

"Brother Benedict has been asking for you. Says he hasn't seen you for several days. Best you attend mass today, don't you think?" says a kind voice from behind him.

Pelonious has been there for days, fingertips bleeding from ceaseless writing. A mountain of paper is piled up in front of him, scrolls scattered all over the floor, echoing his tortured mind.

"Did you hear me, Pelonious? You really should come today. And besides..."

His eyes slowly scan the mess of scrolls and paper around them, noticing the etchings on the walls before descending once more on his piti- ful friend, a bashful monk whose gaunt features portray a man that has not eaten for several days. Whatever happens, he has to get him out of the dark room, even if just to wash and eat something.

"Come, brother. Please. You have to step away from here for a few hours. This isn't at all healthy," the monk says, gently placing his left hand on Pelonious' right shoulder. As soon as he does so, Pelonious turns his head to face him.

The ex-general's eyes are hollow, bereft of life or feeling, and yet blazing with a strange kind of wildness. Suddenly seized with a cold and grip- ping fear, the monk takes a step back and is frozen to the ground for several seconds, too scared to move or speak. He can see that his friend is no more; something else has taken control of his body.

Desperate, the monk wants to plead with his friend to let go of whatever he is searching for, but it is all too clear that it is too late; in front of him is a shell that can no longer be reached. His hands shake a little as he places them on Pelonious' shoulder one last time, smiling nervously before he turns around to leave.

Pelonious sits down again and grabs his writing utensil to resume his beleaguered work but is unable to continue. Why continue when he has already arrived at an unquestionable end? A blunt knife lies on the chaotic piles of paper; he had picked it up a few days earlier as his reality began to take shape, then tossed it aside again, hoping to find an alternative remedy.

He stares at the blade for several seconds as he considers what he is about to do, then plunges it deep into the left side of his chest. In a comatose, yet frenzied state, he chisels around the edges of his heart, undeterred by the searing pain and ferocious gushing of blood.

As his blood-soaked right hand slides along the handle of the blade, he clasps his left hand around it to get a firmer hold, all the while maintaining the intensity of his butchery.

Several minutes later, numb to the desecration around him, he drops the knife, and wrenches out his heart. Should he not be dead? Somehow, he has survived the experience. Staring back at him is the organ that is the orchestrator of all suffering and grief, clenched in his bloodied right hand, still beating. His tunic and everything around him are lost in an orgy of blood.

With a heavy sigh, Pelonious sits. He feels nothing: body, soul, mind – all are dead to feeling or emotion. And yet, he is alive.

For many hours he just sits there, staring at his beating heart.

7

Pearl Street

A cuckoo clock sat proudly on a tall mahogany mantelpiece, undeterred by the many more interesting objects and ornaments in the room: much sought-after paintings by prominent artists from past and present, delicate and priceless vases from different corners of the globe, surreal looking pictures of momentous events that shaped the world, portraits of former Prime Ministers and other global leaders. Every thirty minutes, the clock made a strained winding sound, gathering strength for the final thirty minutes of the hour, determined to keep going, refusing to be retired or left behind. And on the hour, every hour, it re-announced itself as the master of ceremonies, chiming vociferously as its doors opened, making way for the cuckoo to make its grand entrance. Adorned in red, black and yellow feathers, the cuckoo sang as beautifully as ever, serenading the vicinity with its enchanting voice.

Something about the clock fascinated Justina. Its stoic features seemed out of place in a far more modern and refined world, but somehow it still held sway, unflinchingly refusing to be intimidated by the magnificence around it. No matter how exquisite, rare, or expensive other objects in the room were, they stopped whatever they were doing and paid homage to it every hour.

In the centre of the room, separating the brown leather sofa and two armchairs, was a low-lying, charcoal black coffee table with thick, short legs, spanning two metres in width, as though placed there to intimidate waiting guests, causing them to consider the magnitude of the room they were sitting in: the Prime Minister's unofficial waiting room, adjacent to her office. Specifically created to accommodate dignitaries who wanted private meetings away from the glare of the interfering media, it alone had three doors: one leading to the main corridor, another opening directly into her office, and the third to a secret passage, enabling visitors to exit the premises away from prying eyes.

Placed on the centre of the coffee table were a dictionary and a thesaurus. They were peculiar things to have on a table, but apparently, the reason stemmed from the Prime Minister's lack of patience. Famed for her quick wit, intelligence, and remarkable ability to perfectly understand and speak over twelve languages, she had long struggled to manage her frustration when meeting or liaising with those less astute. Rumour had it that after striking a new, far-reaching climate deal with the president of one of the European nations, she signed the agreement, then politely asked her contemporary whether they could step into her office to have their pictures taken for the papers, so that she could proceed to do whatever she had to do next.

She had assessed all possible variables and concluded that the president would sign the treaty once his aids had gone through it. As ever, she was several paces ahead of everyone else. The dictionary and thesaurus were a subtle, inadvertent warning to visitors to be properly prepared; to ensure they were well up-to-speed, not just with the topic of their impending meeting, but with their understanding and use of words.

In the far corner was a picture of some of the most powerful leaders in the world – presidents of the US, China, Russia, France, the German Chancellor, and the president of the increasingly more powerful African Union. Many believe she not only orchestrated the three-day event but determined its direction and outcome. And yet, rather than being at the centre of the picture, she was hovering on the periphery, an ordinary looking black woman, away from sight and attention. To the unknowing eye, she looked like a leader of a smaller and less significant nation, permitted to join the picture as a kind favour.

The day Sarah Atticus Clark won the Conservative party leadership contest, and by default became the British Prime Minister, was momentous to everyone but her. The world took notice as the first black female British Prime Minister gave her first speech.

She spoke eloquently but without fuss or razzmatazz, as was her style, assuring the British public the nation was in safe, prudent hands. Much of the world watched her walk through the hallowed door of 10 Downing Street in the safe knowledge that things would more or less stay the same. The sudden passing of the previous Prime Minister in a hideous helicopter crash had sent shockwaves across Europe and much of the western world; there was dire need for calm assurance and stability. Sarah Clark was a reliable and safe pair of hands, who could be trusted to preserve the status quo. Unknown to them, she would be the last British Prime Minister to reside in 10 Downing Street.

Within three years of her premiership, the seat of power moved from 10 Downing Street to 4 Pearl Street, a huge, modern building that accommodated all the government departments. Despite fierce opposition to the move, she got her way, insisting that, contrary to the public outcry regarding the stupidity of housing all the government departments in one place, there would be no security risks as the building and its vicinity were impenetrable.

She was right; not only had it been built to withstand any kind of armed or ballistic attack but the surrounding area was a fortress nobody in their right mind would dare approach. Nobody really knew where she actually lived. Some said she still secretly resided at number 10, while others claimed she had a sprawling apartment in the new building at 4 Pearl Street.

Known in her inner circle as the 'friendly assassin', Sarah Clark was a woman who nobody ever saw coming. Forever softly spoken, there was nothing forceful or dangerous about her, no 'X-factor'. Though pretty and always sporting her neatly combed afro hair with great pride, her petite, slender stature gave those around her a false sense of security.

Her charm was a supportive and friendly demeanour, one that led most to see her as a trusted ally, as against a dangerous force for change. During her university days, she was elected student union president due to her kind and gentle nature – someone who would put her kind arms around those in need. Within two months of her presidency, she had engineered the student protests that brought an abrupt end to the much-loathed student loans. Throughout the six-month protest, she appealed for peace and calm, urging students to cease their antics and return to learning, but in reality, she had been the silent force behind the movement. To this day, very few people realised that she both planned and determined the outcome.

Within six months of being Prime Minister, she turned her attention to the crime of the slave trade, insisting that Britain had to apologise and pay reparations for the cruelty inflicted on so many Africans between the fifteenth and nineteenth century. Despite much opposition, she not only silenced her opponents and critics but led other European nations to do the same.

Her ruthless determination to get things done knew no bounds. And yet, somehow, in the eyes of her opponents, she remained a seemingly soft touch. No sooner had she overcome one summit was her ruthless determination to get her way swiftly forgotten, almost as though it had never happened.

The daughter of a Nigerian father and Ugandan mother, both of whom were foreign ambassadors to countries in the middle east, she was mainly raised by her grandmother, who lived in a three-bedroom house in Manchester. Her parents loved her but were unable to pay her as much attention as they would have liked. As a result, her greatest influence as a child was her dear grandmother, who doted on her as though she were her very own.

Nana, as she was affectionately called, was a kind, unassuming, but self-assured woman who, though doting on Sarah, meticulously schooled her granddaughter about the machinations of the human mind – specifically, the importance of getting one's way without others realising it. It was during those formative years that Sandie, as she was fondly called, learned the art of masking her true desires behind a veneer of kindness and patience.

She loved and admired her grandmother like no other. Not that she did not love her parents; she did, but she greatly admired her Nana, wanting to be like her in every way, paying attention to her behaviour and mannerisms, soaking it all in like a sponge with water. No matter how big or small, she seized every opportunity to learn her ways, for they always worked; every situation, challenge, obstacle, Nana got her way. When Sandie got into trouble for shoving a female student during her first year of secondary school, Nana had been livid – not because of the act of shoving, but because of her inability to achieve her objective via more subtle means.

"So, you shoved her, Sandie? Shoved? Have you learned anything at all?"

"But she called me a…"

"Quiet! Stop whimpering, girl. Getting emotional and upset gets you nothing, you hear me? Nothing!" She had waited for her words to sink in before continuing. "Now, what should you have done?"

"Smiled and—"

"No, Sandie, what on earth would you be smiling about? She called you a black bitch; what are you smiling about?"

"Sorry, Nana."

"Don't be sorry, girl; think – it's very simple. First, you show that you're hurt by her comment. Yes, look pathetic and stupid if you must, then tell her there was no need to be so rude and abusive. She would have been rude again, no doubt. Then you smile and walk away. Do you know why?"

"I think… I'm not sure, Nana."

"Because you're already planning her downfall. If someone hurts you, you make sure you hurt them back so hard they can never get up again. And nobody must ever know it was you that destroyed them."

Sitting with Nana in the headmaster's office a few days later, Sarah witnessed her grandmother at her very best, weaving a spell over the head with her innocence and charm.

"Once again, I am so sorry for Sandie's behaviour. There really is no excuse, and we fully accept whatever punishment you deem fit, principal."

"Thank you, Ms. Clark; it's refreshing to hear a parent speak as you have done. I always say that we are a reflection of our parents' upbringing. With a guardian such as yourself, Sarah's future can only be bright."

"You're too kind, principal. So, what is her punishment? In fact, I'm still deciding on the one to give her myself. It's just..."

"Please, speak freely, Ms. Clark."

"Well... I just worry, you see."

"About what?"

"The other child... she was obviously wronged by Sandie, but I wonder whether... Oh, never mind."

"Please, Ms. Clark, feel free to voice your concern," said the principal, now slightly leaning forward with furrowed eyes.

"Well, I just wonder whether we might be indirectly harming the other child if she herself isn't punished in some small way. Just concerned about her future."

"Hmmm... I think you have a valid point there, Ms. Clark. I shall definitely consider the matter."

A few days later, both girls were put in detention for two weeks. Riled by her unexpected punishment, Tammy Graham, the other girl, stormed up to Sarah during break-time and shoved her to the ground, screaming abuse and kicking her several times, like a wild, deranged miscreant. She had to be pulled away by several teachers, each with their own bruise to show for their efforts. She was promptly expelled and never seen or heard of again; rumour had it that she never truly recovered from her meltdown and spent much of the proceeding decades in and out of psychiatric care homes. Was she pushed over the edge by what happened, or did she always have psychological issues? Whatever the case, when Sarah returned home with a grazed right knee and swelling above her right eye, the first thing her Nana said was: "As expected. At least that's the end of it."

Liza sat up, moving to the edge of the sofa, yawning as she rubbed her eyes. They had been waiting for over two hours. She had expected some waiting time; it was the Prime Minister, after all, but not two hours – two hours suggested a distinct lack of courtesy, or at the very least, abject disorganisation. Tired of sitting down, she stood up, folding her arms as she slowly made her way towards the thickly veiled window. There she remained, staring out of the window, feeling disconnected from the world on the other side of it. None of it mattered to her anymore; it was merely a collection of people and things that needed to be dealt with, put right... ended. Rolling her right thumb on the inside of her palm, she could feel the heat of her fire, ready to blaze in whatever direction she chose. She could control it now, bend it to her personal whim in any shape or form whenever she chose.

"She'll see you now."

Still seated on the sofa, Justina looked up to see a bespectacled man of average height in a charcoal grey, single-breasted suit. It was as though he had been expertly manufactured by the wooden walls. With his right hand clasped in his left, he remained still for several seconds, enabling Justina to regain her composure. She was not the first to be startled by his entrance. In fact, she had taken it quite well; the thermometer of reactions usually ranged from shrieks and screams to an inability to respond to anything for several slow minutes.

He was especially impressed with the one by the window – not even a flinch; she simply heard his voice and continued staring at whatever it was she was staring at for a few seconds, then nonchalantly turned and walked towards him, although something about her unnerved him a little.

"Coming?" said Liza, pausing by the door to turn to Justina.

"Er, yeah… I mean, yes," replied Justina, still feeling somewhat dishevelled. Such things would not have surprised her in the past, but for some reason, even the smallest things were now capable of shaking her.

The door opened to a short hallway, about twenty-five to thirty metres long, with brown wooden walls either side, imposing themselves on visitors, like erstwhile founders of the Spanish inquisition. The man led them through another door, and suddenly they were in her office. The room was a delicate mix of classic and modern furniture, with the lighting choosing to favour only certain areas, leaving various sections to their own precarious devices. At its head was a large glass table with thick, silver legs, without draws or compartments. The laptop and phone sitting on top of it, the red mahogany chair behind, confirming it to be her work desk. The only other thing on the glass table was a picture frame, facing away from the prying eyes of visitors. Behind the table were two large, rectangular windows, one on either side, adorned with thick, transparent, linen blinds that stretched from the ceiling to the black ceramic floor tiles. A large, antique, black coffee table with two mauve leather sofas on either side hugged the centre of the room.

"Please, take a seat. She'll be down in a few minutes." He was now standing by one of the leather sofas.

"Down?" replied Justina. "Not sure I understand. Is there—"

"Up there," whispered the man as he motioned his head upwards, interrupting Justina to prevent her from disturbing whatever discussion his boss was having with her visitor. On the right-hand side of the room was a staircase, about fifteen steps in all, leading to another landing that incorporated several shelves of books and ample walking space.

They could just about make out her small stature. She was wearing a trouser suit and flat plimsolls, with her right hand placed on the wooden railing. The sparse lighting prevented them from getting a good view of her guest, who was facing away from them. Though visibly taller, all they could make out was a long, black gown with a hood, which, because it was down, revealed a stream of straight, black hair, flowing to the shoulders and beyond. Whatever they were saying was been said in hushed tones, and the person in the gown seemed to be doing most of the talking. Rather than do as the man suggested, Liza made her way to one of the big, rectangular windows and continued her nonchalant gazing.

A man and a woman were sitting on one of the benches in the quadrangle outside – the man eating a sandwich and the woman picking at a box of salad. They did not say a word to each other, focusing only on their food. Liza wondered why they bothered. Why eat together in silence? Neither even looked in the other's direction; surely there were more pleasant ways to spend lunchtime.

Once both had finished eating, they leaned back, staring into the open space in front of them. The man placed his left hand on the metal rims of the bench, and some seconds later, the woman did likewise with her right, both hands inching towards each other until they were lightly touching. There they remained, on the edge of each other, for several seconds, cherishing the fleeting moment before both reluctantly pulled away. Like strangers in an awkward predicament, they sat in silence for another few minutes before the woman turned to say something to the man, who promptly replied, and in an instant, both were up and walking in different directions.

The longer they were being made to wait, the more irritable Liza grew. After some minutes of staring out of the window, with the blinds gently caressing her forehead, she turned her head to the upper landing, hoping to find the Prime Minister was done and ready to attend to them but was distracted by the picture frame on the table. Inside was a picture of a sweet-looking little girl in the arms of an old lady. She could tell from the picture that they were close, a strong bond very few could have or understand. The old lady seemed proud of the little girl, and she, in return, seemed to adore her. The lady was way too old to be the little girl's mother.

The more Liza looked at the picture, the more the relationship intrigued her. But as she allowed her mind to analyse and wonder, she felt the weight of a set of eyes on her – an eerie feeling that caused her heart to miss a beat. As soon as she looked up towards the upper level, the person in the long gown turned her head away, shifting a little as the Prime Minister continued speaking.

Liza tried to get a better view, moving a few inches to her left and straining her eyes, but it was no use, as the angle and the lighting rendered it impossible. In that moment, she realised whoever it was did not want to be recognised, expertly using the room's lighting to dissolve into the shadows.

Suddenly, the Prime Minister turned away and started to descend the staircase. "Please, accept my apology for making you wait so long, ladies; one of those days. Did Michael offer you tea or coffee? You must be Justina," she said, offering her right hand.

"Yes, ma'am, I'm Justina, and she's—"

"Liza, right?" she said warmly, conveying an easy and genuine charm and kindness. "I've heard so much about you two. I feel like an over-excited boyband fan, on the verge of fainting from hysteria. I can assure you the honour is all mine. Care to join us, Liza? You don't have to, of course, so long as you can hear us, and we can hear you."

Still fascinated by the person she left unattended on the upper level, Liza remained where she was, in part listening but mostly trying to get a better sighting of the individual upstairs.

"Tea and coffee please, Michael," said the Prime Minister, leaning over the desk phone. "Do we still have those flaky things? I take it you wouldn't say no to biscuits, ladies. I came across these flaky ones a few days ago. Incredible! You really must try some; you'll never think of biscuits in the same way again. Yes?"

"Sounds great," replied Justina, admiring her perfectly combed, short afro hair. The Prime Minister took pride in who she was and how she looked. She was authentic, unspoilt by the superficial expectations of western culture.

"And you?" she said, looking in Liza's direction.

"Thanks," replied Liza, refusing to move in case the person upstairs mistakenly moved into the wrong kind of lighting.

"Wonderful! Now that's settled, let's get to work. I take it you're prepared for what is about to occur?" she said as she placed herself on the sofa opposite Justina.

Justina leaned forward a little, conscious of the importance of being intelligent and alert. She glanced to her left, unsure of Liza's attention, then turned to face the Prime Minister. She had been groomed for this from such an early age, her life entirely devoted to restoring order and control. And yet, in that moment, words failed her. The magnitude of the meeting was overwhelming her, causing her to hesitate and stutter like a spluttering old engine – most unlike the girl that had always been so sure of herself. Was this another sign of a weakness that had always been there, hidden beneath the veneer of calmness and control, or was it a result of new and unwelcome feelings of doubt? She glanced in Liza's direction again, hoping to be rescued from her moment of shame, but got nothing. "I… think…"

"Yes, we are," said Liza. She made her way towards them, finally deciding to join the meeting. "From what I gather, all forms of emotion will be erased at the end of this month – in two-week's time?"

"That's right, Liza. Please, join us," replied the Prime Minister, patting the empty space next to her. "But, and this is the main reason for this meeting, as I'm sure you know, things rarely go as smoothly as one plans or hopes. In fact, I can categorically say that every success I've had, every decision, has come with some kind of a swerver."

"Swerver?" said Justina, finally regaining her composure.

"Oh, forgive my slang. By 'swerver', I mean challenge, something going wrong. You see, in time you'll come to understand that very few things go according to plan. The world sees the positive outcomes and the results but is unaware of the numerous chinks that occurred along the way; nothing ever goes according to plan."

"I'm not sure I understand you. What could go wrong?" enquired Justina.

"Well, now, let's see... how do I put this?"

"You want us to seize them, don't you? The ones it may not work on," said Liza, comforted in the knowledge that their work will be on-going.

"Yes, but a little more than that. You see, for us to have the peace and order we so desire, for us to rid the world of suffering and grief once and for all, we must ensure that every breathing person is on the same page. For the sake of humanity, there can be no baggage."

A long silence followed. Justina was still unsure of what the Prime Minister was referring to, but a feeling of dread was building up inside her.

"You want us to take them out, right? Kill anyone it doesn't work on?" said Liza, calmly looking into the Prime Minister's eyes, waiting for the answer she craved.

The Prime Minister glanced up towards the upper landing, then slowly lowered her head again. "Unfortunately, to ensure we never go back to the dark days again, we simply must do whatever needs to be done."

Despite her steel and control, Justina had never considered the grave thought of having to kill innocent people. She had killed Annabel, but that was just one person, a means to an end. But this? This sounded like an on-going slaughter of the innocent. "Is there no other way?"

"I really wish there was. The very thought of it keeps me awake at night for hours on end; it is the most painful thing I've ever had to agree to. When Zoldon first pointed it out, I would have none of it. After all, to do such a thing is tantamount to murdering people – a lot of people! But over time, as I'm sure you will, I came to realise that to not do it would be to allow pain and suffering to continue and worsen for centuries to come. In my eyes, that is an even greater crime, don't you think?" She paused again, concerned the two young ladies might not have the wherewithal to do what was required. Liza clearly did not need much convincing, but Justina seemed more than reluctant. "Look – and what I'm about to say mustn't go beyond these walls – every single person in this building has already given their lives to this cause... literally."

"You mean they're—"

"No, not what you think, but in terms of having already sacrificed their feelings, hopes, aspirations for the greater good. I won't go into details – I'm sure Zoldon will elaborate – but every person here has already been neutered, all freed of their various emotions. To the best of my knowledge, it worked perfectly on all of them. Although, only time will tell as to the accuracy of my observations – no doubt there'll be a few still clinging on to their former weaknesses, but that is where you two come in."

There was nothing forceful or cold about her words or manner. Rather, she conveyed genuine anguish about the painstaking decision she found herself forced to make. She pursed her lips, closing her moist eyes for a few seconds before continuing.

"I know this must be very difficult for you both. It is the last thing I want. Unfortunately—"

"There's no other way," said Liza, growing impatient with the conversation. Someone had to ensure things worked as planned, and it might as well be them. "I agree, some will resist."

The Prime Minister took a deep breath, then slowly exhaled before turning to Liza. "No, there isn't. Ahh, Michael, what took you so long?"

"We'd ran out of the biscuits you requested for, ma'am, so I sent someone to buy some more."

"Oh, very good, Michael, thank you. Now, ladies, you simply must try these; they really are quite incredible!"

As the Prime Minister leaned forward towards Justina, with tray in hand, Liza took the opportunity to get a better glimpse of the person on the upper landing. But when she looked up, there was nobody there.

8

A Night Out

"How did you find this place?" asked Justina, standing with Liza opposite a queue of twenty people or so. "I would never have guessed there was anything remotely interesting around here, let alone a popular bar."

"That's one of the things I love about it," Liza answered, excitedly watching the queue bustle before her. "To everyone else, it's just an interesting looking door with a weird name, on the side of the high street. Strangely enough, it was my mum that first brought me, ages ago – about a month into our first year. Think she wanted to show me that Oxford would be fun, or something. Must have done her research. Anyway, never seen her here since."

"How did she know you'd like it?"

"She's my mum, I guess she has a fair idea of the kind of place I'd like."

Justina liked it when Liza spoke more freely. The dark cloud that forever hovered above her momentarily drifted away. It always came back, of course, but during those precious few hours, her company was far more enjoyable. It was strange for her to feel such relief whenever the other Liza surfaced. After all, for so long, she had been the one in charge, so to speak; in control of her emotions and whatever situation she found herself in. But over the years, Liza had grown more withdrawn, darker, moody – an uneasy presence that often unsettled her. Something had clearly shifted; even her appearance was a little different – all in black as always, but the stilettoes, tight leather trousers and the loose-fitting black blouse gave her a slightly lighter feel.

They stood there, watching the queue of people for several seconds, ladies in long coats and high heels, others braving the biting cold weather in short length dresses, skirts, and light frocks, determined to celebrate their hard-earned physiques at whatever cost. On the other side were a cluster of smokers, a couple visibly well-inebriated, chatting and laughing the night away.

"So, are we going in, then?" asked Justina, beginning to wonder why they were looking on like curious voyeurs.

"Yeah, of course; just waiting… Ah, there he is," Liza replied as a handsome-looking man with a long, black ponytail appeared at the door. They crossed the street and headed straight to the front of the queue, envious eyes stripping them bare.

"Hey, you," said Liza as she kissed her friend on the cheek. "Rob, this is my friend, Justina, Jus, this is Rob."

"Hi, nice to meet you, Rob," said Justina, leaning forward to shake his hand.

"Pleasure to meet you too, Jus. Come on, follow me guys."

Much to Justina's surprise, they proceeded to descend a steep and narrow, well-lit staircase. At the bottom was another door that led them to a cosy-yet-vibrant bar and lounge, sparsely lit to create a relaxed, private ambiance. She could never have imagined such a scene from the High Street. It was as though every trendy-but-down-to-Earth individual in the city was there; all thirty of them. They all seemed to know each other, basking in their seemingly members-only bar, safe from the pestering tentacles of real life. They were special, handpicked by the owner himself to enjoy their own private paradise. Some were at the bar, chatting and flirting with the barmen and women, others were seated in comfy looking leather chairs and sofas at tables, hidden away in various secluded sections.

"Is it always this busy?" asked Justina.

"Sorry?" replied Liza, unable to hear over the music and chatter.

"The bar, is it always like this? It's so busy. But I love it!"

"Oh yeah, most nights, apart from Mondays. Came here on a Monday once and I'm pretty sure I was the only person here that night. Didn't bother me much, though. I quite liked it like that, actually. Rob and I ended up drinking all night – it took me about a week to recover. Look, over there, I've spotted a free table. Quick, let's nab it before someone else does," said Liza, swiftly heading towards the available table. They made their way to the far corner of the lounge area, passing several alcohol-induced conversations on the way, ranging from heated arguments about politics to the pandemic of racism and hate on social media. Not the kind of meaningful chatter one would expect in such a trendy bar, ultimately making the scene more endearing.

"I love this place," said Justina as they arrived at the table. "It's trendy and chic, but also real: real people, real conversations. When we were waiting outside, I feared it would be full of superficial hipsters. Nice find!"

"Yeah, know what you mean. It's a nice mix in here. Personally, I like the lighting the most. You can sit in a corner on your own sometimes and not be noticed or bothered by anyone."

"You would say that, wouldn't you?" said Justina, chuckling about Liza's penchant for preferring her own company to that of others. "So, Rob... Anything I should know?"

"Huh? Me and Rob? Don't be silly! Just friends. Well, now we are anyway."

"What, you mean you two once had a..."

"Ages ago. Just the one time. We were off our heads. It was fun, but we both agreed it should never happen again."

"And has it?"

"Nope. Been there, done that. Now just friends. Besides, who has time for dating anyway? Got enough on our plates."

"Yea, guess you're right," said Justina, again wondering whether dating her Scottish friend was such a good idea. She liked him, no doubt about that. She found his strange nervousness endearing and always felt so at ease with him. She often wondered what life would be like if she was just... normal – no mission to worry about, open to the vagaries of love like any other naïve individual. She noticed a couple to their right. From the way they were subconsciously mirroring each other's movements, she could tell they were in the early stages of a budding romance; both sets of eyes were hypnotically fixed on the other, fingers gingerly touching, testing the waters of their new-found affection. Every now and then, one would look away nervously, as though gathering breath before plunging back into their crush-infected ocean. She knew how they felt. If only she could surrender to it, herself.

"Sad, isn't it?" said Liza, obstructing Justina's wishful thinking.

"Sorry?"

"It's sad, seeing people fall for each other like that. Never lasts. Always ends in tears. Always!"

For a moment, Justina was tempted to ask Liza to stop being so negative but remembered her place just in time. "Yeah, true. I guess they don't know any better," she muttered, quickly snapping out of her precarious state. "That reminds me, are we going to address the elephant in the room, or are we going to continue to pretend yesterday didn't happen?"

Liza did not reply for several seconds. She seemed distracted by something over Justina's shoulder. For a brief moment, the glare in her eyes announced the return of her cloud. Justina turned her head to see what had caught her attention but noticed nothing in particular. By the time she turned back, Liza was ready to talk again.

"To be honest, I wasn't all that surprised. I mean, I've known they can take human form for quite a while. Raphael did it once at school. Took the form of an old man – caretaker or something. Kind of makes sense that Zoldon is Carlisle; same character really. And it explains the disappearances during school trips. Always thought that a little odd, don't you think?"

"Yes, I agree. But I can't lie, I was quite shocked. Especially as—"

"What? Because you've known him for longer?" interrupted Liza, invading Justina's space as she leaned forward. The glare in her eyes was back – two opposites teetering on the edge, as though a battle was raging inside of her. Quickly, Justina resorted to what she knew. She calmly sat upright, using her right index finger to slowly and continuously draw a circle on the table, each circumference restoring her steely self-control. It was what was needed; she could not allow herself to be intimidated by Liza. "Yes, that is exactly what I meant. How you take it is up to you."

Sensing an impasse, Liza retreated back into her chair and in the blink of an eye, the nicer version of herself was back. "You know, it really doesn't matter; not as much as you think, anyway. You may have known him since you were little, just like I came across Raphael when I was a kid, but what good is that now? What I mean is, all that really matters is what happens now, and what happens next. Doesn't mean the past isn't important. We just need to let it go a little and focus on the now."

Although a little taken aback by the flippant manner with which Liza consigned the past to realms of irrelevance, Justina could not argue with her. Her viewpoint was somewhat callous, but overall, it was right, intelligent, and wise. Once again, she could not help sensing a shift in the dynamics of their association.

"You know, the more I think about it, the more I like it," said Liza, easing the tension.

"Like what?"

"Carlisle being Zoldon. At least now we know he's always here. It's like... do you get the feeling that the two realms are merging? Feels like it's all becoming one. Like we're reaching the climax."

"Yes, I know what you mean. That's also how I feel. Especially after meeting Clark – the PM, I mean. Feels like something big is finally about to happen. I still find it amazing that there are so many of us; that, I definitely didn't expect, not even in the slightest. It's like he's been planning this for centuries. I guess maybe he has."

"Weird that meeting, wasn't it? To think the PM is also in on it; basically placed there by Zoldon. I wonder how long she's known him. Probably from a young age, like you. Chess pieces, aren't we? But no biggie, not as if we're being forced into it."

"What did you think of her? The PM, I mean," asked Justina, still perturbed by a meeting that strangely left her with more questions than answers. "Very direct, wasn't she? Almost unnerving, the way she was so matter of fact about everything. Like a mini-Carlisle."

"I kind of liked that, no pissing around. 'Yes, you two have got powers, but I'm the PM, and this is how things will be done.' And yet..."

"What?"

"Kind of felt she wasn't really the one calling the shots."

"Well, of course she isn't, Zoldon is," said Justina, giving a faint laugh.

"No, I know that. I'm talking about the person in the long robe on the upper landing. Such a powerful presence. I could sense it, feel it. Couldn't you?"

"Yes, like whoever it was was really the one in charge."

"No, more than that. It was like the PM was tense, scared even. Didn't you notice her turning around slightly every now and again, like she was checking to make sure she was saying the right things?"

"Yes, I did notice that. At first, I thought she was just wondering what the person was doing, like we were."

"Who do you think it was?" asked Liza, fascinated by what she was sure was a new and darker force.

"No idea. No doubt we'll come across him or her again, though."

"Is your friend still coming? Thought you said he'd be here by eleven."

"He is – just sent me a message saying he's running a little late. Should be here soon though." Still feeling uneasy about Liza meeting her Alex, Justina could not help wondering about the poor timing. Considering what they were about to do, it was probably the worst possible time for Liza to meet Alex. After all, he could appear to be a weak link of sorts – a distraction, or worse still, evidence of the turmoil that was steadily brewing inside of her. She was entertaining the possibility of the very notions they were seeking to destroy. It would not take long for her hypocrisy to be revealed.

"When did you say you guys met?"

"A while back now," replied Justina, suddenly taking more interest in their surroundings.

"How come you never mentioned him 'til recently?"

"You're kidding me, right?" laughed Justina. "Not as though we chat about personal stuff much."

"Yeah, fair point. So, you're just friends, then?" asked Liza, her eyes landing on Justina's and staying put for several seconds, causing her long-time nemesis to squirm in fear, like prey caught in the trap of a predator. The sight of Justina's unease was confirmation of something she had long desired.

"Of course, anything more would be a little silly, wouldn't it?"

"Indeed! Just so long as you're aware of that," replied Liza, allowing Justina a temporary escape from her snare.

"Oh look, there he is. He looks totally lost. Better go fetch him before he drowns."

Relieved by the temporary respite that Alex's entrance brought her, Justina jumped to her feet to make her way towards the entrance, a journey which proved far trickier than it looked. He was standing just a few feet from the door, rooted to the ground and straining his eyes as he searched for the only face he desired to see. The bar was not his type of place at all; too busy and noisy for his liking. If it were up to him, he would turn around and head straight out again, but for his fondness of Justina. After much meandering and squeezing through several small groups and a handful of couples, she reached her man. "Hello, you."

"Hey you, too. Another few seconds and I'd have had to scarper. So many people! Like a wee spot of chaos. How the hell do you get a drink?"

"Drink! I knew there was something missing," replied Justina, raising her voice to overcome the hurdle of noise.

"Eh?"

"Oh, sorry," she continued, laughing at herself. "Just that we've been here, chatting away for almost an hour, and not once did we think to get a drink."

"How can ye do that? You need the hard stuff just to cope in here."

His comment made her laugh, although she could not quite tell whether she was laughing because of his comment or flirting in natural response to his authentic attire. She loved the fact that he just... looked normal; dark blue jeans with no fades or rips, a black collared shirt, and a dark, navy blue V-neck jumper – not even the vaguest hint of a fashion statement. He somehow seemed more real than all the other men in the room – calmer, truer, more mature. She had missed his accent and sense of humour, unloaded and harmless – a perfect breath of fresh air. "Right, come with me."

"Where to?"

"To the bar, silly. I'm going to get us some shots. Should help with the noise." She grabbed his hand and barged through the scrum in front of her, apologising countless times but not really meaning it. She was practically breathless by the time they reached the bar, a dizzy mix of exerted energy and excitement. She often felt like a different person when she was with him, forgetting who she was and the gazillion things that troubled her mind. Once again, she had reverted to the sweet little girl who doted on her family. All that mattered was him. With their hands still firmly clasped, she felt as though they were the only ones there; the noise had faded away, and the bodies were faceless. He pulled her towards him, his gentle smile lighting up his blue eyes. "Sorry I was late. Thought it best to be cool and keep you waiting."

"Right! As if you have it in you," replied Justina, giggling like a star-struck child.

"What do you mean, woman? I already did it."

"You were late, but it doesn't mean you have it in you to be cool. Sorry, Alex, cool just isn't you," she replied, chuckling at her own joke. Alex laughed along with her. She was the only person that could put him down without making him feel inept or inadequate. It was what he liked about her; she had a way of teasing his nervousness out of him. For a few seconds they gazed into each other's eyes, care- and trouble free. He leaned in to do what she had been wanting him to do since he arrived. But as she tilted her head to the left in anticipation of his kiss, it suddenly dawned on her that Liza was watching their every move, and in a flash, their island for two was gone. She pulled back a little and stepped back, turning to face the bar.

"Are you okay?"

"Yes, of course, just didn't want to kiss in front of all these people. You know what I'm like when I get started," she replied, laughing nervously.

"Aye, fair point, I'll let you off. Now, how many drams we getting?"

"I was thinking of getting us three shots of tequila each. What do you reckon?"

"Tequila? So, it's one of those nights? Count me in, woman."

Justina's sixth sense was accurate. Liza's protruding eyes had followed them all the way from the entrance to the bar. She had noticed everything: the hand holding, loving gaze, the near passionate kiss. So, they *were* more than just friends. The fact that Justina lied to her confirmed what she suspected some minutes ago: she was scared. But was she simply worried about the consequences of her careless actions, or scared about what Liza might do to her? She hoped it was the latter. What was she thinking? How could she be so... foolish, giving herself to the very thing they were about to destroy? It angered her, made her feel betrayed. As she sat at the table, her feet tapping faster and faster, the dark cloud returned to its rightful place. She welcomed it, allowing it to stay, but waved the fury that was building inside away; now was not the time – she had something else in mind.

"Shots! You read my mind! And you must be Alex. Jus told me so much about... Actually, no, she hasn't. It seems she kept you under wraps for quite some time," said Liza, keeping herself in check.

"Is that so? Something I should know?" said Alex, turning to Justina with an exaggerated inquisitive expression.

"Don't read into it – just a case of wanting things to grow before blurting my mouth off."

"Hmmm... wanting things to grow. Good to know you're taking 'us' so seriously."

"Stop! You know what I mean. Just didn't want to jinx it."

"Hmmm... you 'didn't want to jinx it', 'wanting things to grow'; sounds to me like the early stages of an actual relationship," said Liza, laughing along to maintain her pretence. Justina's coyness was yet more confirmation of her hypocrisy and betrayal; she had clearly lost her way. "So, Alex, tell me all, how did you guys meet? How long have you guys been dating? Have you—"

"We're just friends, taking things slow for now," said Justina, stopping Liza mid-sentence. Even though she and Alex had not yet spent a night together, there was no point allowing Liza to know just how close they had grown; to allow such a thing was tantamount to suicide. Alex turned to look at her, the faint frown on his face conveying his concerns. She smiled back at him, gently squeezing his hand.

"Aye, she's right, Liza. Taking things slow for now. Nae point running before we can walk, aye? Right, first shot on the count of three then, ready?"

Each grabbed a shot glass and waited for the count. "One, two, three, down the hatch."

"Yeah, I get it, makes sense," said Liza, downing another shot of tequila before biting into a slice of lemon. "But you still haven't told me about when you guys first met. Wait, is that... Hey, I love this song. Come on, you can tell me all about it on the dance floor." Liza grabbed Alex's hand before he had a chance to respond.

They made their way to the dance floor, which was not really a dance floor at all, but a small space in the centre of the room where people congregated to move rhythmically to songs they liked. There was very little room to fully express oneself when the bar was full, but all punters respected the tiny space as a hallowed place for sporadic limb movement.

Staring at the remaining shots on the table, Justina contemplated taking her third one. She had downed her second as Liza led Alex to dance, but her gut instinct told her to leave the third one alone. She needed to keep her wits about her; something felt off – she could barely see them. Every now and then she caught a glimpse of Alex's head or spotted one of Liza's flailing arms, but she had no idea what they were doing. Yes, they were dancing, but what were they actually doing? Just dancing? Dancing and talking? It was the talking that concerned her, she did not want Liza getting too close to Alex. The more she knew about him, the greater the danger he would be in.

Fortunately, just then, a small group of revellers decided they had had enough of standing and plumped themselves on the chairs of a nearby table. Now, Justina could see them; Liza dancing energetically, sporadically moving backwards and forwards, and every now and again getting Alex to twirl her and pull her close. Each time she did so, he quickly stepped back, looking even more hesitant and nervous than usual. She was flirting. Why? What was she playing at? It verged on embarrassing. The tequila had obviously blinded her from seeing the reality of Alex's discomfort.

Others looked on, entertained by Liza's flirty twirls, 'whoop-whooping' whenever she made her move. Song after song they danced, Liza becoming increasingly out of control and Alex looking like someone who wanted the earth to swallow him up. Every time he attempted to leave, she pulled him back, pulling him close and jigging her body as if to entice him. Unsure of what to do, but knowing she had to do something to rescue him, Justina got up from her chair and walked towards the dancing area, then hovered on the fringes for several minutes, smiling and dancing along with them.

"Hey, just gonna stand there, or are you gonna join us? Come on, woman!" said Alex loudly, hoping she could hear him. She accepted his invitation and joined them, instantly putting a stop to Liza's antics. Alex grabbed her hand and turned to face her, leaving Liza looking like a spare part. She continued to dance with them for a little while longer but knew her game was up. After some time, she returned to her table and promptly consumed the remaining shots of tequila.

Sat at the table on her own for the next twenty minutes, the room began to swirl around her as the tequila seized her senses. And as the room swirled, her cloud darkened. Suddenly, she grabbed her bag and headed towards the exit, unapologetically barging past people with sour disdain.

"Wait, I think Liza's leaving," said Justina, releasing her hands. She had quite forgotten herself, allowing her heart to dance freely in endless moments of recklessness.

"What's that?"

"Liza, she's leaving," replied Justina, swiftly walking away.

By the time she reached the exit door, Liza had gone. She ran up the staircase, tripping over a couple in a warm embrace. On arriving outside, she looked to her right, only to see an empty street. The only sign of life was a beggar under a sleeping bag. When she looked left, she saw Liza, trudging down the street in her stilettoes.

"Liza! Liza, wait!" shouted Justina as she chased after her. Liza did not respond. "Liza, where are you going?"

"Home," said Liza, now just a few metres away.

"You could have said goodbye, don't you think?"

"And ruin your romantic evening?" replied Liza, turning full circle.

"What are you talking about? I told you we're just—"

"Cut the crap, Jus. Stop fucking lying."

Justina's heart jumped. Her palms were sweating. She was unsure whether it was the tequila or her heightened nerves talking. Maybe both. Unable to reply, her world began to move in slow motion, as though her end had come.

Now eerily calm, Liza walked slowly towards Justina, then stopped a few inches in front of her. "You're a hypocrite, Justina. Now you're going to experience it all over again." She stood there, still, silent, allowing her cold words to take full effect, then turned and walked away.

Frozen to the pavement for several minutes, Justina considered the ramifications of giving in to a weakness she had always detested. She was on the edge of a precipice, and all she could see in front of her was pain and destruction. There was only one thing she could do. When she finally turned to head back, she was startled to see a silhouette of the same figure she had seen at the Prime Minister's office in the far distance, adorned with the same floor-length cloak. Same imposing presence.

"Hey!" shouted Justina as she began to run towards it. But no sooner had she started, the figure turned around and disappeared.

9

Turning Point

"Kill them all," said Liza, her words reverberating through the corridors of Zoldon's mind. He had what he wanted: the ruthless focus and control of a young girl he had groomed from childhood – and now, Raphael's tempestuous apprentice, who he sensed was a smouldering volcano that would be unstoppable.

But his concern about his brother's retaliation meant his satisfaction was short-lived. Raphael may have been crippled, his followers consumed by flames in one fell swoop, but he knew where Zoldon and his cohort were based. Raphael had nothing to lose, and that made him dangerous.

For much of the coming weeks, Zoldon and a handful of others searched for a new home.

But despite venturing into previously unknown regions of the outer realm, nothing quite sufficed. A few locations came close, but it was clear Zoldon would not compromise with whatever picture he had in his head. Weeks passed, months, and more months. The intensity of their search was matched only by a frenzied-like drive to exterminate every dragon, big or small, that was not in his camp. It was the next phase, one that needed to be concluded before anything else. The more dragons they found and destroyed, the greater his belief that there were more out there, plotting to thwart his plan. Over time, he developed a deep-rooted fear of marauders lurking in the dark, plotting and waiting, ready to pounce at any given moment. Not a day went by without more dying; some were possibly future obstructions, but mostly they were innocent neutrals who simply wanted to live their lives in peace. Each day presented a new finding, a new chase, more lives to end.

It was during one such skirmish that they came across what would become their new home. They were searching the eastern parts of the outer realm as a handful of neutrals had fled in that direction the day before.

"Can you see anything?" asked Justina. They were hiding behind a nest of trees, on the edge of a forest. They had been drawn to a secluded part of a thick forest because of the gaping wide circumference that had somehow sprouted in the middle of it. As if looking entirely out of place was not enough, a disorderly mesh of green and brown leaves stretched across the area, and beneath the dull but still crisp leaves was a thin layer of grass, creating a picture-perfect scene of autumnal residue. Rows of trees circled the edge – attentive, watching… waiting. The air stilled with a silence that screamed concealment.

Zoldon's dark eyes scanned the vicinity, penetrating deep into the fortress of trees on the other side in anticipation of a possible ambush. Only when he was convinced that they were alone did he return his attention to the mysterious sight of grass and leaves in front of them. He bowed his head towards the ground and slowly inhaled. The others around him waited in silence.

"Something about this place... doesn't seem.... Justina, Liza, climb down and take a look. But be careful."

The girls climbed down, unsure where to begin – whether to prowl around the edges or plunge straight in. After some seconds of tipping her toes around the perimeter, Liza stepped onto the circle, took a step forward, and then another. Justina didn't follow, opting to prepare herself for a likely reprisal. Cold as ice, she clenched both her fists, then calmly loosened them. Nothing happened.

Liza continued walking until she got to the middle, then turned back to them, looking a little confused.

Justina walked slowly around the edge, her focus on the leaves and grass only occasionally interrupted by a glance at the other side. She stopped, turned to face the circle and kicked gently at it, using the tip of her shoe to feel the edge.

Sensing they may have fallen for a ruse, she crouched down, knelt on her left knee and used her hands to feel the edge. Finding something, she lifted up her hands, pulling up a layer of grass and leaves. "It's just a cover. They must be down here."

"Just as I sensed. Liza, help her remove the layer. The rest of you, make a wide perimeter around this area. Nobody is to approach, and none are to leave," said Zoldon, turning to the dozen or so dragons that accompanied them. They nodded in quiet obedience, ascending skywards in different directions before strategically placing themselves in various vantage points – some on the top of the trees, a few hovering high up in the sky, and others on the ground in the thick of the forest.

Much heavier than they imagined it would be, it took several minutes for Justina and Liza to pull back the cover, revealing a huge pit with steps leading down.

"Shall we…?"

"Yes, both of you, go down there and look around. I want to know how many are down there."

Wondering how the concrete steps came about, Liza followed Justina down the pit, eagerly anticipating whatever awaited them. Daylight faded into memory as the stairwell stifled the air around them. A dim light illuminated the distance.

Counting every step, Justina took her time. With nothing on either side to lean on, the only way to steady herself was to tread carefully. Two hundred and fifty, two fifty-one... two fifty-three… two fifty-four… two fifty-five... two fifty-six... two fifty-seven.

Their steps became slower the further they descended, the decreasing light increasing the threat of danger.

Finally, they arrived at the bottom. Three wide passages stood in front of them: one to their right, another on the left and one directly in front. Small cauldrons of burning flames, about fifteen metres apart, ran along each passage.

"What now?"

"Shhhhh..." hissed Justina, hushing Liza's faint whisper. "Can you hear that?"

"Hear what?"

Both remained still, allowing their silence to focus their senses. An ensemble of voices could be heard from the passage on their right.

"This way." Justina turned to the right-hand passage.

Liza followed, the gentle beating of her heart unaffected by a strange sensation that wormed its way up her right arm. As they walked along the passage, the voices grew louder, revealing an anxiety-fuelled conversation between a mesh of large shadows:

"I don't understand. One minute you say that you're sure no-one saw you, and the next you're saying they may have seen you fly in this direction."

"No, you're not getting me. What I meant is that they may have seen me fly in this direction, eastwards, towards the forest, but I'm pretty sure nobody saw me descend the pit."

"Yes, but 'pretty sure' doesn't exactly banish all doubts, does it? Might as well say you may or may not have been followed."

"I really don't know why you guys are having a go at me. It wasn't only me, was it? What about them? Why aren't you interrogating them as well?"

Four dragons stood behind her, desperately hoping that her remarks about any interrogation concerning their own possible failures would be succinctly forgotten.

"Enough!" echoed a sterner and more authoritative voice. The chatter ceased immediately, allowing the silence to soothe jangled nerves. The silhouette of a larger being slithered towards them like molten lava. "I'm sick of this bickering. We all knew the risks we took when we decided to go off on our own. The reality is that we will always be living on borrowed time. Every time we go out there, every time we return, when we're asleep, awake even, we're in danger. Zoldon's slaughtering of those dragons won't be his last. There's no point blaming anyone. We live each day as it comes."

"I just... We're so lucky we found this place... We need to do all we can to protect it; we *have* to."

"And that is what we have been doing. Every day, doing our best to prevent this place from being found. But a time will come when it will be. Mark my words: this isn't going to last forever."

Justina spotted two more silhouettes of winged beasts a little distance behind them, stationary and scared. She could sense it: they were no different to the others; the fear of being found coursed through their veins. She turned to Liza and nodded in the direction of where they came.

Liza's widened eyes failed to respond. The tingling sensation on the tips of her outstretched hands was in sync with the festering force of energy and rage that had seized her.

"Liza!" Justina whispered a little louder. "Not now." She firmly gripped Liza's shoulders. "We need to head back and let him know first."

As though overpowered by Justina's firm grip, the tempest that had been gathering subsided. Liza nodded in agreement and followed her accomplice. Pausing momentarily at the foot of the long stairwell, they heard more voices from the other two passages.

"What do you mean, it's hard to tell?" asked Zoldon, irritated by the lack of clarity.

"I mean just that. I thought there were just about a dozen or so, but on our way out, we heard more voices from the other two passages, so it's—"

"Two passages? What do you mean?"

166

"At the bottom of the stairwell there are three passages, each one heading in a different direction. We went down the one on the right because that's where we initially heard voices coming from. It was when we went down that passage that we saw who I'm pretty sure are the leaders of the group. They were arguing."

"About what?"

"Whether or not some of them were seen. They're scared of being found. But on the way back, we heard more voices coming from the other two passages. Either way, I don't think they'll be much of a problem for us."

Zoldon took a small step forward, gazing at the descent for several seconds before slowly scanning the vicinity again. There was something he liked about it; aside from the cover afforded by the forest landscape, not too many would think to venture this far east. He looked up and gave a nod to one of the dragons guarding the perimeter, receiving an answering nod in return. He turned to Justina, who immediately climbed onto his back, ready for another necessary culling. Once settled, she turned to instruct Liza to do likewise, only to find her already set.

"No need for anyone else; the four of us are enough," Justina said.

"The rest of you stay here and be on your guard. Who knows how many more there may be around here," commanded Zoldon.

Before long, they embraced the welcome of the darkness as they glided down the descent. As they approached the bottom, Zoldon slowed down a little and turned to Abaddon, who immediately inched ahead, leading them down the right-hand passage.

The strange fuzzy sensation seized Liza's body once more. She understood it now and relished what came with it. It was as though something inside her that had been suppressed for so long was finally free, accepted, and cherished. The thrill of the energy coursing through her veins was different to what she had experienced before. She felt liberated, free to embrace the darker side of herself – her real self.

As the dim lights grew a little brighter, their targets were revealed, still in anxious discussion. Liza raised her arms and released a powerful, rage-filled, violent surge that shook the walls and the ground beneath them, throwing the hapless dragons in various directions.

Before any of them knew what was going on, another powerful surge hit them, this time from Justina, causing them to crash into the walls with such force that most were instantly concussed and unable to move.

Desperate to inflict more pain, Liza continued to batter them with the violence of her power, sending surge after surge, pinning their bodies to the walls with ruthless venom. Catching sight of a tall stone pillar to the right, Liza grinned. Its length and width excited her as she knew the kind of pain and damage such a huge object could do. But, just as she steered her right arm in its direction, she hesitated; something inside her resisted. Though small and almost insignificant, it was enough to make her pause.

With nothing more to do in their particular part of the pit, Justina and Zoldon looked on, waiting for Liza to pull her trigger.

"Whatever resistance you're feeling is not you, Liza – not who you are. Let it go once and for all," Justina said.

Still hesitant, Liza froze in mid-destruction, unwilling to let go of the few remaining remnants of someone she once knew.

"Do it!" shouted Justina, her eyes blazing with authority and steel.

Liza shut her eyes, her chest slowly puffing out before gradually deflating again, releasing whatever doubt and hesitation remained. She twisted her outstretched right hand and pointed her index finger to the dragons. In an instant, the pillar crashed into them, shattering bones and crushing bodies in one fell swoop.

"Never hesitate to do what needs to be done, Liza. Ever!" said Justina, irritated by Liza's hesitancy. "Destroy or be destroyed. There can never be room for sentiment. Understand?"

Liza nodded her head, still staring at the devastation in front of her – a devastation she caused. For a fleeting moment, she was troubled by the fact that she enjoyed it, relished the pain she inflicted on others. It was the reason she hesitated; she had looked in the mirror and was shaken by the sight of her real self.

The ease with which Liza threw the pillar did not go unnoticed. "Justina is right; feelings and sentiment can only put you in danger. The more you let go, the greater your powers grow," said Zoldon, fascinated by Liza's potential; it was just a turn of the wrist and the pointing of a finger. "Now, let's complete our task. Did you say there were voices coming from the other two passages?"

"Yes," replied Justina. "We need to head back towards the entrance."

Two female dragons were idly chatting by the entrance of a large, open concrete space. In front of them were over a dozen dragons, young and old, whiling away the day in various ways. The bigger space, adorned with more lit cauldrons of fire, and the voracious giggling of young dragons in merry play, gave it a safer and more cheerful ambiance.

The young ones were playing various games of mischief as the adults watched and chatted amongst themselves, lounging on their stomachs in blissful ignorance of the fate of those down the other passage. This was their little haven, a place for their children to grow without thoughts and rumours of war and pestilence. Here, in this happy place, they could forge their own peaceful, new world.

"You must be so proud of your twins, Agie – playful but gentle, never too rough or too silly. It's like they were born naturally wise or something," commented one of the adult dragons. She was portly, with kind gentle eyes, complete with a motherly nature that cherished every opportunity to watch over and nurture the young.

"Thanks, Minnie. And at least there's no kingdom for them to fight over, so hopefully they'll remain peaceful," replied Agie, laughing at her own joke.

"Eh? Not sure I understand. Why are you laughing?" asked Minnie.

"She's referring to the legend of the twins, Minnie," added another, a male. A blank expression filled Minnie's face. "You mean, you've never heard the story of the twins?"

"I've no idea what you're talking about. What twins?"

"Right, I guess I'd better tell you, then. Not as if we have a busy day ahead or anything. As the tale goes—"

"Wait! Is this a true story or just a tale? Did what you're about to tell me actually happen?"

"As far as I know, yes. But nobody really knows for sure. Anyway, the queen of a great and powerful kingdom—"

"Wait! What queen? Was it a kingdom in our realm or what?"

"No, Minnie, in the inner realm. No more questions; just listen," said the male dragon. He chuckled; the anathema of her impatient nature and that of the twins was one that made the mind boggle. "Right, as I was saying, the queen of a great and powerful kingdom, the name of which now seems to have slipped my mind, and I blame your interruptions for that, by the way.

So, twins, a boy and a girl, born to a powerful king and queen. They were raised to rule the kingdom together – equal power and authority. Both were schooled in the art of leadership and governance. But when they got older, in their late teens, I think, the parents changed their minds, deciding the boy should be king..."

"Why?"

"Why what?"

"Why did they change their mind?"

"Oh, I don't know, Minnie! Maybe they felt he would make a better ruler. Just listen!"

"Just asking, 'cause…"

"Minnie!" they all shouted at once, exasperated by their friend's ceaseless questions.

"Right, so the boy – Leo, I think his name was – was chosen to be king. And as soon as they made that decision, the girl, Julia, was left on the side-lines – basically ignored; all the attention went to the boy. So, fast forward a few years, and Leo is crowned king. His sister didn't attend the coronation. In fact, from that day she was never seen again. Many years later, Leo's kingdom is invaded by an evil emperor whose army had conquered nations across the entire face of the earth. Apparently, this emperor had dark magical powers – lifting huge castle gates with a flick of his hands, decimating lives with his eyes and stuff. It was even said that his army was enchanted. Nobody ever saw their faces – all in black armour from head to toe, with bronze masks covering their faces. Nobody ever saw the emperor's face either. Needless to say, Leo's army, powerful though it was, was no match for that of the emperor."

"What happened to him? Sorry."

"After Leo surrendered his kingdom, the emperor, upon walking into Leo's palace, made the king and his men kneel before him. He then took off his mask – something he never ever did. It was the other twin, Julia."

"What? Julia? How?"

"Who knows? Many believe she always possessed mysterious powers, and that she was groomed and trained by a powerful sorcerer."

"Oh my, that's a shocking sto... No... please... please; you can't! I'm begging you, please don't..." pleaded Minnie, her face ashen with fright.

"What is it?" asked Agie, turning her head to ascertain the cause of her friend's sudden fear.

Before she could do so, her body was consumed by a blaze of fire.

Horrified by the sight of their friend burning and melting in front of them, Minnie and the two others were unable to move. Tongues of violent flames lashed out at them, engulfing them, searing and tearing their skin to shreds. The pathetic shrieks of babies crying out for their mothers echoed through the passage as they attempted to scramble to safety, each one pulled back and inevitably reduced to a heap of burnt flesh.

"Over there!" shouted Liza, pointing to a handful of dragons attempting to flee. "Don't let them get away!"

Abaddon breathed out yet another burst of volcanic flames, destroying everything in its path. Some attempted to climb up the walls, desperate to find solace from the avalanche of scorching violence that was inflicting them. But it was no use; one by one they fell into the cruel arms of the blaze of fury beneath them.

"And there – look!" shouted Liza, jumping off Abaddon's back before releasing a brutal force of energy that threw several dragons across the room, splattering into the wall in a mesh of flesh and bones.

As Zoldon burned another batch to cinder, Liza raised both arms and diverted the furnace towards the dragons she had just thwarted, piling on flame after flame as they pleaded for mercy. Recognising their already dead state, Zoldon withdrew his fire, but the savagery of the furnace did not relent, growing hotter and more vicious as Liza released wave after wave of frenzied surges, creating a large ball of fire that engulfed everything in its path.

Justina jumped off Zoldon's back and made her way towards her accomplice, stopping just behind her. Her upper lip curled a little as she allowed Liza to revel in her devastation for a few more seconds, before gently placing her right hand on the other's left shoulder.

"That's enough." Justina felt the force of energy wane but did not remove her hand until it ceased completely.

Breathing heavily, Liza turned to Justina, eyes glaring with pent-up rage. Charred remains of various sizes lay scattered across the floor as the putrid stench of burnt flesh spread its ghastly tentacles, stifling the air like a boa constrictor squeezing the air out of its prey. Gradually descending from pernicious heights of unfathomable rage, the whites of Liza's eyes began to emerge, replacing the red glow that had temporarily seized them.

Her heart returned to a normal rhythm once more as she assessed the remnants of her slaughter, this time bereft of remorse or tears.

Zoldon scanned the vicinity, assessing its size and structure. Aside from the clumsy attempt to conceal its existence, the location was perfect; nobody would expect them to come that far east. "This will do just nicely."

10

Cries Of Conscience

The bunker, as it was known, became Zoldon's fortress. He and his followers migrated there shortly after the slaughter. They spent the first few days removing waste and debris before gutting the place entirely.

Tearing down the passage walls was Justina's idea. She pointed out that having different passages and spaces would encourage cliques and scheming; it was better to have everyone in full view. They created a large, open space, spanning two acres or so, but even after the renovation was complete, they still did not move inside. On Zoldon's insistence, they spent several more days sleeping outside during the night, his reasoning being that the spirits of the dead needed to be given more time to vacate the premises – a passive exorcism that had to take place.

Deep down, he was simply paying his respects. Despite a ruthless focus on his objective, the killing of other dragons had never been something he enjoyed. This one in particular seemed to affect him. No regrets, of course – just a touch of sadness that it had to be done at all. If Raphael was not so naïve, there would have been no need for such actions. His brother was to blame; the more dragons they killed, the more he resented him.

Two weeks passed before they finally moved in, on a wet, windy morning. Zoldon was the last to enter, preferring to watch his followers descend to their new home. Once every single one of them was inside, he stood to his feet and unfurled his wings, gently flapping them as he rose skywards, rising far above the trees. Uppermost on his mind was the birds-eye view of the bunker, for he had an important decision to make.

As he suspected, even the most imbecilic individual would know there was something down there, something that could be neither ignored nor left to chance. They had ventured to a part of the outer realm few would expect, and yet here they were, in plain sight. A part of him wanted it so, to be spotted and attacked – get it over and done with once and for all. If only his brother had the tenacity. In the end, he left it exactly as it was: no covering or camouflage, daring his enemies to attack.

*

After taking a walk in the forest one afternoon, something she found herself doing frequently as she became more and more marginalised, Justina returned to find Zoldon, Liza and Abaddon in quiet discussion. As she had not quite entered the big hall, she was out of sight, thus able to study their demeanour for some minutes.

They were quite at ease with one another, certainly more so than whenever she was with them. She wondered whether they were discussing her, whether Liza had informed them of her friend, Alex, but she knew that was not Liza's style; over the years, she had come to realise that Liza would rather openly seize power, rather than steal it sneaking in through the back door. Justina's mind went back to when they killed the first handful of dragons in that very same spot, how she had scolded Liza for hesitating. She recalled being a little concerned by it, only to witness something else entirely some minutes later. It was in that very moment, when Liza almost single-handedly decimated dozens of dragons, that she realised it was better to allow Liza's rage to roam more freely as opposed to suppressing it.

Justina was proud of her creation, of who she was fast becoming. She had decided there and then that she would unleash Liza's rage more often. What she did not realise was that she had opened her very own Pandora's box. The more Liza's rage was allowed to surface, the greater her power grew, and the more her power increased, the more estranged they became.

Not that they had ever been close, but at least they used to converse free of tension. Maybe that was the problem: she had wanted a relationship on her terms, one in which she was the one in control, pulling the strings. Did she in some way resent Liza deep down? Or was it the other way round? It was something she had never considered before. Was it possible that Liza resented her for releasing her dark spirit? It would certainly explain the blatant contempt and the constant mood swings. It was as though she hated her for setting her on a path that she knew could only go one way.

This was her fault, not Liza's. In any case, why did this concern her so much? Why should any of it concern her? After all, was this not what she wanted all along? Only, for some time now, much of what they were doing was not resting so easy with her.

"Ahh, Justina, you're back. Come, join us," said Zoldon, looking in Justina's direction.

"Coming," she replied, gathering herself together, clenching and unclenching her fists several times as she made her way towards them, decluttering her mind of memories and questions.

"How are you feeling?" asked Zoldon, referring to the migraine Justina had complained about before leaving them.

"A little better; think the fresh air helped a little." She had taken to using migraines as an excuse to get away whenever she needed to. The voices that seized her senses some moments after meeting Alex for the first time had taken to calling more regularly, growing louder and increasing in intensity. However, on this occasion, she had actually had a splitting headache, and the fresh air had eased the constant throbbing in her head.

"Good. We were just finalising plans for the next week."

"Finalising plans for the next week." She could not help dwelling on those words. Planning such things was something he would never have even considered doing without her before; she was fast becoming a spare part, reluctantly included as a form of respect for past services. That was not really what troubled her, though; her chief concern was that she preferred it that way, looking in instead of being in the thick of it.

"So, it is next week, then?"

"Yes, we'll have Elias in the next couple of days as we now know exactly where he is. You and Liza will..." His words began to fade as an acute din sounded in her ears, echoing in her head like a distant thunder, growing louder and louder as it approached her mind's eye. She knew what was about to follow, and there was very little she could do to stop it. Taking a small step back, she pressed her toes into the soles of her shoes, squeezing hard in a vain attempt to maintain her composure. Her only option was to somehow prevent it from occurring in front of them. She shut her eyes tight for a few seconds to halt the tidal wave that was fast approaching, but it was no use.

When she opened them again, she noticed Liza staring straight at her. Nothing in her expression suggested she knew what was going on, but there was an air of suspicion in her glare. Zoldon was still talking, unaware of the siege in her head. She had to get away.

"Oh dear, it seems to have started again," she blurted.

Now excruciatingly loud, the din had settled at the front of her head, piling on so much pressure on her eye sockets that she felt as though they would explode. And then the voices came.

In that moment, she knew she had to leave, turning around and ambling away.

"Help us", "please, help us", "why are you doing this?", "please, not the children", "take us instead", "I beg of you, show mercy, please", "Mummy, it hurts", "please, Dad, make them stop", "Mummy, I'm scared", "not the children.", "please, not the children", "I don't understand, why are you doing this?", "it hurts, mummy, please make them stop.".

Over and over again they screamed, different voices expressing various forms of physical and emotional torment. The more they screamed and shrieked, the more she lost her balance, causing her to trip over herself. With her eyes still shut tight to stem the mass eruption, she scrambled to her feet, feeling her way across the hall, waiting for the inside of her eyelids to sense the light on the stairway.

"Are you okay, Justina? Justina!"

"Yes, I mean, no... it's... it's the migraine again."

"Liza, maybe you should go with her and..."

"No; better to leave her. From what I've heard about migraines, the last thing she'll want is a reason to have to talk or open her eyes," said Abaddon.

Upon reaching the foot of the stairwell, she collapsed on all fours, unable to withstand the thousands of voices that had seized her mind, begging and groaning for their lives, like she was killing them repeatedly. As she scrambled up the stairs on hands and knees, she pleaded for them to stop.

"Why should we? You showed us no mercy. Why should we show you mercy?", "Yes, why should we?", "You did this to us", "You did this to yourself.", "No! No mercy!"

The more they screamed and shrieked, the more her mind raced, painting vivid pictures of the scenes of her killings. She felt as though her mind was bleeding and desperately wanted it to stop. She wanted to stop thinking, stop seeing. For a few moments, she contemplated taking her own life to stop the noise. By the time she reached the top of the stairwell, death seemed the only viable option.

Still on all fours, and panting and feeling her way, she scrambled to her feet and staggered into the forest, in part hoping for some respite and in part searching for something to end her life with. Unable to tell which direction she was going, she kept moving, staggering, stumbling, scrambling, crawling through the forest, like a wounded animal at the gates of death, until she eventually collapsed at the foot of a tree, covering both ears with her hands and placing her head between her knees, hoping for her head to implode or her mind to bleed out.

The image of a dying mother squeezing the life out of her child to ease the agony of her suffering scythed her heart in two. As her child breathed his last, the dragon lifted her wing to gaze at her precious creature. Her heartache, pain, suffering – it was too much to take.

Justina opened her eyes, hoping the vision would disappear. Voices of grief and anguish continued to torment her as she lifted her head, searching for something sharp or heavy. Nothing. In desperation, she raised her right hand and pointed it at one of several trees in front of her.

As its roots lifted out of the ground, the voices quietened, drifting away like a horrific storm. It made little difference to her decision as there was no reason for them not to return. What she and Liza had done could not be undone.

With the tree fully uprooted, she steadied her hand in preparation for her final act. But just as she took aim at herself, she caught sight of a young boy in the distance. His brown-blond hair was familiar, as was his stature and gait.

Even though he was stood several metres away, she could see the sadness in his eyes.

Swinging her right arm, she sent the tree into a nest of others and gingerly got back on her feet, ears still ringing. She staggered towards the boy in the distance, swaying from side to side as she struggled to regain her senses. At first, she seemed to be making little progress, as the distance remained the same, but all of a sudden, he was ten feet away, grey-blue eyes, parting on the right side of his head – a sight she had longed for since that tragic day at her friend's house. Gates of tears, closed for so many years, opened once more as she gazed at her brother.

"Is... is it really you?"

He did not answer.

"It is you... isn't it?"

Still no answer. She recognised his mood; forlorn and bereft with sadness, eyes soaked with tears.

"Why are you doing this, Jus?"

"Doing... doing what?"

"You know. Stop pretending."

"Know what? I don't understand."

"Look around you, Jus. Look... all around you." He was not the same child she had once known; he was more grown up, using bigger words. She did as he asked and looked. All around them were heaps of corpses of dragons and humans. She momentarily lost her footing as her heart skipped a beat, causing her to feel numb and silencing the sound around her. The world drifted into slow motion as she assessed the destruction around them – thousands and thousands of dead humans and dragons, stretching as far as her eyes could see.

"You did this."

"But I... I don't understand. We've only been... I mean... we're trying to..."

"This is how it will end, Jus; this is the result of what you're doing – it can only lead to this."

"I... but I... I thought..." She was like the little girl at her friend's house again, alone, lost and scared. She had always believed her cause to be true and honourable, doing what was best for humankind.

"It can only ever lead to this." And suddenly he was gone, out of her life once more.

Justina dropped to her knees and stared at browned leaves and twigs for several minutes.

Her body trembled as years and years of imprisoned emotions gushed through her once-impenetrable dam. Despite the circumstance, it was good to see him again, to see a face she had forcefully removed from her consciousness, folded up neatly with other painful memories and placed in a small box, concealed by several larger boxes of different sizes. Not since the day of the funeral had she allowed herself to dwell on her family. She hated the way she felt – a dreadful feeling of loss and pining that would never go away. It frightened her to think she would never get better. Zoldon had given her an alternative, one that enabled her to put every drop of her well of grief and anger into a mission that would not only cure her but ensure nobody ever felt the way she did again. And from that moment she had never looked back; it was part of her steely resolve and control – an ability to block out anything that could deter her focus. Each passing day provided another layer of concealment, covering an open wound that would never heal.

A mishmash of memories flooded her mind – fun memories, happy memories, sad ones, and angry ones, finally freed from an unjust imprisonment. On and on they poured like vengeful waves of discord, never to be confined again. Emotions she had assumed she would never experience again took hold of her – sadness, grief, anger, fear – possessing her as forcefully as they had done on the day she lost her family.

Taking several deep breaths in the hope of thwarting the sense of panic that was fast seizing her, Justina got to her feet to regain some composure, but as soon as she did so, the forest began to spin around her, circling faster and faster, making it even more difficult for her to catch her breath and causing further disorientation. On and on it spun, like a sadistic torturer, as she struggled to regain her balance. She tried propping herself on a tree and holding tight to one of its branches until she could no longer withstand it, finally falling to her hands and knees.

The spinning continued as she gasped for breath, closing her eyes to somehow wish it away. Was it the spinning she wanted to stop or the avalanche of truth that was forcing its way into her consciousness? The pain that she had felt on the day her family died had never left her; she had merely stored it away, pretending it had never happened. Yet, it was good to feel such pain and anguish – it made her feel alive again, to yearn, to grieve, even to cry.

She pictured the little girl in the garden on the day of the funeral, her entire world destroyed in a fleeting moment. Lost, alone, terrified of an unknown future. Did that little girl simply take the easy option? Giving in to her anger and fear and taking a route of certainty, as against allowing her life to unfold naturally? She had an opportunity to curtail her grief and she took it. Who could blame her? Would not most people do the same? Surely, nobody wants loss or fear, but is that not what life is about? Giving hope a chance, to keep going no matter what?

That little girl would not be the first or the last to experience such fear and uncertainty.

Had Zoldon taken advantage of her fragile state of mind? Deep down, she knew she was also at fault; she had wanted it. Try as she might to prevent such alien thoughts and emotions, she was entirely unable to do so. Before long, images of the charred remains of dragons and humans coloured her mind. There were thousands of them; tragic heaps of murdered corpses stretching across the wasteland. She could hear their desperate cries for help – their screaming, their pleading…

Justina buried her head in her lap, using her arms to cover it in a desperate attempt to quieten the noise, but it was no use; the voices grew louder and louder until she could no longer withstand them, clambering to her feet to somehow escape.

With both eyes shut tight and her hands covering her ears, she staggered through the forest for what seemed like hours – though was only really a matter of minutes – crashing into trees, tree stumps, rocks, and fallen branches, often collapsing to the ground.

Despite the pain and the cuts that accompanied each collision and fall, she kept her eyes shut, for fear of the voices growing even louder. Still, she soldiered on, blindly scrambling through unknown territory. Even if she did open her eyes, she would have no idea where she was.

The voices did not relent, lashing at her mind with no mercy. The only way to make them stop was to sever her head from her neck. As the reality of her only escape route grew clearer, she arrested her stagger and opened her eyes in search of something to use. Nothing… but maybe there was another way.

With the din in her ears as loud as ever, she raised her arms and pointed both hands towards a tall and muscular tree, about twenty metres to her right, then, using the little strength she had left, she swung downwards to her left. The tree yielded, crashing onto her with great force. A lesser mortal would have died in an instant, but all she managed to do was knock herself out. At least her mind was free from the harrowing voices.

It was not until the next morning that she stirred, waking up to the same screams and groans that had tortured her the day before. A sharp, searing pain coursed through her body, from the tips of her toes to the sides of her head, reminding her of her futile attempt to end her life. She was sad to still be alive and had reached the very end of herself.

Everything she had lived for and had believed in had been based on a lie – a lie she had forged by a desire to rid herself of her pain and grief.

If only the tree had killed her.

But maybe it was what she deserved; death would have been an easy way out.

The tree was even larger than she thought, with thick and heavy branches. She made a half-hearted attempt to move, but it was no use. The only way she could escape from beneath its weight would be to use her power, but her right arm was trapped by her side and her left too weak and in pain to summon the required surge.

For hours she simply lay there in agony, plagued by the voices in her head. All around her were tall, imposing trees, peering into her soul like an inquisition, invading her privacy without a shred of remorse. She spotted a tear on one of them. She figured it must have been hit by the reverberations of her earlier actions. It was teetering slightly – all it needed was another surge, and it would crash on top of her. Surely one more heavy hit would do the trick.

Struggling, Justina gathered the little strength that remained and raised her left arm a few inches above her hip, hand shaking from the strain. It was no use; she had nothing left. She lowered her arm again and received the cursory additional pain for her exertion.

Like a sadistic tease, the tree continued to sway.

After some time, she accepted her bitter reality: there was nothing she could do except lie there and take whatever came her way. Once in a while, the voices would stop – a break in transmission that in itself was a form of torture, for she knew they would always come back, louder and stronger than before. In those brief moments, she drifted into sleep, only to be brutally woken up again minutes later.

As dusk's shadows descended, the voices grew louder still, creating an unbearable orchestra of bleating sirens, bellowing louder and louder as the night wore on. No transmissions, no respite. Despite the unbearable din of noise, she could hear them quite clearly – hundreds, thousands of voices: "please, help us", "why are you doing this?", "we did you no harm", "my babies, my poor babies", "you killed my children", "how could you do such a thing?", "I don't understand – why did you do this?", "why are you doing this?", "how could you do this?", "we did you no harm", "we were just living our lives", "the children, why did you have to kill the children?", "you killed my mummy and daddy", "you killed my mummy", "why did you kill my mummy?", "why did you kill my daddy?"

The voices blared constantly, searing through her head, like a pneumatic drill smashing through concrete. She tried closing her eyes, gritting her teeth, screaming for them to stop, but to no avail; their voices of anguish continued to tear her body and soul. By midnight, her exhaustion had taken a form of mild insanity. She no longer knew whether she was awake or asleep. As far as she could tell, the voices no longer gave her any respite, whether conscious or unconscious. The only thing she knew for sure was that the only way to block them out was to scream louder than them – a brief and unsustainable solution that became her only form of escape.

She screamed as loud as she could for several seconds, causing her body to convulse and drowning the voices – a moment of bliss. Then, as soon as the air in her lungs was spent, the voices came back, as loud and merciless as before. Tears rolled freely down her face as she wondered how long her peril would go on for.

She yearned for her life to end; it was the only way out of her hell.

"Ask for their forgiveness."

Despite her frazzled mental state, this statement startled Justina. She could not tell whether it came from inside her head or elsewhere. It had a little more authority than the other voices. In an instant, she dismissed it as yet another addition to the thousands of voices inflicting her never-ending torture.

"You must ask them to forgive you," came the voice again.

Despite its authoritative nature, she sensed no anger or malice in it. This time, she opened her eyes, sensing the voice came from outside her head. Was somebody else there? She darted her eyes left to right, scanning the vicinity as best she could for sign of life. But there was nothing. In spite of this, the voices did not relent.

As she shut her eyes in preparation for more violent screams, the voice repeated its proverb.

"Ask them to forgive you."

She finally allowed herself to consider the question that had been gnawing away at her sub-conscious: Was she sorry?

For as long as she could remember, she had always believed her mission to be an honourable one, for the overall good of humankind. But was it?

Did she not feel her heart pound when she saw her brother again? It was painful, but she felt alive. And to be told by her own brother that she was the cause of so much death and suffering...

Images of her long-dead family littered her once-impenetrable mind – playing in the garden with her brother, arguing with him about what to watch on TV, pestering Mum in the kitchen, Dad's bedtime stories, all conjuring an unwelcome duet of sadness and longing.

And Alex – her heart skipped a beat whenever she thought about him.

Struggling to steady her mind, she laboured to realign her thoughts with the real question at hand: was she sorry for ending so many innocent lives?

A distant memory revealed itself – a petrified female baby dragon staring in silence at its dead mother, then realising she herself was in imminent danger and attempting to scramble for safety, hoping her detractors would let her be, turning her head to see whether she was being hounded. Her sad, panic-stricken eyes caught those of Justina's, distraught and fearful of what would happen next, pleading for it all to stop. The confusion – why was this happening? What had they done wrong? Nothing; they were simply bathed in fire for no other reason than being alive. The memory hit a nerve, opening a pit of regret and remorse. Unable to escape herself, she closed her eyes, appalled by the person she had become.

"Sorry," she gasped, unbelieving of any right to forgiveness. She had reached her end. Her heart began to beat faster and faster as furious torrents of guilt and shame coursed through her, sending her body into a frantic mess of convulsions.

"I'm sorry!" she screamed as an army of unleashed tears flooded her eyes. "I'M SORRY!"

She screamed louder, her voice echoing through the forest. Again and again, she yelled her apology until finally, sobbing profusely as the little strength she had waned, she drifted into an unconscious state. "Please... forgive me."

*

Nature absorbed Justina's words, aware of the possible ramifications of her moment of enlightenment as her drained mind enforced a deep sleep that tarried throughout the night – and the following morning.

It was mid-afternoon when her eyes finally stirred, the glow of the day's light caressing her eyelids. The voices had ceased, leaving behind a still and eerie silence.

For several minutes, she kept her eyes closed, appreciating the peace and quiet and weary of the possibility of the trauma starting all over again should she open them.

She tried as best she could to keep the events of the previous two days and nights at bay, holding on to her respite for as long as possible, but it did not take long for her memory to trigger, reminding her of her acceptance of the ills of her actions, of her moment of remorse; there was no hiding from it.

She wondered where she was – obviously in the forest, but where exactly? She had been gone for several days, so how come the others had not found or come across her? How were her screams not heard?

After some time, she summoned the courage to open her eyes, daring to hope the worst was over. A sea of ghostly bodies, humans and dragons, were stood in front of her.

Although a little startled at first, she was not so surprised, as deep down she knew the likelihood of her tormentors simply disappearing was slim.

A long stand-off followed, both parties staring at each other in expectation of the other breaking the silence. She did not know what to say; she had said she was sorry.

The shame she had felt the night before reacquainted itself. Everything was as it was before, the only difference now was that she could see them, and where once they were tormenting her with shrieks and groans, they now furthered her suffering with a sustained and vengeful silence.

Would they forever be in her sight? Would she wake up to their sorrow every day?

She dared not speak; no manner of words could justify or redeem her actions. Her heart began to beat faster again as her mind connected once more with the grotesque nature of her killings, reminding her also of the beast she had created. Liza's malevolence was her creation; she had manipulated her, moulded her into the evil she had become.

"You have to undo what you've done." The young boy in the middle was speaking for them. Her brother was their speaker.

"Are you with Mum and Dad? Where are they?" She was aware of the selfishness of her response but could not help herself; she longed to see their faces. Her questions were ignored, slamming into a transparent wall and trickling to the bottom like the insides of a raw egg.

"You must undo everything you've done, Jus." He clearly looked like her brother – same eyes, nose, colour, and hair texture, but a veneer of anger and disappointment was cast over him, obscuring their blood ties.

Recognising the foolishness of her enquiry, she attempted to respond. "I meant what I said last night; I was wrong, selfish, and heartless... but I'm not sure what you mean. How can any of it be undone?"

"Elias. You must rescue Elias. He's the key to all this."

"Elias? Who's—"

"That's just it, Jus! You really have no idea what you've done, do you? And now you're not even involved in their scheming. They captured Elias because he's the one they'll use to remove hope and love for good."

"But… how?"

"They will use his speed. It's all about resetting the universe. By circling the core between the outer and the inner realm seven times, they can reshape everything in whatever manner they wish. You must get Elias back."

"But what if I'm unable to?"

"Then the lost lives of those you see behind me will be nothing compared with what will happen in the future." He seemed agitated, irritated by her lack of conviction.

"You mean, they still—"

"They will kill anyone they suspect to still feel any type of emotion. She will kill thousands more. You made her this way, and now she's uncontrollable."

This part she understood; Liza was more than capable of doing just that – she would revel in it. And he was right: Liza was her doing.

Beads of sweat surfaced on her forehead, shimmering in the morning light before foraging south, towards the tip of her nose. She used her right hand to wipe them off, coming to the sudden realisation that her hand was free. Surprised, she glanced downwards, assessing the rest of her body. The tree that had pinned her down was no longer on top of her. She looked towards her brother in appreciation but soon realised her recent freedom of movement was nothing to do with him. Surely, she had not somehow freed herself. With what strength or power? Last she checked, she had had none. Despite the mass of bodies in front of her, her mind raced, trying to make sense of it.

"It's up to you, Jus. Or this..." He turned his head to the spirits of humans and dragons behind him, then turned to face her again, "...and so many more will all be on your head."

For a moment, she wondered what happened when people die. Do they stay the same age, or do they keep aging? The person speaking with her was not the same young boy she used to know.

She closed her eyes; now was not the time to get emotional again. She had a decision to make. The only decision she knew was right was the one she was the most reluctant to make. Afraid to venture down the right path, she opened her eyes again, hoping to find some sort of compromise, but they were gone. Dragons, humans, children, adults, dissolved into thin air, as though they were never there.

"He still loves you. He always will. But he isn't the same boy you once knew. Your brother, I mean."

It was the same voice she had heard earlier. Still at a loss as to where it was coming from, she sat up and was relieved to feel very little pain –

no broken bones, just a dull throbbing on her chest and arms.

Her eyes darted back and forth, searching through trees and branches. Gently lifting her left knee and pushing her right hand into the ground, she slowly got to her feet.

"Watching a sibling commit the most heinous acts will do that to a person." It was coming from behind her. It was a forlorn, almost broken voice, but there was something strangely familiar about it.

Justina turned slowly, the pit in her stomach growing deeper and wider.

Immediately, the source of the voice took a step back. She had never seen him up close before but recognised the dark green skin and the mark on his forehead – not as clear as it once was, but still very present. He took another step back, now merely a shadow of the once-magnificent beast she had seen from afar. He was leaner, more brittle. Despite the assuredness of his statements, he seemed hesitant, nervous even. His eyes twitched, betraying a cold and raw fear of the danger she presented. Could it really be him? The same one so many trusted and relied on? Whom even Zoldon feared?

"I won't harm you. I… Are you Raphael?"

His eyes wandered, veering away like a lost soul. It had been long since he heard someone say his name. It reminded him of who he once was, piling more misery on the shame that now haunted him.

"You are, aren't you? We searched for you for so many years. We looked everywhere. Where were you hiding? I meant what I said, by the way; I mean you no harm. Besides, I get the feeling you're the reason I'm no longer trapped under that tree." She could feel her babbling getting out of control, but she could not help herself.

She had never been this close to him before. Although he had always been her enemy, she had always admired him, revered him even. Despite Zoldon winning the war on all fronts, she had always sensed a heavy shroud of anxiety hanging over him. It was the reason they pursued his death with such vigour. Her master's fear of his enemy gave him a god-like status, an invisible and untouchable foe that could strike at any moment, a legendary opponent that could not be snared.

And here he was, standing right in front of her, but not as the great and valiant leader she had always imagined him to be.

"How did you know the voices would stop if I asked for their forgiveness?"

"Because we're all connected." He looked straight at her again, buoyed by her question. "The living and the dead; we're all connected. The reason they reached out to you is because they sense there is still some good in you. It seems I may have been wrong about you all along."

"But what can I possibly do? It's just me."

With a heavy sigh, his eyes veered away again. Reluctantly, he turned around, weary of the danger he was in. She had been missing for three days, and Zoldon's followers would no doubt be searching for her. Besides, she was right: it was just her. What could she possibly do to stop the juggernaut that Zoldon had at his disposal? There was a time when he would not have given such doubts a second thought.

He unfurled his wings, accepting another lost cause, but something stirred inside him.

"I know how things look. Trust me... I, too, think it's an impossible task, but the impossible is all we have. Remember, you are not alone."

His wings began to lift him up, and she watched him rise above the trees, gliding into the distance until she could see him no more.

*

Aware of his brother's pursuit, Raphael had been on the run for longer than he could remember, opting for a nomadic existence. Too many had died because of him, scorched to death by angry flames. It was quite straight-forward at first; he knew the outer realm better than most – the best places to hide, areas few dared to venture, places none knew existed.

He had needed to disappear, hoping Zoldon would eventually relent, but deep down he knew it was unlikely his brother would rest until he laid eyes on his dead corpse.

He spent a year hiding in uninhabitable marshlands, another on hazardous mountains most would consider to be death traps, some months at the bottom of an abandoned stream, all the while losing touch with himself until years later he had become a shadow with no purpose. His was a meaningless existence, waiting for time to make its final call. Most of those he had been close to or regarded to be of the same ilk had suffered cruel deaths. He often felt like a coward; running and hiding, hiding and running. His brother had won, and all that remained was for him to die. He desired it more than anything, but death continued to elude him, teasing him with near misses and refusing to sign off. The eastern part of the forest was his latest hiding place. He had heard a rumour that his brother's new lair was also in the same forest, but he figured the best place to hide was in plain sight; nobody would expect it. Besides, tens of miles of dense forest lay between the underground cave he had dug and the location of his pursuers.

For six months, he had hidden in his dark, waterlogged cave, burdened with sadness and regret, often wondering how he had gotten things so badly wrong – his brother, the gathering, Liza… one hapless mistake after another. Not a day passed when he did not think – could not think – of that terrifying day, hundreds of lives cut short because they dared to desire a world of love, hope, and peace. Was his ideal so foolish?

And Liza – he had put so much hope in her, invested so much of himself, only for her to become the most cruel and malevolent one of them all. He should have known better, read the signals, and taken heed. The image of her on Abaddon's back haunted him every day, reminding him of his naïvety.

In time, he caved in, yielding to the unending accusations in his head and accepting his fate.

He should never have encouraged the others to oppose his brother; it had all been for nothing.

After several months of self-confinement, he started to venture out a little more, half hoping to be captured. Glad to get some air, he traversed the forest for some time until he perched himself on a thick branch of a tall tree, high up enough to be undetected from the ground, but out of aerial view. And there he sat, staring in limbo for several hours until a crunching of twigs and leaves seized his attention. He leaned his head forward to ascertain the cause of the commotion, but a nest of leaves and branches obscured his vision, and so he moved slightly to his right to get a better view.

Still unable to secure a clear sighting, the ominous sounds of crunching leaves grew louder, confirming his suspicions that someone was walking through the forest. The crunching was too light to be that of a dragon's, but that only made him more nervous; dragons, he could possibly reason with, but humans, particularly the likes of Zoldon's two accomplices, were an altogether different level of risk.

Just as he readied himself to make his escape, he caught sight of an individual wondering aimlessly through the forest, staggering from tree to tree with hands over both ears. The person seemed to be in some discomfort, swooning and swaying like a wounded animal before crashing to the ground, head buried in both knees.

His heart burned with a natural desire to help, but something about the mousey-blonde hair caused him to remain frozen still, afraid of drawing attention to himself. Upon getting up again and turning around, he finally caught a glimpse of the individual's face, confirming his worst fears.

In an instant, images of his former comrades flashed through his mind – burning, pleading, dying. A cold shiver engrossed his spine, causing him to become rooted to the branch, unable to move. When last he had seen her, she had been sat on Zoldon's back, delighting in the murder of countless innocent dragons. He feared her – that was obvious – but another emotion stirred his heart, one he had never thought possible: hate. He resented her for turning Liza, for so cruelly killing dragons that had attended what they believed would be a peaceful meeting.

Yet, his was a hate with no substance, a toothless tiger. He no longer dared to believe in himself; too much had gone against him, too many lives lost because they heeded his call to place their faith in him. Just the day before, he had lost his last remaining friend and ally, captured by Abaddon and Liza.

Although he had not been there when Elias was taken, he still blamed himself; everyone close to him had either been killed or taken. The more he looked, the more he realised Justina was in anguish. As his bitterness towards her intensified, he breathed in, determined to have his revenge, but as faint whiskers of flames began to rasp on the surface of his nostrils, she screamed.

He could see the agony etched on her face as she crawled along the ground. The desperation and pain in her voice caused him to think again, allowing his kind nature to surface.

On hands and knees, she scrambled to a nearby tree before resuming her tortured position. To his surprise, she raised both her hands and used her powers to fell a tree, plunging it straight into herself. In an instant, she was pinned to the ground and knocked unconscious. He knew her desire, understood and empathised with it. But why? Why try to kill herself? What was she hearing that made her want to end it all?

Once more he breathed in, this time sending forth a luminous flame that fizzed and stirred as it formed a wide, transparent dome around the immediate area. Slowly, he descended, landing beside her, still aware of the danger she posed.

A whirl of emotions circled his mind as he stared at her. She had killed so many – surely, the sensible thing to do was to finish her off. He could not; his heart would not allow it. He grabbed the tree with his jaws and tossed it aside, allowing her to breathe a little easier. A bright shining light began to emanate from the distance, moving closer and closer, revealing thousands of ghostly bodies and faces of dragons and humans. It became clear: he knew the cause of her suffering.

"As soon as we sensed her doubts, we had to reach her somehow. We must convince her to undo all she's done," said a young boy.

"But... how?" asked Raphael.

"Have you forgotten everything, Raphael? Not only did you give up on who you are but you seemed to have lost your understanding."

"It's just... how can she possibly...?"

"That is why we're here. Listen very carefully to what I have to say…"

*

"The voices will never leave you, Justina. How you navigate them from now on is up to you."

Like a noose around her neck, Raphael's final words to Justina before he departed clung to her, tightening their grip the more she considered them.

Would they forever haunt her? Torment her daily until her mind imploded? What did he mean? It had been several hours since she heard them, and yet she could sense their presence, humming below the surface of her consciousness, waiting to strike at any given moment. What did they expect her to do? Fight Zoldon and Liza on her own? Such a notion was foolhardy, especially considering Liza's new powers.

Justina shuddered at the thought, recognising a reality she had been trying to ignore – she feared Liza, not just because of her newfound ability to burn anything in her way to cinder, but because of something more sinister. There was a darkness about her, a bottomless pit of bile and hate she dared not approach. Justina no longer understood her – how she thought, what she desired, who she was. Liza had become a book that could no longer be read or disseminated. Justina had seen it coming for some time but had allowed her ego to distort the truth, telling herself *she* was the one in control, that Liza was under her influence, that Liza was nothing more than her creation. It was all too clear now that Liza had taken her place as the weapon of choice in Zoldon's endgame, an uncontrollable force that he was ready to unleash, regardless of the ramifications.

Justina felt like a weak and spent force in comparison. How could she possibly oppose them? Such a thought was futile; all she could do was hope they would not go too far. But even if they did, what could she do to stop them? Nothing. The only viable option was to tag along and hope for the best, whatever that was.

She started to wonder where she was. Was she getting closer or was she heading further away? She was fairly sure when she departed that she was meant to turn left, but maybe she had turned left because it was the easiest route to turn without taking the risk of coming across him again. There was nothing she recognised – she saw countless rocks and boulders, buried under an endless sea of brown leaves and fallen branches, trees stretching out as far as her tired eyes could see.

After some time, she came to a huge open ditch. At first, she thought it was the new base, but the sight of dark, gurgling water brimming inside it caused her to think again. How could she not remember traversing such a wide ditch? Her eyes narrowed as they glared at the water's surface. How could she have evaded it?

For several minutes she peered at it, wondering what would have happened to her had she fallen in. A part of her wished she had, reunited with her family once more.

"You need to get back, Jus," she muttered to herself, snapping out of her trance.

She resumed her journey, hoping her instinct to go left was more than just her fear of bumping into Raphael again. For hours she walked through a forest she did not recognise, stopping every now and then to rest her feet, but never for long, as she dreaded the thought of spending another night alone in it.

The voices were still quiet, as though waiting to see what she would do upon getting back. Deep down she knew but did not want it to ruminate, so as not to upset her uninvited guests.

In time, the shades of night began to encircle her, reducing her frantic pace to a hesitant crawl, feeling her way through the dense forest as her eyes became redundant. Utterly exhausted, she slumped to the ground, surrendering to whatever the blackness of the night brought with it.

Straining her eyes one last time to assess her surroundings, she turned her head side to side – nothing but a thick fog of darkness. Better to close her eyes.

Her brother had looked so upset with her, disappointed, aghast – ashamed of who she had become. Shutting it out was the only way she could stop the hurt and quench of the pain that so cruelly seized her all those years ago. Had she just taken the easy way out? Succumbing to hate and anger instead of navigating her way through the hell she had been placed in? What else could she have done? What would he have done? Could he have coped any better? She wondered why she had not seen her parents in the crowd of ghosts that had besmirched her; they were probably too hurt and disappointed in her. Their little girl had turned into a monster, a mass murderer of innocent lives.

Struggling with her thoughts, she drifted into sleep, all too aware it could be her last.

"What makes you think she'll do the right thing?" came a voice.

Justina was right in sensing the voices had not left her. All around her were souls of the departed, many of whom had died by her hands. They had been following her, watching... waiting.

"What other choice do we have?" said another.

"I know my sister. I'm sure…"

"You *used* to know your sister. Was she slaying people for fun before you died?"

216

"No... I mean... she's in there somewhere; I can feel it."

"I hope so, dear son. For all our sakes, I really hope so." Her husband put his arm around her, his loving eyes comforting her, trying as best he could to convince her everything would be alright, that their daughter would come through.

"I, too, sensed a small stirring when we spoke, but I fear she may be too afraid to shift her stance. All we can do is hope," said Raphael. He had followed all day, ready to somehow steer her back in the right direction in case she turned the wrong way. At one point, he was sure she saw his reflection in the water at the ditch. She lingered there, staring, as though encouraging him to tell her what to do. For a moment he wanted to but quickly came to his senses. The decision had to be hers, and hers alone.

"Is she safe here?" asked another.

"She has almost reached the lair. It's right in front of her, but she couldn't see it because of the dark."

"Yes, but is she safe?" asked Justina's mother.

"This area is surrounded by her... *Zoldon's* followers. At worst, they will protect her. Besides, I will watch over her."

All night he watched her – they all watched her – protecting their two realms' one and only hope. Only when dawn's gentle rays began to paint the forest with strips of light did the throng leave her. Raphael retreated, positioning himself outside the perimeter of dragons guarding the lair.

Justina stirred a little, then drifted back into sleep. After some minutes, she stirred again. A ray of light was massaging her left eye, making it more difficult to pretend it was still night-time. She kept her eyes shut; to open them meant another day of doubts and questions she would rather not face.

11

Elias

"We've been looking for you, Miss," sounded a voice, ending her brief moment of illusion. Justina opened her eyes to find two dragons peering down at her. Behind them were four more, positioned by the entrance, with another half a dozen perched on top of the towers around the perimeter, standing guard, as though an attack was imminent.

The towers were new; Zoldon had obviously had a change of mind. It was as though he was inviting – *daring* his brother to attack. If only he knew he had nothing to worry about. Squinting her eyes to get a better view of her surroundings, Justina slowly rose to her feet, dusting the leaves and dirt that had kept her company during the night. Her pulse quickened as she considered how she would explain her absence. She still did not know exactly how long she had been away, but she was fairly sure it was at least three to four days. What would she tell them? Where had she been? Why?

"Where are they?" she asked.

"Inside. A lot has happened since we last saw you," replied one of the dragons.

Why did he say that? Was he implying something, or just giving her an update? She felt like even more of an outsider than before. The voices in her head were fast turning her into an imposter. Could they tell what was going on inside her? She needed to get a grip and get inside.

"Take me to them," she said, asserting her authority.

But there was no response. Rather, the dragons took their time, inhaling and exhaling slowly as their eyes dissected her mind.

A little taken aback, she repeated herself, this time more forcefully, calling their bluff; it was all she had left. "I said, take me to them!"

Both turned around at once. "This way, Miss."

They led her to the entrance and descended the steps, which were now lit all the way down by burning flames in dark brown pots of clay. Upon reaching the bottom of the stairs, her eyes marvelled at what lay in front of them. There were no longer three dark passages, but one great hall, containing hundreds of dragons, mingling, discussing, planning, preparing – a den of intense activity.

Cone-shaped pestles with luminous flames hung symmetrically along the concrete walls. She was comforted that Zoldon had heeded her advice; it made her feel a little less irrelevant.

Maybe she was not under suspicion after all. Maybe the feeling of dread that had fastened itself to her was as a result of something else. She had felt an acidic reaction in her stomach as soon as they entered, causing it to churn in nervous discomfort. She could hear the clumping of the soles of her boots on the concrete floor, each step cementing her loneliness, but why, she did not know. After all, she was the same person; nothing had changed. Some things had occurred, but she was the same. She longed to get her position back, for Zoldon to rely on her again, for everything to return to the way it was before. It was up to her. She would display a renewed conviction for the cause.

But where had she been? She still was not sure what to say. How was she going to explain her disappearance?

Many dragons acknowledged her as they proceeded towards the back of the hall, some even bowing a little, honouring the return of a prodigal child.

"Ahh, Justina, we sent several search parties, but none of them could find you. Care to tell us where you've been?" Zoldon was perched on a large marble slab, flanked by Abaddon on one side, on his right a sinister-looking figure in a long, hooded, black cape that shielded much of the face.

Justina's spine quivered as she wondered who it was, but she soon recognised the tips of Liza's black boots, an imposing new cloak conveying her heightened status. Her renewed conviction began to wane as her heart skipped several beats. Once more, she felt like an outsider looking in, or worse, an outsider facing imminent interrogation. They were in mid-discussion – Zoldon's head leaning slightly to his right, with eyes gazing downwards, whilst Liza spoke in a hushed tone. Something had either happened or was about to happen. Were they talking about her? Did they somehow know about her dalliance with the departed souls of their enemies?

She breathed in and out again, slowly, reminding herself she had done nothing wrong. Yes, she was approached by the other side, but nothing happened; she had walked away.

"Ahh, Justina, where have you been? One minute you said you weren't feeling well, and the next you disappear for four days. Anything we should know?"

"Sorry? Oh, nothing at all, just needed to get myself together... to feel better, I mean."

"And how are you feeling now?"

"Much better. At least, the migraines seemed to have stopped, anyway."

"Yes, until next time, I suppose," commented Zoldon. He fixed his piercing eyes on hers, laying siege to her shaky defences.

Whatever courage she had managed to muster was fast evaporating. She could feel Liza's brooding eyes, searching and probing.

"Let's hope that's the last of it. You guys look as though you're concerned about something. What's happened?" It was all she could do, change the topic and channel their focus on the matter at hand.

A long silence followed, with both parties waiting for the other to speak. Was that a tinge of disappointment she sensed in his eyes, or was she being too self-conscious? Out of the blue, Zoldon rose to his feet and began to slowly walk towards her, eyes still fixed on hers, stopping just a few inches in front of her.

He paused, waiting, lingering. "Come with me; something I want to show you. You too, Liza."

For some seconds, Justina's feet remained glued to the ground, unable to move for fear of what lay ahead. Where was he taking her?

Liza followed, passing without so much as a glance in her direction. She turned to follow them, only for Zoldon to stop after a dozen or so paces.

"Lower the cage," said Zoldon.

Two dragons grabbed an iron chain with their mouths and began to pull, taking backward steps as they did so.

Justina looked up to see a large metal cage descending from above. Judging by the visible strain on the dragons' necks, whatever was in the cage was large and heavy.

"Quickly!" shouted Abaddon.

Two more dragons joined in to help lower the cage faster. As it neared the ground, its occupant became more visible.

It was a dragon, pinned to the floor by the heavy chains around it – body, legs, feet, mouth. Only its eyes and nose were free.

The cage finally landed on the ground, placing the prisoner's eyes directly in front of Justina. It stirred a little upon seeing her, eyes blazing with hatred and resentment. She wondered why it reacted to her so quickly. Did it know her? For a moment, she shuddered at the thought that it might be Raphael; maybe they had heard their conversation. But it was not him – different eyes.

"Who's this? Why is—"

"…It not dead like the others?" Liza's eyes were searching again, looking for signs of fear or guilt.

"Elias is the final piece of the jigsaw," said Zoldon.

"I don't understand. What... who is he?"

"In order to destroy love and hope, we must turn back time in our own image," said Zoldon.

"I still don't get it. How?"

"Elias is the fastest of all dragons. To say he flies at the speed of light would be to do him an injustice. He's always been the key. One of you – Liza – will ride him seven times around the perimeter of our two realms, and by so doing, everything will be reversed; humankind will be reduced to gormless corpses, devoid of sense or feeling."

The anger that was bulging in Elias' eyes some moments ago had subsided, replaced by a sad recognition of his unfortunate fate; after all he had fought for, he would be the one to end it all. Memories of his unwavering commitment to the cause floated aimlessly through his mind, reminding him of his folly. He should have known there would only be one outcome as he watched his friends and kin burned alive on that fateful day. The probability of the meeting being a trap had been all too apparent to him; it was the reason he went out of his way to convince Raphael to delay his arrival.

*

"I'm not sure I understand you. Why do you want us to avoid the meeting?"

"I'm not saying we shouldn't turn up, Raphael. I just think we should assess things first, from afar. Just to make sure."

"That's what I don't understand. Make sure of what?"

"There's something I... something just doesn't seem right. We need to be careful."

"No, Elias. How can I expect others to attend, if I don't turn up myself? Such a thing would be hypocritical and foolhardy. No; we will go as planned."

226

"But can't we—"

"No, Elias! I've made my decision, and it's final." Raphael turned to leave. There was only one way to prevent the disaster he feared, and that was to resolve things amicably. For both humankind and dragons to survive, a truce with Zoldon was paramount. The fact that Elias did not understand that irritated him.

"Raphael, wait!"

"Yes, what now?"

Elias paused, the guilt of what he was about to say rising inside him like a festering volcano. He loved Raphael like no other, not just as his leader, but like an older brother. But he sensed his friend and mentor was being naïve.

"I see your point. I really do. Everyone looks up to you, as do I. I'm probably overthinking things. You have to be there, of course you do."

"Precisely!"

"And I want to... I *will* be by your side, no matter what. But in this instance, I think I need a little help. Maybe we could visit Zebulun's grave together? I think it will give me the courage I'm so obviously lacking at present. Can we visit him before we go to the meeting? It will help me reconnect with why we're doing all this."

"If that's what it will take to steady those nerves of yours, then of course we can."

"Thank you. I feel sure it will help me a great deal."

Much to Raphael's grievance, Elias arrived at Zebulun's grave some thirty minutes later than planned, and as a result, he and his leader escaped Zoldon's heinous ploy. As they witnessed the massacre of their comrades, he sensed Raphael's shame for not dying with the rest; to have escaped was as though he was part of the plan. They looked for him, cried out his name, hoping to be rescued from their agonising peril. But help did not come. Help was watching them from a distance, distraught and ashamed.

"What have you done, Liza? What have you done?" said Raphael.

The young girl he had placed so much faith in had turned before his very eyes, yielded to a part of her he always knew existed but never dared to contemplate. How could she come back from such a terrible deed? In that moment, his hopes and ideals began to melt away. All he had taught her eviscerated in an instant. Time came to a shuddering halt, and everything was still. There was nothing else to resort to; she was the last glimmer of light in a perennial darkness that would consume all he longed for. He withdrew his wings from Elias' shoulder as the realisation of what his friend had done became apparent. His breath quickened as a steady stream of resentment flowed through him.

"This is why you turned up late? You did so on purpose?"

"I tried to warn you, but you wouldn't listen."

"And so you decided to trick me? Keep me safe with your deceptive ploy in the knowledge of... Look! Look at them! They are dying because of me!"

"Yes, but if only—"

"If only what? I would rather have died with them than be here, hiding like a coward as our comrades perish. If you think this is a good thing you've done, then you really don't know me at all."

"Yes, but whilst you're alive, there is still hope, Raphael."

"Hope? Hope? You dare speak of hope? Hope has just been slaughtered before our very eyes!"

"That's what I don't get. You told us Liza was the key, the one who would help us win this war, but now look at her."

Raphael stepped forward, leaning his head towards Elias, his nostrils flaring, rasps of flames flickering in his now open mouth. "What is it you're trying to say, Elias? Go on, spit it out."

Despite the dangerous territory he was treading on, Elias refused to back down. Why should he? His friend needed to be told the truth. "You put so much faith in her, and for what? Look at her, Raphael! She's killed them all. They're dead because of her... because of you. Not only did you train her but you wouldn't listen to reason. Instead, you allowed your ideals to blind you."

There: he had said it. Whatever happened next did not matter; he was ready to die – Raphael could do whatever he wanted to him. But as soon as the final word poured out, a cold numbness engulfed him as the constricting fangs of guilt began to circle. "I... I'm sorry, Raphael... it's just... I was..."

"Speaking the truth." Elias' words were ringing in his ears, carrying with them an unbearable weight. Raphael took a step back and lowered his head. The flames that had been sizzling in his mouth retreated in shame. In silence, he remained still, crestfallen eyes fixed to the ground, lamenting his fatal errors.

After some minutes, Elias, wracked with guilt, attempted to console him. "This isn't the end, Raphael. We mustn't give up. There must be another way."

Raphael did not reply; he could not. He had stood on the edge of an abyss and fallen headfirst. Slowly, he turned around, unfurled his wings and set off into the distance.

Wanting to apologise, Elias prepared to chase after him, but his body refused to respond. He knew his words had been harsh, insensitive to the turmoil his friend was experiencing. But deep down, he knew he had spoken the truth, and it needed to be said.

Raphael's angry reaction irritated him, causing him to wonder whether he was any different from his brother; hundreds had died, and yet all Raphael could think of was his own pride.

For several hours, he remained at the top of the hill, staring at the charred bodies below, wanting to descend to see whether any survived, but he was too wary of being seen to dare. Whenever he thought he saw a body stir, he scanned the horizon for signs of Zoldon's followers and always felt sure he saw something, shadows lurking in the background, waiting to pounce.

Zoldon would have known his brother was not amongst the dead and would no doubt have ordered a few of his soldiers to stay behind, hidden behind trees and crevices, waiting for their moment of glory. The fact that he could not help the wounded and dying magnified his guilt. Maybe he was a coward after all.

Only when the murmurings of the night began to descend did he decide to leave, making his way back to the dark cove that had become their home away from home. He hoped to find his friend there waiting for him, ready to make amends, but there was nobody there. What had once been a hive of activity was now barren and lifeless – an empty morsel.

Under the heavy blanket of darkness, he feared for his friend's life. What if he had been taken? What if... No, not Raphael; surely, he would not? He wanted to go and search for him, but to do so would have been suicidal. Besides, where would he even begin? The least he could do was to stay awake and keep a look out. For several hours, he battled sleep's arrows, drifting in and out, cursing himself for being weak and cowardly whenever he woke up. Eventually, nature's weighty hands had their way, sending him into a deep and troubled sleep.

Elias was awoken by light plops of water, dripping from the roof of the cove. At first, he kept his eyes shut, hoping it had all been a bad dream, but the silence around him spoke otherwise.

Daylight brought with it a fresh armoury of courage, and the whereabouts of Raphael suddenly became all too clear to him. In an instant he set off, surging through the skies like a possessed rod of lightning, hoping and praying his worst fears were not about to materialise. It was not long before his heart began to beat less feverishly, enabling him to breathe more easily. There in the distance was his friend, frantically looking for something amongst the dead.

For some seconds, a horrendous outcome that Elias had not considered was unravelling itself. A cold shiver scurried down his spine as he contemplated the possibility that Raphael had lost his mind. What could he possibly be looking for in that sorrowful heap of charred remains? But as he got closer, the picture became clearer; he was digging, not looking, using his feet, wings and even his head to dig as wide and deep as possible. Ever a beacon of light, he was showing his love and devotion to his departed comrades in the only way available to him.

It was too late to apologise and plead for their forgiveness but not too late to pay homage and respect, an act of love few would even consider, putting his own life at risk for the sake of those no longer present.

In that moment, Elias was rekindled with the unquestionable reason for his admiration and loyalty to his friend. With his heart warmed with renewed faith, he descended towards him, landing a few feet away from the mass grave.

Sensing his presence, Raphael paused, raising his head a little, then continued to unearth the soil around him. Elias surveyed the grave's perimeter, then started to dig, widening the circumference of the open tomb.

In silence, they dug all day. Occasionally, they paused for a break, resting on their hinds, engrossed in their pathetic thoughts – fond memories, regret, remorse. Not one word was spoken between them that afternoon. And when they were done digging, they dragged and pulled body after body for several more hours, placing them in the grave they had created, their faces mired in sweat and tears. The night was pitch-black by the time they were done covering the open pit, but darkness no longer concerned them.

They sat by the grave throughout the night, mourning lost friends and relatives.

By the time daylight arrived, their well of tears had run dry, and the reality of the abject nothingness that lay on the horizon of a faceless future was all too apparent.

"Forgive me, Elias; this is all my fault, I see that now."

Shocked to see him standing right in front of him, Elias jolted, almost tripping over himself.

"You have always been a dear and loyal friend. You simply wanted to protect me. I see that now."

"Raphael, I'm so—"

"No need to say anything, my friend. I should never have doubted you."

"All those things I said… I didn't mean them to come out that way. I've always looked up to you. I always will."

"And I you, my friend... more than you know." Raphael's eyes were beginning to drown in his tears. He took a deep breath, hoping to rein in the sorrow inside him. "But I fear this is the end of our road, my dear friend."

"End of... what do you mean? We can't just give up!"

"There's no other way, Elias." Raphael's voice was calm, almost whisper-like. "We both know there is nothing more we can do to stop this."

Elias could not respond, for deep down he, too, had acknowledged the reality that their war was lost. As he finally allowed their obvious demise to register, his body began to shake, exorcising years of unfulfilled hope. He wanted to hold his friend and cry but feared the well of tears that had filled his eyes would never cease, and so he looked up to the skies for solace, desperately trying to keep himself together.

"I will always hold you in my heart, my friend... and it is for that reason that we must part ways. It's safer that way... for your sake. I would never forgive myself if something happened to you because of me."

Elias continued to gaze upwards, unable to face what was about to occur. He dared not; how would he cope without his dear friend? What sense of direction could he possibly find without his leader and mentor? Maybe he should not have tricked him, after all.

A lone figure sat astride a light grey dragon, beyond the hills opposite them. Clad in a dark brown cape, the only noticeable feature were the tips of the red boots at the foot of the gown. The dragon's light grey skin made it look different to all the others. Its torso was smoother, less reptilian even. They had also been there the day before, witnessing Zoldon's mass assassination. In perfect stillness, the hooded figure and its beast studied Elias and Raphael, as though analysing an enemy's weakness.

"That right there is why they can never win this war: too weak, too... sentimental," said the dragon, unnerved by what he had just seen.

"Hmmm... you mean, you wouldn't do the same for me?" the rider asked.

"That's different."

"Not so different, my love. Not so different at all. But I'm beginning to understand why this must be done."

"So, now you agree with Zoldon?" asked the dragon.

"Not agree exactly, just understand. Why should people have to suffer forever? If hearts and minds are the weak points of human beings, then… I guess my father was right."

The dragon tilted his head back a little, unsure of how to phrase what he was about to say.

"Do you think you'll ever be able to forgive him? Pelonious, I mean…"

The heart of the individual beneath the cloak began to beat faster at the hearing of the name. It had been long since it was last uttered… centuries. But no amount of time could heal the damage done.

Raphael was never the same after that day. Belief, conviction, fight; all began to drain out of him, dimming the light until all that was left was an abandoned hollow shell, bereft of life or hope.

His friend also died that day.

In time, they parted ways, Raphael insisting that it was safer for all if he sojourned alone, but such was his love for his leader that Elias never strayed too far, often keeping an eye on him without his knowledge, watching, guarding, protecting him from his pursuers. Why Raphael chose to venture so close to his brother's new lair was a mystery to him – so close to those who wanted him dead. Was he still clinging to his hope that Zoldon would somehow have a change of mind? The very notion seemed ludicrous. Still, he continued to watch over him from afar. The Raphael he used to know was long gone, and in his place was a feeble replica living a pipe dream. He saw Justina, wandering the forest like a deranged animal, screaming for help, their sworn enemy in as vulnerable a state as they could ever wish for. And yet, there he was, watching over her.

Raphael's zeal for love had once again led to another's demise – his own, snared by his enemies as he watched over his friend.

*

Feeling another's sadness and pain was not something Justina was accustomed to. Conscious of the rising tide of emotion in her eyes, she looked up towards the ceiling. "Is this thing stable?"

"The cage? Yes, of course it is; it was made especially for him," replied Zoldon.

"Good. If he's the key, then we can't afford any mishaps. And you're sure there aren't any others out there?"

"We have guards stationed right across the forest. Only a fool would dare try to enter. Liza, it's time. You know what to do."

Liza nodded, her hood shielding the smirk on her face. Without a word, she turned around and made her exit.

"She is also the key. Her ability to blaze is not the only new power she possesses."

"What do you mean?"

"She can now control minds, Justina. No matter how much Elias tries to resist, she can make him fly as fast and in whatever direction she wishes. I sensed it in her a long time ago. It just needed a little coaxing."

A still silence consumed Justina's senses as the walls began to inch towards her, robbing her of space and air. Had she been reading her thoughts all along? Her knees buckled in response to her feigning body.

"Are you okay?"

"Yes, I'm fine. Just feel a little dizzy. Probably a side effect of the migraine or something."

"Yes, probably. I think it's best if you get some rest, Justina." Zoldon turned around to return to his palatial seat. "We have everything in order. Take the day off. Tomorrow is a big day."

She was a bystander now, looking in from the outside. All she could do was watch, agree and hope they would not turn on her.

12

Alex

Seated on a blue plastic seat in a waiting room in Glasgow's Queen Elizabeth University Hospital was an eleven-year-old boy. He had been there for several hours, replaying the video of his mother's sudden collapse in his head over and over again, blaming himself for not being able to help her.

If only he had not said he was hungry. He should have known she was not feeling well – the signs were there; they had always been there. The room had started to spin again, accompanying the latest surge of anxiety and worry that had been whirling inside of him like a crazed revolving door.

Placing his head in his trembling hands, his breathing quickened as he tried to contain his emotions. The more the mental video played, the more his breathing grew faint and shallow. The circling panic accelerated into a feverish spin.

He leaned forward, pushing his tear-soaked palms into his eyes. It seemed to help, as the spin reduced to a slow circling once more, encouraging the echoes of vomit that had been gathering at the back of his throat to retreat. It was all he could do to keep himself together.

Mentally and emotionally exhausted, he wanted to rest his weary back on the upright of the chair, but he dared not; it was not the first time the swirling had seized him, and, after so many episodes, he knew the next one would not be too far away. Head in hands was all he could do to delay the inevitable a little.

"Poor boy. How long has he been sitting there?" whispered a nurse.

The receptionist withdrew his head from the screen in which it was buried and turned to the nurse, confusion addressing his weary eyes.

"The wee boy! How long has he been waiting? I'm sure I saw him sitting there hours ago," whispered the nurse a little louder.

"Oh yes, him – he's been here for hours, at least five or six. His mum collapsed, I think. He was the one that called the ambulance and everything. Can you imagine? To have to go through something like that. Such a good kid as well; so well-behaved."

"So, nobody's with him? Dad, brother, relatives?"

"We've been trying to get hold of his dad all day, but there's no answer. Left several messages but he hasn't called back. Honestly, some people, eh? For a kid like that to have to go through such a thing on his own. Any idea what's wrong with her? His mum, I mean."

"Not sure, but from the look on the faces of the doctors I saw coming out of the room a few hours back, it doesn't look too promising. Poor thing. Has he eaten?"

"I've asked him a few times now, but he just looks at me and shakes his head, then places his head in his hands again. Been shaking like a leaf all day. I dread to think what he's going through."

"Er… excuse me, I'm looking for my wife. And my son. Yes, wee boy as well, if you've seen him." The man's glazed eyes were vacant and bloodshot. Clutching his flat cap, the whites of his knuckles were fraught with tension and uncertainty. He leaned forward, then took a small step back, conscious of invading the others' space. The nurse leaned back a little, removing her head from the firing line of the stale whisky that was freely seeping out of his pores.

"What's your wife's name, sir?"

"Julie... Julie Spires. I... Have you seen a wee boy? Little fella, black hair. I think... Alex? Alex, is that you, son?" He turned to head towards the young boy but abruptly stopped, putting on his cap, then taking it off again. His legs refused to move, preferring to stay where they were, uncertain of what lay ahead.

Now with a better view, the receptionist eyed him up and down, then whispered something to the nurse, eyebrows furrowed in disappointment.

Finally, his legs responded as he summoned enough courage to continue. He made his way to his little boy and sat himself beside him, lifting his left arm, then bringing it down again and clasping both hands together. The last time they were together was two days earlier, and he had raised his left arm for an altogether different reason. The boy removed his hands from his face and turned to the person sitting next to him. It was him, the one who only ever showed up when he had to.

"They've been calling you all day; where have you been, Dad?"

"Oh, I... I'm so sorry, Alex, I..." There was nothing he could say. If he told him the truth, it would simply confirm what he was sure his son already knew. The last time he saw him was in the kitchen, shouting obscenities at his mother, telling her how useless she was. He had been upset about having the same thing for dinner three days running, conveniently forgetting that there would be nothing at all on the table were it not for his wife's job.

"I'm tired of this damn food, woman. Can't you make anything else?" His face was a few inches from hers, the stench of cheap whisky pouring from his breath.

She did not reply; there was no point in reasoning with him when he was in such a condition.

"I asked you a question; answer me, woman!"

She still did not answer.

He felt insulted by her silence – it rendered his remaining shreds of masculinity impotent. He raised his hand to hit her; it was all he had left.

"Leave her alone!" shouted Alex, shoving his father away from his mother. "Leave her alone! She's trying her best. What about you? All you do is drink and shout."

Unprepared for his son's audacity, he paused, took a couple of steps back, allowing the words to ring in his alcohol-impaired ears, then lunged at his wife, left arm raised in preparation for its cowardly onslaught, but he stumbled, crashing to the floor in a calamitous thud. And so, the last few drops of dignity spilled out of his already empty cup. Slowly, he got to his feet, put on his cap and made for the kitchen door, leaving the house via the back garden. Unsure of what to do, he made his way to the only place he understood – the one place he could depend on.

"Bottle, please, Sue," he said, making his way to the far corner of the pub.

"Jim, I can't give you…"

"Woman, bottle." Before long, his worries had dissipated, forced into flight by rivers of brown liquor. He proceeded to drink himself into oblivion. A few regulars he knew joined him for a short while but left as closing time approached. By the end of the night, his head was placed on the table, alongside his flailing left arm. "Another, please, Sue," he said, jolting out of his drunken trance.

"Sorry, Jim, that's your lot. You still owe us from last night. And besides, it's closing time. Go on, best be having ye."

A feeble grunt was all she got in reply.

She waited a few more seconds, then gave a heavy sigh before positioning herself beside him, gently putting one arm around him and the other under his arm pit to slowly lift him up. He was heavy, weighed down with whisky and his numerous troubles. She beckoned the doorman to give her a hand, and together they escorted him to the door.

"I said I want another, Sue. Another bottle, damn ye."

"Not tonight, Jim. Maybe tomorrow. Right now, ye need yer bed, me friend."

"What shall I do with him?" whispered the doorman.

"Aye, I heard that. Get me anodda one, that's what ye canni do, get me anodda," said Jim, trying to untangle himself from the barman's arms.

"Not tonight, me friend. I told ya, tomorrow," said Sue. She leaned towards the doorman and whispered: "Put him in a taxi. Number four, Doyle Street."

The doorman heeded his boss' instruction and took Jim outside. They stood on the pavement for a few minutes, waiting for a taxi, Jim swooning, swearing, groaning, and protesting his ill treatment. Seeing a passing taxi, the doorman flagged it down, then leaned forward to give the driver the address.

"Four Doyle Street. Can you help me make sure he goes inside when he gets there?"

"Hey, leave me be. I ain't goin' nout. Leave me be, I say," said Jim, raising his voice to convey his displeasure.

"Jim, I need to get ye home, man," said the doorman.

"I said, leave me be, man. Don' wanna go home." Finally managing to free himself, he staggered away, breaking into a short sprint in case the doorman was chasing him.

"Leave him, Jack. Best get yourself home," said Sue.

"Are you sure, Sue? I can find him, ye know."

"Nah, nout you cannnie do when he's like that. I'm sure he'll be back ready for more tomorrow. Go on, get ye'self home, lad."

The sound of inebriated chatter and the rumblings of broken bottles emanated from the dark alley that Jim had ran into. Sue leaned forward;

a cold, gentle breeze brushed the fringe of her shoulder-length grey hair as her eyes strained behind her black, thick-rimmed glasses. A cluster of light drops of rain landed on her glasses, meandering and criss-crossing until her already imperfect sight became fatally handicapped. "Oh, Jim," she sighed before going back inside.

Jim spent the night with a handful of other drunks, drowning their grievances and sorrows with whatever they could find. As ever, he managed to make his way back to The Stag, plonking himself on a stack of black bin bags outside the back entrance. There he remained, unconscious throughout the night and for much of the following day.

"Look at the state o' ye," came a voice. "And answer ye phone, for Pete's sake."

"Huh?" His eyes were still closed, oblivious to the heavy pellets of rain laying siege to them. Swinging his head from side to side, as though being tormented by ravenous demons, he swatted his left arm, hoping the unwelcome disturbance would leave him in peace.

"Answer ye phone, ye pillock; it's been ringing non-stop. Wouldn't even have known you were out here, were it not for that bleedin' thing.

249

Go on, answer it," said Sue, picking up the phone and thrusting it to his left ear.

Alex kept his head buried deep in his hands. He knew he was sat there next to him; he could smell him – stale whisky and urine. It made him want to vomit. The angst and disgust at the pit of his stomach encouraged him to lash out at him, tell him what a terrible husband he was, tell him how ashamed he was to have him as a father. But deep down, he did not want to be alone. Even the drunken excuse for a man sitting beside him was better than nothing. Simply ignoring him would do for now.

In a feeble attempt to console him, Jim placed his hand on Alex's back, as rigid and unresponsive as it was. He removed it again, unsure of what to do with himself. He looked about him, searching for someone to give him some answers as to the whereabouts and condition of his wife but remained frozen to the chair, his tongue unable to mouth the requisite words.

He leaned forward, peered at the back of his son's head, opened his mouth, then quickly shut it again and leaned back. He tried to recall his last words before leaving the house the previous day, but his memory was a mangled web of disorder and confusion.

All he could muster was being woken up by Sue. Yearning for some coffee to perk himself up, he searched his soggy pockets, but all he could feel was rain-sodden tissues and a dirty hanky. He leaned forward again, trying to sum up the courage to ask his son for some loose change, then recoiled once more. When would this end? What kind of life was he living?

"Mr. Spires?"

Alex withdrew his head from his hands and faced the direction from which the voice came.

Jim straightened and got to his feet, still swaying a little.

"This way, please; you may see her now. But you should know that she's still unconscious. I fear the fall may have done irreparable damage to her cranium." His middle-class English accent seemed alien to both of them, but they were able to understand him, nonetheless. They followed him down the corridor, passing several rooms, every now and then getting a glimpse of the ghostly-looking patients that were strewn on numerous beds inside, a final stop for dying patients.

"In here," said the doctor. "Feel free to hold her hand and talk to her if you want to. In fact, I always recommend it; you'd be surprised how much an unconscious patient can hear. I've heard

251

some incredible stories, I can tell you." He seemed more engrossed in tales of the unconscious than the likelihood of Mrs. Spires making a recovery.

With his head bowed, Alex approached the bedside, delaying his sighting of his mum for as long as possible. His hands trembled as he sat on the chair by the bed. His head was shaking when he finally looked upon her, tears streaming down his cheeks.

"Ma! Ma, please, wake up, Ma."

"I don't think she can—"

"You heard what he said!" Finally, Alex laid eyes on the wretched man beside him. He wanted to hit him, throw him out and tell him never to return, but somehow, he still needed him; he could not go through this on his own.

"Erm, Mr. Spires, can I have a quick word?" enquired the doctor.

Alex turned to him, unsure of which Mr. Spires he was referring to.

"Spires senior, I mean. You stay there with your mum, young man. Remember to talk to her; she can hear you."

Alex watched his father lumber up to the doctor, fixing his gaze on them as they stepped out of the room. He continued watching them for several seconds, trying to make out what they were saying but could not make anything out. He turned to his mother again and held her hand.

It was barely warm; life had already begun to make its exit. His eyes gazed at her; even then, with multiple tubes going in and out of her, he could see those little dimples he had always adored. He would often pinch them whenever he got the chance – especially when he was younger. He would pounce on her whilst she was reading him a story and squeeze, giggling as she protested and attempted to remove her cheeks from the grip of his stubby little fingers.

"Oi, stop that, ye little devil," she would say. "I'll nay read ye story if ye don't stop."

But he would carry on anyway, unable to resist the opportunity to tease. He loved the reaction it caused – her face seized by spasms of endless giggles, her body quivering like an electric eel. In those moments, she lost all coordination in her body. It was as though she was being tickled under the arm by a thousand feathers.

For a moment, the sides of his lips curled, warming to the memory. He wondered how much of her was left. The tubes in her nose and mouth suggested she could not breathe on her own – the machine on the other side seemed to be breathing for her. In-out, in-out, in-out, in unison with the heaving of her chest. Whatever it was, he did not like it. It made him feel as though his mother was not the same anymore, like a part of her had been taken away. Could she hear him? He squeezed her hand a little, hoping for some kind of reaction, but none came.

Her eyes seemed to flicker every now and then, and he wondered, *hoped,* it meant she was waking up. But she didn't; they remained closed. If only he had done something, insisted that she go to the doctor's that time, then maybe this would never have happened. He should have made her go. He had given in to her assurance too easily. He had thought about telling his father but feared he would use it against her, blame her for her own sickness. He blamed her for everything – work, money, life, everything was her fault. Alex could never understand how or why. As far as he could see, his father was the problem – no job, always drunk, shouting, threatening, hitting. Alex had pleaded with his mother once for them to leave him, to run away and never come back, and for a moment he felt sure he caught a glimpse of an agreement, but for some reason, one he could never understand, she felt an obligation to stay.

"He needs us. We cannie abandon him, me boy. He needs us."

He could not get that day out of his head. This was his fault. He should have done something when he saw it…

"Mum, we're running late, we need to go," said Alex.

"Hold your horses, wee fella. Why the big rush? Oh, don't tell me, it isn't because of your wee new friend, is it? What's her name now... hmmm... Amy?" She ruffled his hair, enjoying the rare opportunity to tease her son. A rush of blood warmed and reddened his cheeks. He swiftly rejected her suggestion, turning around to pick up his bag.

"Don't be silly, Ma; she's me friend, that's all."

"Ma wee boy has got his first cruuuuush," teased his mother. Again, she ruffled his hair, with both hands this time.

He stepped away from her in defiance, but his now plum-coloured cheeks told a different story. "Mum, stop. We have to go."

"Okay, okay, let's get you to Amy, then," replied Julie, ruffling his hair one final time.

She cleared her throat as she picked up the keys from the table, then coughed. "Think I need some water before we go. One sec," she said as she picked up a glass and made her way to the kitchen sink.

Alex sighed, inconvenienced by the further delay.

His mother turned on the tap and let it run before placing the glass under it. By then, the coughing was more frequent, causing her to wince and splutter. She switched off the tap and made her way to the chairs at the table, the glass shaking in her hand as the cough grew worse.

"Ma, you okay?" asked Alex.

Unable to withstand the discomfort rising from her throat, she dropped the glass before she got to the table, creating a puddle of shattered glass and water. She continued to cough uncontrollably, unable to stop it.

"Ma, what is it? What can I do?" asked Alex.

She pointed at the box of tissues on the counter, and Alex rushed to get them, panic-stricken by the sight of his mother doubled over the table.

"Sit down, Ma," he said as he handed her the box.

She stayed on her feet, aware of what might happen if she sat down. She withdrew some tissues from the box and placed them over her mouth as another round of coughing gathered momentum.

And that was when he noticed the smattering of blood on the tissues.

Only then, sitting by her side as she lay unconscious in a hospital bed, did he realise the lack of surprise on her face when it had happened. Her eyes had searched for somewhere to hide, like someone whose guilty secret had suddenly been revealed.

"Ma, that's—"

"Just a bit of blood, darling; nothing to worry about."

"But—"

"Trust me, love, it's just a wee cough, that's all; perfectly normal. Let's keep this to ourselves, eh? Just between us. Don't want Dad getting all flustered and worried for nothing, do we?"

But he knew there was nothing normal about it. How could it be normal to cough up blood? Despite his protestations, she insisted on staying put.

"I'll hear no more of it, love. Now, let's get ye to school. Don't want to keep the wee lass waiting now, do ye?"

The fit had subsided. She picked up a brush and swept broken bits of glass into the dustpan, scanning the surroundings for unseen pieces. "Right, come on, let's be having ye," she said, pouring the broken pieces into the bin. She grabbed her car key and headed out of the kitchen.

The conviction of her actions assured him a little, but deep down, he knew there was something wrong. Despite a sinking feeling weighing down his stomach like a lead balloon all day, the uneasy episode eventually drifted away.

"I'm sorry, Ma; this is all my fault. I should have known, should have taken ye in. It's all my fault." He was talking to her now, taking the doctor's advice, hoping his mother could hear how sorry he was. If he had not been so selfish, he would have made her go. But all he could think about was Amy Snowdon – his mother was right, he did like her. His eyes were watery again, showing signs of another outpouring of grief-stricken emotions.

He raised his head and looked towards the ceiling, pleading with whoever was up there to help his mother, to make him sick instead – it was his fault, and he deserved it. His mouth opened, but words failed him. The tears his eyes had released swam into his trembling lips as his grip tightened. Squeezing her hand more was all he could do to contain himself. Only when he realised that he might be doing her harm did he ease off, lowering his head once more. The stillness of her body worried him; it suggested she was already gone, never to open her eyes or speak again. He sat there for a while, staring at her, longing for another chance to look after her, hating himself for allowing her sickness to worsen.

He looked up again, and this time, the words he had been searching for gushed out. "God, please, don't let her die. Let her live, and I promise I will look after her every day for the rest of me life. Please, God."

He hoped it was enough. Surely, God would save her. She was the most incredible person, and God knew how much he needed her. Surely, He would not take her away from him.

After some time, he remembered that the doctor had asked his father to speak with him. He glanced at the door, but the only two people behind the glass pane were a pair of nurses escorting an elderly woman along the corridor – no sign of the excitable doctor and the odorous man with a hangover. He wondered where they were and why they were taking so long. What was he telling him?

As yet more anxiety began to furrow, Alex got to his feet and made for the door, pushing it gently before stepping outside, turning his head right, and then left. He could see his father some metres away with his back turned to him. He was staring at something on the floor, holding the white metal railing on the wall with his left hand.

Still drunk, Alex thought, disgust rising inside him. Something made him want to confirm his suspicions so, hesitantly, he walked towards the older man, careful not to alert him to his presence. The closer he got, the more he noticed how much his whole body was shaking. And then he heard him:

"Oh God, no, please, no."

There and then, he knew his mother would not make it; his feet froze to the ground. In that moment, Alex pitied his father, felt his pain, but he was just as much to blame; he was never there, preferring the company of copious bottles of whisky to his wife and child. Alex turned around again to make as much use of whatever time his mother had left – tell her how he felt, how much he loved her, and how sorry he was.

He also wanted to tell her not to worry about him, that he would be okay, but he didn't want to lie. Upon entering the room, his eyes were greeted with the miraculous sight of his mother's outstretched arms, still flat on her back with half-open eyes beckoning him to come to her. God had answered his prayer. He ran to her and grabbed her hand.

"Ma, Ma, are you okay, Ma? Can ye hear me? I've been worried sick."

"Shhh... my beautiful boy," she said, doing her best to lower his expectations gently.

She turned her eyes to her left, head following as best it could.

He followed her stare, wondering what she wanted him to see. On the side table were the rosary beads that never left her side. He picked them up and placed them in her hands, but she put them back in his and closed his hand.

"They're yours now," she said. Her voice was faint and weak. "Look after them for me. They will watch over you."

She started to cough, spluttering for some seconds before her eyes closed for the final time. The only person he truly loved, taken from him. A downpour of emotions flooded his senses as his world came to a shattering end.

Seconds later, the odorous man entered the room, crestfallen with his bitter reality. Alex wanted to scream at him, but he was unable to. Instead, he ran to him in a desperate search for solace.

"You're gonna be okay, son. We're gonna be okay," his father said as tears rained down his stained cheeks. He had made a promise to himself, whilst sniffling in the corridor, to make the necessary changes in his life to look after their boy.

*

Jim embraced his promise. All bottles and cans of liquor were disposed of. In one fell swoop, their home became an alcohol-free zone. He cleaned up his act, staying away from anything and anyone that could turn him back to the poison that had very nearly destroyed his life.

Most of all, he focused on his son's well-being, putting him first in everything he did. He swallowed his pride and found a job in a warehouse, sorting parcels and arranging boxes for collection. It was a huge downgrade from his previous position of a senior PR executive – a job he loved dearly, right until the day he was laid off. For over a year, he had tried to get another job but was unable to get so much as an interview. In time, he could predict the exact words of his rejection letters: "Unfortunately, we are not able to accommodate you at this time", "Whilst we are very impressed with your CV, we feel you are over-qualified for this role", "We will keep your file and contact you when a suitable position be-comes available", "Your resumé is very impres-sive, and you certainly have the requisite experi-ence that we're looking for, but we feel the role is better suited to someone a little younger"... As each letter eroded his confidence and belief, he be-gan to doubt himself. His wife suggested he make do with something a little more menial for a while, to keep himself busy and help with the bills, but his pride would not let him. Before long, doubt turned to self-pity and anger, which inevitably morphed into self-loathing.

Now, it was time to dismiss his pride, and fo-cus on what mattered: taking care of his son. Their relationship remained a little uneasy, but it was a far cry from what it had been before. They chat-ted during dinners, watched TV together once in a while and Alex even brought his friends home sometimes.

The first time he did so, Jim had been so excited that he spent over an hour chatting with them, telling stories of his youth, and for a mo-ment he noticed a contented glare in Alex's eyes. For the best part of a year, life seemed to smile at them, mercifully bestowing hope and comfort, but it all changed on the anniversary of Julie's death.

Struck with an acute sense of guilt and loss, he fought with his demons throughout the day, telling himself it would pass, to keep going, that things were already getting better, apologising to Julie for giving up on himself, for treating her so terribly. Before he knew it, the self-loathing had returned, ridiculing him for the worthless job he was doing. And with it came a desire to drown the reality of his status. The more he fought it, the more he yearned. He tried so hard, using all his willpower to resist it, but like throwing a ball as hard as one can high up into the air, willpower alone will only get one so far; the ball will always come down.

Hours later, standing at the bar of The Stag, Jim was rolling his thumb around the rim of a shot glass, staring at the brown liquid inside. He had reached a crossroad: keep heading in the direction he had been travelling for the past year and never turn back, or veer left or right. Either turning would lead to an inevitable downward spiral and possible destruction, but maybe he could just branch a little, just a few yards right, then return to his original path. The acidic reaction in his stomach intensified, making him breathless with anticipation. He told himself it would be just the one – get it over and done with, and move on; surely, one drink would not hurt. Several hours later, he stumbled through the front door, clutching the coats and jackets on the railing to steady himself. Unable to regain his balance, he fell to the ground, bringing the railing down with him. Consumed with guilt, he shut his eyes, wondering how he had erred so badly. When he opened them again, there in front of him was Alex.

"Alex, me dear boy, it's nothing to worry about, just a..."

Alex turned and walked away, accepting the harsh reality of his broken life. It would not be the last time his father broke his promise. Over the coming weeks, he steadily slid back to his old ways, and before long, he was out of a job, dismissed for constantly turning up to work late and reeking of alcohol. He would often go missing, spending days and nights in pubs and dark alleys, leaving Alex to fend for himself.

A huge chasm emerged inside Alex, and it was not too long before it yearned to be filled. He began to skip school, idly wandering around parks, searching for other things to fill his day. Sometimes, he would simply sit on a bench and stare into the abyss of a meaningless existence; at other times, he would skulk around the play areas. On one such day, whilst sat on a swing, he noticed three boys on the far side of the park. They looked to be the same age as him – it comforted him to know that he was not the only one playing truant. He studied them for a while, kicking a ball around, sitting on the bench having a smoke, drinking something from a brown bag. They seemed happy and carefree – and they had each other.

He longed to know them, befriend them, be a part of their group, but he dared not approach them.

Day after day, he propped himself on the same swing as parents of toddlers tutted under their breath, watching friends he wished he had. Then one day, one of them stood up with a cigarette in hand and waved at him. Startled, he turned around to see who was behind him, but there was nobody there. Surely, he was not waving at him.

He decided to do nothing, so as not to make a fool of himself. Again, the boy waved. He seemed to be calling him over. Alex turned his head again. Nobody there. Maybe he *was* waving at him. He considered all the possibilities – they were waving at somebody he had not seen, mocking him, wanting to play a game of two against two, maybe beat him up. He decided to risk it; at worst, he would be beaten up and learn not to fall for such pranks in the future. The closer he got to them, the faster his heart raced. Fears aside, he felt alive.

"What's your name?" asked the tall, ginger-haired one.

"Alex," he muttered. He had wanted to speak louder, but the bag of nerves, excitement, and fear that had burst open in his stomach had stifled his voice.

"Eh?" said the ginger-haired one.

"Alex," he replied, this time forcing more sound from his throat.

"Do ye like footy, Alex?"

"Aye," he replied, relieved that he was, in fact, not about to get a beating.

"Right, you two against me and Alex. This is Tom, and this weirdo over here is Finn, me wee brother."

"Hi," said Alex, still a little nervous. "My name's Alex."

"Aye, we know that," he said. The other two laughed. They seemed to follow his lead. Alex laughed too, recognising his docile comment. "So, what's your—"

"Oh, my name's Jamie, but you can call me Jamie." The other two laughed again. He was definitely the leader of the pack, and the other two looked up to him.

They played a somewhat physical two-versus-two for over an hour, Tom and Finn testing Alex's mettle. The more he coped with their rough tackles, the more respect he gained, especially from Jamie. By the time they finished, the long summer's day's sun had begun to disappear over the horizon.

"Fancy a puff, Alex?" said Jamie, holding a joint in his hand. Alex had never smoked cannabis before; he had never indulged in *any* kind of drugs. For a brief second, he hesitated, but the desire to belong overpowered him.

"Aye, sure," he replied. Jamie lit the joint and took a couple of puffs. Finn stretched out his hand to take it from him but was reprimanded by his brother.

"Manners, brother; have some respect." He handed the joint to Alex, who took it sheepishly, conscious of the six pairs of eyes studying him.

He put the tip to his mouth and took a small drag. It scratched and tickled his throat, causing him to break into a coughing fit. The others laughed, Tom doubled over, unable to control himself.

"Don't worry, Alex; we've all been there. First time sucks. You'll get used to it," said Jamie.

A feeling of relief spread through his body, accompanying the hazy sensation that had suddenly engulfed him. It proved to be a long night of laughter and mischief – getting stoned, drinking and stealing from the local corner shop. At the end of the night, Jamie insisted they walk Alex home.

"See ye tomorrow?" said Jamie.

"Aye," replied Alex, giggling as he struggled to put his key in the keyhole. When he stepped inside, he smiled, then laughed as he recollected some of the night's adventures. He felt happy, an emotion he had not experienced in a long while.

Over the coming years, he spent less and less time at school, preferring to hang out with his new friends. The great thing about his father's inability to be a parent was that it had created a vacuum, one wherein he could do whatever he wished. He was answerable only to himself. They would spend the days larking about in various parks, getting high on whatever they could get their hands on, having to scarper whenever they spotted a police officer. At night, they hung around the market square, often venturing into nearby grocery stores to steal cans of beer. Sometimes Alex spotted his father, walking in a zig-zag towards the alley. The others laughed whenever they saw him.

"Look at him, pissed as shite!"

They would point and ridicule him, calling him names, and Alex would laugh along with them, retreating into the shadows.

He had just turned sixteen when he first got arrested. They had heard rumours about the police's new drive to reduce truancy but had evaded them on so many occasions that they believed they were invincible.

It was mid-morning on a cold winter's day. The four of them were sitting around the edges of a park bench – Tom and Finn on opposite arms, and Jamie and Alex on the top of the back. The weed they were smoking was particularly strong, and as such, their alertness severely dimmed. Upon finishing their joint, they decided to walk to the shops to buy snacks to satisfy the inevitable attack of the munchies. Little did they know that two police officers were following them, with the female officer speaking into her walkie-talkie. When they got to the side of the road, a police van screeched to a halt in front of them, and out jumped three police officers. They turned to run but found another two officers directly behind them. They looked at each other, contemplated the possibility of making a dash for it anyway but decided against it, the disconnect between brains and limbs being too vast.

"Are you in possession of illegal drugs?" asked the female officer.

"Nah, ain't carryin' nothin'," said Jamie.

"Are you sure about that, lad?" She knew they were; it was not the first time they had seen them – they had had eyes on them for some time.

"Aye, 'course I'm sure. Go on, check me if ye like," said Jamie.

She accepted his offer and found a bag of weed in his jacket pocket. The other officers frisked Tom and Finn but found nothing.

"And ye? Got anything on ye?" asked the female officer.

"Just a tiny bit," said Alex, removing a small wrap of cling-film from his jacket pocket.

"Right, as I'm sure ye know, weed and drugs are illegal in Scotland, so we'll be taking ye in. Step into the van please. No, not ye two. The two of you can go. And go to school, for Pete's sake."

Alex had never been in a police van before, let alone a station. His pulse was racing; he felt as though he was going on a wild adventure. His glazed and reddened eyes caught Jamie's. Jamie nodded at him, and Alex nodded back, feeling quite proud of himself. By the time they arrived, the effects of the weed had started to wear off. No longer feeling quite so triumphant, they were marched into the station and asked to hand over their valuables – neck chains, watches, coins. Alex took off the rosary beads that he always wore on his neck and put them in the see-through bag.

They were led to different cells and simply left there. Alex thought he would be able to sleep, but he was wrong; he lay awake all night, growing increasingly frustrated by the four walls around him. Maybe it was time to take life a little more seriously.

They were released in the morning and told to go home.

"Let that be a cautionary warning to ye both," said the officer in charge. It was as if they had just wanted them to take some time out, make them consider their ways.

Two weeks later, Alex was staring at the floor of another cell, his breathing deep and heavy as his heart struggled to accommodate his body's excessive demand for oxygen. The floor looked grey and cold, giving no comfort to his wretched demise. He had never realised there was so much anger inside him. He wondered where it came from and why it had taken so long to come out.

He replayed the incident over in his mind, searching for clues of his pent-up anger.

It had just been another night, no different to any other. Jamie, Finn, and he were kicking an empty can about in the alley opposite the grocery store. They had not seen much of Tom since they were arrested for possession of drugs some weeks back; it seemed to have scared him into taking a different path. Whenever they did see him, he would stop to chat for a few minutes, then make some excuse to leave. They never tried to persuade him otherwise. Deep down, they admired his courage to seek another path.

The grocery store looked busier than usual for early evening, leading Jamie to suggest the inevitable.

"Hey, Alex, check it out. Like a Friday night, whadya think?"

Alex took a few steps towards the store to get a better view. It was teeming with people buying groceries and beverages on their way back from work. The portly fellow behind the counter looked different to the one that was usually there. "Yeah, know what ye mean, but I reckon we just use your fake ID. That wee fella looks shagged out; be a cinch."

"Just what I was thinking." Jamie put his hand in his jacket pocket, and a glint appeared in his eyes as he withdrew the ID. "Come on, let's go, you go first, and I'll follow in a wee second."

Alex made his way to the shop, lowering his eyelids and pulling his face cap down to avoid the cameras. He entered and proceeded to feign interest in various items in the frozen foods section. He picked up some frozen sausages and read the label: "Richmond – special Irish recipe made with subtle flavours of nutmeg and pepper." He put it down, walked a few paces and picked up a packet of fish fingers: "Birdseye Wholegrain, 12 Fish Fingers, 360g."

All the while, the portly man at the counter was keeping half an eye on him – despite the queue of impatient customers lined up in front of him, he had noticed the dodgy-looking teenager with the baseball cap walking in some minutes ago.

Jamie had entered the store now and was waiting in the queue. Conscious of the fact that his eyes were probably fairly red and musty as a result of smoking weed for much of the day, he fixed his gaze on the shoulders of the man in front of him, denying all temptation to allow them to stray. He could hear the couple behind him whispering and giggling and wondered whether they were making fun of him – after some minutes, he felt sure of it. Did he look funny, maybe his flies were undone? He gently placed his fingers on the zipper of his trousers. They were fine.

More minutes passed as the queue inched forward. The gentleman with the shoulders bought a lighter, then asked for some Camel Lights, which the portly shop assistant took an eternity to find. By the time it was his turn, he had almost forgotten what he wanted to buy.

"Yes, sir," said the large man.

"Err, yea, bottle of Grouse, please," said Jamie.

"ID, please, sir."

Jamie reached into his pocket, pulled out his ID and handed it to him. A still and unnerving silence descended as dozens of eyes drilled an enormous hole in the back of his head.

The man brought the ID closer to his furrowed eyes and peered at it for many elongated seconds, as though he was inspecting a group of suspects at a police station. He veered his eyes left to analyse Jamie's features, then peered at the ID card again.

Jamie began to grow increasingly irritated, feeling the idiot in front of him was being over-zealous, looking for a reason to say no.

Finally, he returned the card to him and turned to pick up the requested bottle. "Do you want a bag, sir?" he asked.

Jamie nodded.

The man put the bottle in the bag and was about to hand it over, when all of a sudden, he pulled back and asked to see the ID card again. The couple behind him were no longer whispering. Everything was silent. A sense of indignation began to worm its way through his body.

"Why? Ye just seen it, man. What's ye problem?"

"Sorry, sir, I need to see it again."

"Why?"

"Because it's my right. I have to make sure you're not underage. If we sell to the underage, we get in big trouble."

"Well, no. I ain't showing ye again."

"Then I'm afraid I cannot serve you, sir."

Now irate, Jamie started to shout. "What's ye fucking problem? I already showed it to ye. What's your fucking problem?"

"Sir, I must ask you to please leave."

"No! I want me fucking drink. Give it me na!"

"Sir, if you don't leave, I will have to—"

"Have to what? Eh? Eh? Have to what? What the fuck are ye gonna do? We can stay here as long as we fucking like! What, our money not good enough for ye?" Jamie turned to find Alex standing next to him, stunned by his friend's outburst. He never thought he had it in him. "Give us our fucking drink, man."

"No," said the man, standing firm. Two other assistants had made their way to the back of the counter as the other customers gingerly stepped back.

"We're not going anywhere until you give us our fucking drink!" shouted Alex, pacing around the counter, eyes glaring like an angry beast.

"If you don't leave we will have to call the—"

"Go on then, call the fucking police! Ye think we give a shit?"

Jamie attempted to place a hand on Alex's shoulder, but Alex shrugged it off, grabbing several items on the counter and throwing them at the shop assistants. He then started to kick everything in sight, shouting all manner of obscenities as he did so.

"Hey, hey, Alex, that's enough. We can buy our booze somewhere else, let's go."

"Fuck the lot of ye!" shouted Alex, walking down the aisle to kick several more shelves, creating a pile of beaten goods on the floor. "Fuck the lot of ye! Ye hear me? Fuck the fucking lot of ye!" He continued shouting as Jamie dragged him out of the shop. The portly man was already on the phone reporting the incident.

"Hey, hey, Alex, calm down, man," said Jamie, leading him down the street.

"Who the fuck do they think they are? They're not better than us. Fuck 'em!" said Alex. He was struggling to restrain the river of anger rushing through him. Suddenly, he pulled himself away from Jamie's arms and ran towards the shop, picking up a brick along the way.

"Hey!"

The shopkeepers and the customers turned to him.

"Yeah, ye, all of ye, take this, ye fucking tosspots," Alex shouted, throwing the brick at the window.

The glass front of the shop shattered as customers screamed and jumped for cover.

"Not feeling so high and mighty now, are ye?" he bellowed, raging at the world.

Jamie grabbed him and pulled him away. "We need to get out of here, na!" he said.

They turned to run, but already they saw a police van heading towards them. They turned back to run in the other direction but were blocked by the three shop assistants. A big tussle ensued, the two boys kicking and punching wildly, and the shop assistants giving their all to restrain them for long enough for the police to arrive.

"Ye two again," said the same female officer as she cuffed them. "This time ye really are in the shite."

Alex spent all night in the cell, whilst the duty officer tried to reach his father. Another rainswept day was in full motion by the time they reached him. Too hungover to make his way to the station, he told them he was too unwell to go out and pleaded with them to have someone bring his son home.

It was a few minutes past noon when the doorbell rang. Still in his dressing gown, he shuffled to the door, head still ringing.

"Mr. Spires?" enquired the officer.

"Yes," he replied in a muffled voice. He cleared his throat. Why was there a police officer standing in the doorway? His mind raced, trying to recollect what he may or may not have done the night before. "Yes, that's me, how can I...?"

"You asked us to help you bring your son home," said the officer, stepping aside to reveal Alex standing behind him.

"Oh yes, of course! That's right, you brought the wee fella home. Thank ye. I haven't been well for some time now, ye see," he said, recognising the concerned expression on the officer's face.

The officer hesitated, weary of the lack of daylight in the house. "How long have you been unwell?"

"A few weeks na. Don't know what it is; probably just a bug or som'in." He was struggling to pronounce his words, and his legs were wobbling.

"Right, anyway, here's your boy. I should mention that he's in quite a bit of trouble, and there'll most likely be a criminal case."

"Criminal... hear that, boy? Criminal court case! What the hell have you been up to?"

Alex's eyes were numb and unresponsive, leaning into the distance, marooned in limbo like an abandoned vessel.

"Eh? Eh? What have you got to say for yourself, boy?"

"Well, I'll be off then. You'll be hearing from us soon," said the officer. He glanced at Alex and assessed his father's condition before reluctantly leaving.

Alex was already halfway up the stairs by the time his father closed the door.

"Hey! Hey! I'm talking to ye. Come back now, boy!"

Alex paused briefly, clutching the banister tight, then continued to his bedroom, slamming the door behind him.

Jim thought about going upstairs to admonish him, but his legs were too weak. He ambled to the sitting room and proceeded to pass out on the sofa.

It had been a while since Alex had last been in his bedroom. He had spent the past several months criss-crossing between alleys, parks and Jamie's house. They usually returned to Jamie's when they needed a bed and a bath.

His bedroom looked bereft of life, an empty shell of yesteryear's ghosts. He stood by the door, staring at his bed as the walls closed in, trapping him in his thoughts. Still gripped with anger, he yanked off his top and with it the rosary beads that hung on his neck. The chain broke, scattering the beads across the floor.

In a panic, he began to pick them up as images of his dying mother garnished his mind. His anger subsided, allowing the bitter grief that lay concealed beneath to finally emerge. Only after he had picked up every bead did he stop, hunched on the floor with his mother's dying wish in his hands.

As the tears flowed and his body trembled, he held the beads tight to the side of his head, hating the sorry, confused mess his life had become.

*

"Aye, but dad, you need to always make sure you take them first thing every morning, not every few days. Otherwise, they won't work properly."

Now diluted with a half glass of English, his accent was not as strong as it was when he lived in Glasgow. His neck was corked to the right, with the phone merged between his right ear and shoulder as he washed glasses and cups with a jet-powered hose. "Aye, exactly, every morning. And don't forget to keep doing your morning walk; it will help you," he continued, placing the washed drinking glasses on the dish rack. "Yea, I'm good. College's going well. Working at a café to earn a little extra cash. Listen, I've gotta go, but I'll be seeing you in a few days, okay? Great, see you soon, Pops."

Alex leaned towards the counter to his right and propped his head towards it, easing his phone onto the surface and placing the remaining glasses and cups on the rack, then grabbed his mother's rosary beads and rolled them onto his wrist.

He thought about her for a moment, her smile warming his heart, then proceeded to wipe the tables.

Mid-afternoon was usually quiet in the café during the week, as most clientele were either in lecture halls, the library or on the sports fields. It was the best time to listen and sing along to his favourite songs whilst going about his chores, wiping, scrubbing, sweeping, arranging, and whatever else needed to be done to make the café more inviting.

His voice bellowed songs from Travis' "Invisible Man" album, reaching a heartfelt climax when his mother's favourite – Sing – came up, unaware of Justina's entrance at the start of the second stanza. Her pulse danced and skipped merrily with his voice as she watched him sing and sway in his own little world. She longed to share in his freedom, to revel in music with him without care or worry. If only there was another way.

"But if you sing, sing, sing, sing, for the love you brought won't mean a thing... Oh my God, how long have you been standing there?"

"Hmmm... let's see now... let's just say long enough to know that you really do "sing" quite well." She had wanted to tease him a little but did not want to waste the little time they had left.

"Aye, that's what me mum always said. Maybe in another life, eh?"

"Nothing stopping you from making it happen in this lifetime! Seriously, your voice is amazing! You should think about giving it a go."

"Maybe after Uni. At least the degree will give me options. An Oxford degree, no less!"

If only he knew how little time he had, thought Justina.

"Fancy a walk? Thought it might be nice to enjoy the sunshine together."

"Great! That would be "awesome", as ye Americans like to say." He removed his pinny and returned the cleaning utensils to the cupboard, washed and dried his hands, then grabbed both her hands and affectionately placed his lips on hers. "Wanted to do that as soon as I saw ye."

"So why didn't you?"

"Because my hands were dirty."

"What've your hands got to do with it?"

"I wanted both – hands and lips. Just call me greedy and be done with it."

They giggled as they gazed into each other's eyes, her heart temporarily free of its troubles.

"Right, come on then, gorgeous, let's go find this sunshiny thing you were talking about."

Justina giggled again. He had a way of making her feel like a kid.

They walked through town and on to Christ Church Meadows, basking in the warm haze of a midsummer's day. Every now and then, a gentle breeze massaged the tiny hairs on her arms, accentuating her surreal contentment. She wondered whether anyone else was as perfectly in love as they were.

Love – a word she never thought she would entertain; but there it was, hollering at her like a long-lost friend, endearing her to its magical charm. She embraced it, cherished it, allowed it to smother her with its overbearing arms. She would have been happy for time to stop, suspending them in a moment of perpetual bliss. But all the while, at the pit of her stomach were danger's ominous shadows, lurking before their inevitable siege. Deep down, she knew nothing good ever lasted; all good things were temporary. *This* was temporary, and now she had walked into her own cocoon of vulnerability with eyes wide open. Was she even being fair, knowing all too well that it would all come to an abrupt end in a matter of hours?

She tried to swat away their impending reality, but no matter how hard she hit, tomorrow kept returning. The thought of destroying what they had filled her with sadness and remorse, and soon enough, her previously content heart was agape with solemnity. The sun's radiance, which had effortlessly skimmed off the warm glow of her face, was suddenly being pulled into the aggrieved turmoil of her heart.

"Ye okay, love?" asked Alex, noticing her downcast expression.

Her lips twitched, but her tongue refused to respond, unsure of what it was expected to say.

"Hey, something the matter?"

"Nothing, I'm fine. Just something I saw. Reminded me of something I used to do with my family whenever we went to the park."

Alex squeezed her hand gently, unsure of what to say. It was a topic he had been wanting to bring up, yet he had not wanted to pry. He understood more than most how tragic it was to lose someone so dear before their time. To remain silent would have seemed uncaring.

"You never really told me what happened. I know it must be really difficult to talk about, but you know you can with me, don't you?"

She squeezed back a little harder and forced a smile, feeling guilty about using her family as an excuse. She narrated her childhood to him, the fun, arguments, tantrums, laughter, long joyful nights around campfires, and their tragic death.

He had always thought his story was tragic, which in many ways it was – his mother, Jenny, his father's struggles – but it was child's play compared to hers. At least he kind of saw his coming. "God! I don't know what to say. I'm so sorry, Jus."

He wanted to cry for her, hold her close and comfort her, but his fingers remained rigidly entwined in hers.

They walked in silence, contemplating the cruelty of life, so adept at luring people into an unsustainable joy.

"What about you? You never really talk about your people."

"Oh, you know, the usual stuff that most people know. We Scots are a proud and passionate people. I think it goes way back to the time when—"

"Nooo, silly, I meant your family... and Jenn."

"Oh yes, my mum and dad were both born in Scotland. I guess that's what makes me Scottish as well. In fact—"

"Stooop!" She was giggling again, her troubles floating out of her fragile window.

"What?"

"Stop being silly! I'm being serious. Tell me now!"

"Okay, okay! You really are quite demanding, aren't you?"

He told her about his broken childhood: his mother's early death, and how it led to him taking a path that almost destroyed his life before it got going – the drugs, the violence, the two years he spent in an institution for young offenders.

Her spine tingled with anxiety as his story unravelled, shaken by thoughts of his angry childhood. Was there an ugly side of him lurking beneath his gentle veneer? She eased her hand out of his and pushed them firmly into her linen trousers. No matter how wonderful things could be, they never lasted. Adversity was the only certainty. And yet, he somehow found his way back. Flipped the page and found another path. So much so, that he even found love at his first university. She wondered how much of his past Jenn experienced. In that moment, it was clear an opportunity had presented itself.

"Hey, are you okay?" he asked, in the knowledge his transparency may have put her off.

"Yeah, fine, just… look, I'm not judging, I'm really not; people deal with things in different ways, and I couldn't possibly imagine how difficult it must have been for you. It's just..."

"Aye?" his accent seemed to come out stronger whenever fear knocked at the door.

"I... I'm not sure I know how to handle what you've just told me. To be honest, it's kind of freaked me out, the violence and stuff."

"Jus, it's from me past. Everyone has a past; things they did that they now regret."

"Yes, I know. I really do get it. But... I don't know, I just think I need a little time to dwell on it. I have such strong feelings for you. I need to be sure that your past is really your past."

There, she had said it. It was cruel, but the opportunity was too good to waste. Whatever she would choose to do the next day needed to be done without worrying about him.

A couple of veins grazed the side of his head, rustled into shape by the unexpected downturn of their conversation. Another shattered dream, stifling the air of his hopes.

"Wow! You really are judging me, aren't ye?"

"No, I'm not. I promise I'm not. I just need some time to take it all in."

"So, what are ye saying? You want to call it quits?"

"No, not saying that. But I think we need to take a break. I just... need a little space to get my head around everything you told me."

A sad tension smeared his face as they walked back in silence, Justina already considering what she would do the next day. Whatever the case, a temporary break up was the best option; she needed a clear head, needed to keep him safe. He may have taken a wrong turn, but he found his way back.

She did not enter the café with him, choosing instead to say goodbye at the door. Their eyes met one last time, hovering precariously with longing and regret.

"Right then, so, I guess I'll see ye when I see ye," he said. He kept his hands in his pockets.

"Yeah, maybe soon. Just need a little time to think."

"Bye then." He turned the latch and entered.

"Bye." She watched the door close, wondering whether their happy chapter had come to an end. It was not what she wanted, but it was necessary.

13

Reset

Sarah Clark had spent much of the morning mining her in-tray – assiduously dissecting document after document, analysing pros and cons, hidden agendas and various eventualities. It was what she enjoyed most, sifting through the ins and outs of numerous possibilities with steadfast diligence. As the long hand of the clock lunged past twelve, she needled her right temple with her tired fingers and removed her glasses. The nervous tension that had been building up inside her all morning had reached its crescendo and could no longer be ignored or swatted aside.

Her phone rang, shaking her out of her daze. She glanced at it. Identity withheld. It was not a day for unexpected or unwelcome conversations, and so she rose from her seat and walked towards the window, allowing the ringer to fade away unattended. Whoever it was seemed to not want to give up. It rang again, this time for much longer. She hated it when people did that. Why could they not just take the hint? After five rings, the person either does not wish to speak with you or they are away from their phone. Suddenly, realising who it was, she ran to her desk and answered. They spoke for several heightened minutes, persuading, defending, remonstrating, assuring, as she paced up and down her office.

When the call ended, she walked to her chair and slumped into it, weighed down by the numerous consequences of the preceding hours. She stared at her phone, loosely balanced on her right palm, then heaved a heavy sigh before putting it down.

Five small vials lay in perfect formation on the right-hand corner of the table, waiting to be relieved of the red, congealed liquid inside them – one for her and one for each of her four assistants. She considered the possibility that she may have missed someone out but quickly reminded herself of the importance of a swift, clean break from the past; no room for more than one leader in her new world. A comatose proletariat would be governed by an all-knowing few – a handful of sacrificial lambs, leaving themselves open to the perils of hope and grief. It was a heavy but necessary price for unity and peace. In time, humankind would rise again, paving the way for an entirely new world made in her image.

She went over the phone conversation again in her head. Why so agitated about one of the girls? "There's more to this than you know" – what did she mean by that? Was she missing something? And the way she turned her back to them as soon as they walked in. What was she hiding? She had known this particular friend since college, and they never kept secrets from each other. Sarah wondered what was being kept from her – and why was her friend starting to keep secrets now?

Deep in her thoughts, she was oblivious to the knocking on the door. She leaned forward, checked her watch, and reclined again, then got up to walk to the window. A handful of individuals were standing in a circle smoking cigarettes. Four seemed quite jovial and chatty, but the lanky one with the blue and white striped shirt looked a little lost at sea, pensive and downcast, as though troubled by something. Nothing had changed; it obviously had not happened yet. She checked her watch again and made for her desk.

She pressed the intercom switch. "Michael, please come."

There was no answer.

"Michael, are you there?"

Still no answer.

"Where the devil is he?" she muttered to herself.

Irritated by her assistant's disappearance, she walked briskly to the door and yanked it open, ready to shout his name, only to find him standing in front of her, knuckles wrapped in preparation for another round of loud knocking.

"Oh, where the hell have you been?"

"Right here, Prime Minister. I've been knocking on your door for the past five minutes."

"So why didn't you... Oh, never mind, come in, come in." Her throat was beginning to tighten, and a faint migraine had placed itself on the right side of her head. She picked up her phone again and put it down, checked her watch, and walked to the window.

"How can I help you, Prime Minister?"

"What?"

"You said you were looking for me."

"Oh yes, yes, I was… Come over here for a second."

He walked over and stood beside her, still waiting for her instructions.

"Don't just stand there gawping at me, Michael. Look! Out there!"

"Yes, ma'am?"

"What do you see?"

"A group of people chatting, ma'am."

"What else do you see?" Her eyes started to ache as the migraine grew more audacious, expanding its territory like a vicious plague. She rubbed her temples and turned to pick up her glasses. "Look at them, Michael! How do they seem to you?"

"Well, they... they're just chatting, Prime Minister, nothing out of the ordinary." He wished she would just spell it out instead of making him feel like an imbecile.

"What about that one? The lanky one on the right. Seem okay to you?" The lanky man in the striped shirt was inhaling hard on his cigarette, staring at the grey mass of concrete beneath him as the others continued their merry conversation.

"Well… I guess he looks a little troubled or something. No different to most people, as we're

297

all troubled by one thing or another. I don't understand the significance, Prime Minister."

"He looks troubled, Michael. Troubled!"

"But… oh, now I get you." The penny had
finally dropped. "I guess it hasn't happened yet."

"Obviously! But it should have by now." She
checked her phone again before realising that doing so was pointless.

"Prime Minister, shouldn't we have taken
those by now? It's the reason I was knocking. You
said noon."

"Yes, that's true." She was starting to feel dishevelled, unbalanced by uncertainty. "Yes, very
true. Call the other three and let's hope it won't all
come to be a disastrous waste."

"Sorry, did you say 'three', Prime Minister?"

"Yes, three of my most senior advisors. You
don't expect just the two of us to build a new
world, do you?"

"But the agreement with—"

"Michael." She needled her right temple with
increasing intensity. "Agreements are simply a
convenience of a moment in time. They come and
they go. You really think I'll allow dragons to rule
over us for eternity?"

Some minutes later, the Prime Minister and her most trusted aides were gathered in a circle in the centre of the room with vials in hands.

"Remember, for them this is the endgame. But for us, this is just the beginning."

Four large wheels had been attached to the four corners of the cage. An anxious silence preyed on the hall as eight dragons pulled on the metal chains that were fastened to their bodies. The weight of the cage and its inhabitant were etched on their strained miens as they marched in step towards the exit. Pausing to gather their strength at the foot of the stairwell, they redoubled their effort as they ascended the stairs, gritting their teeth as the climb unfolded.

Elias growled and roared his defiance, but his dulled eyes betrayed him.

Walking alongside the dejected prisoner, Justina glanced in his direction, pitying his terrible ordeal, feeling more and more like an intruder – finally acknowledging the wrong that was being done enhanced the steady flow of guilt that was gushing inside her.

By the time they reached the entrance, Elias' chin was on the floor of the cage as he lay prostrate in surrender to his fate. Her eyes darted from left to right, certain someone would try to rescue him, but the stillness of the terrain corrected her optimism. She glanced at him again, hoping to see a glint in his eye, but they were closed; even he was not expecting a rescue. How could such an important member of Raphael's followers be so abandoned?

"Keep going!" shouted Abaddon. "To the top of the east hill. They'll meet us there." It was obvious who 'they' were: Zoldon and Liza, his new right-hand. Her meteoric rise did not bother Justina so much anymore – nor did their private discussions, secret plans, cruel schemes, and the pretence of including her. Justina had not seen Liza since she left the day before. She adjusted her pace, taking smaller steps for Abaddon to unwittingly catch up with her. She had never really spoken with him before, but the days of seeing him as slightly lower rank had scuttled away some time ago.

"Who will be meeting us there?"

"You're supposed to be beside the cage. Stick to the plan." His eyes remained on the cage. "Liza and Zoldon. Get back up there, Justina. Focus on your task, and worry not about those of others," he said, addressing her as though she was a foot soldier.

Biting into her bottom lip, she increased her pace and caught up with the cage, resenting him for his disdain. Elias' eyes were still closed. The dreary, fattened clouds released a light drizzle and, for some minutes, threatened to impede their progress with more weighty clumps of rain, but they held back, recognising their folly. On and on, they marched and trudged in silence, stopping only when they reached the top of the east hill.

The cage door was unfastened, and finally Elias' eyes opened, wondering why they had stopped. Noticing the cage door had been lifted, he surveyed his new surroundings. He still did not know what they wanted to do with him. He shut his eyes again and awaited the nefarious actions of his captors. Justina wanted him to at least try to escape, but his sad resignation was clear to see.

*

A dark silhouette emerged from the shadows, gulping the air beneath it like a venomous beast. A cold shiver trickled up Justina's spine as she looked up to see a shrouded figure astride her old friend. As they neared, the others on the ground bowed in reverence, welcoming their two masters. It was what he had always wanted – what *she* had always wanted.

Perfectly still throughout the descent, Liza masterfully jumped off Zoldon's back before his claws touched the ground. She stood still, assessing the creature in the cage, oblivious to all around her.

Zoldon walked slowly to her side before nodding in her direction.

Liza marched to the cage, half-raised her right arm and flicked her hand to the right. The chains and shackles pinning Elias to the floor broke as the cage's spikes instantly keeled and fell to the ground. She paused just a few feet from him, and Elias' eyelids flickered violently before eventually lifting, revealing a wild and frenzied nature beneath them. A fire alighted around him, a few centimetres away from his body, as she slowly circled her right thumb around her right index finger. In a matter of seconds, the fire was fully ablaze, obscuring him from view. Liza circled the cage, all the while seizing his mind with her hypnotic gaze. She drew the fire closer to him, sizzling his flesh like meat on a stake.

Elias did not move; only his eyes carried the spark of life. Unencumbered by the restless flames, Liza crouched in front of him and stretched out her hand to pet him, whispering something in his direction. As soon as she stood up again, the flames faded into the same unknown that they had come from.

Justina shuddered, wondering how such a person could possibly be overcome.

The forest's trees cowered in the distance, sensing a moment in time that would turn the world on its head. The light drizzle had returned, this time more constant, smearing its hazy mist across the horizon with no signs of abating. Hundreds of dragons gathered around the mound below, their claws digging into the rain-soaked grass as they waited in expectation. They came to witness a day they had long desired. For years they had battled, losing loved ones, killing foes that were once friends, burning entire regions to cinder, and now their dream was being realised. Everything they believed in was about to manifest.

Zoldon signalled Justina to come to him before glancing at the dragons below. This day could not have arrived without their loyalty and conviction. They had left their homes and followed him without question or doubt. Not once did they flinch from their duties, no matter how awry or gruesome. He welcomed the churl of gratitude bristling inside of him. His eyes darted around, left to right, up and down, hoping to spot the presence of an old accomplice, but he saw nothing. He was proud of all his followers, grateful for all they had done, but her presence was what he desired the most, to have her witness what she always deemed impossible – the mission she walked away from.

His mind drifted back to the moment Pelonious' frozen heart sensed her presence. Having not given so much as a stir for hundreds of years, it thumped with excitement, as though meeting its true owner. He had not expected it – had not even considered it. But right there and then, he recognised the immense and irreversible power of blood and time. No matter how long, the two would always find their way.

"You're with me today," he said to Justina.

It had been a while since she rode with him, and the thought of it made her a little nervous, especially now. She climbed onto his back and sat in silence, unsure of what to say.

Abaddon stood beside them, proud and awaiting further instructions.

"No sign of them?" enquired Zoldon.

"Siras and Mara? No, not yet. But I'm sure they're lurking somewhere." He did not particularly like Siras. Why, despite Abaddon's unflinching loyalty to him, would Zoldon still ask of Siras?

Liza looked to Zoldon, who nodded. She turned around and marched swiftly towards Elias before effortlessly springing onto his back. His frenetic eyes screamed and shouted, but there was nothing they could do to extinguish the power that now took over him. She leaned forward and whispered in his ears, and, in an instant, his eyes blazed in frantic fury as his unfurled wings propelled them towards the skies.

"You stay here and keep an eye on things," said Zoldon, tetchy and anxious.

"With pleasure." He watched them ascend, gathering speed as they chased after Liza and Elias.

Unable to make any gain on Elias, Zoldon slowed down, recognising the futility of his attempt to catch up with them. Liza knew she was to wait for him, so why try to fly at an impossible speed? "Are you okay?" he asked, his raised voice slicing through the billowing of the wind.

"Yes, I'm fine, thank you for asking," Justina replied, over-doing her politeness. She wanted to believe everything was okay, that nothing had changed, but the voices in her head said otherwise. They were no longer accusing her; rather, a hesitant pact had taken place.

"I've sensed a reluctance in you during the past few days, Justina. Is something the matter?"

"Sorry? Say that again?" She had heard what he said but needed time to prepare her response.

"Is there something troubling you? You haven't been yourself for some time."

"Not at all. Just taking a back seat as you suggested. I know this is Liza's moment, and I'm okay with that."

Zoldon narrowed his eyes, unconvinced by her willing acceptance.

She lowered her head and stared at the moving blur of patches and dots beneath them and wondered what Alex was doing – probably finishing his final lecture of the day and heading to the café. She did not handle things well the day before – she was too curt and sudden. She shouldn't have made him feel so judged, but it needed to be done to keep him out of harm's way. If only she was with him and not about to do something so damnable. He would never remember who she was. Worse still, he would be incapable of feeling anything for her. And yet, her heart would continue to ache for his. She was destined to be the loser in all of this, haunted by memories of what was and plagued by the remorse of what would never be.

The drizzle transcended into a torrential downpour. Justina lowered her head further to shield her face from its violent outburst, crouching behind Zoldon's neck. All the while, the voices rose in their thousands, assuring her that they were with her, willing her to be brave. She wondered what they meant. How could they possibly help her? They were the voices of the dead – what use was that? But no matter how much she applied logic to her situation, deep down she knew.

Zoldon slowed, allowing the winds to guide his outstretched wings to their final destination. Sensing the shift in momentum, Justina raised her head a little, braving the clouds' cold, biting arrows. Straining her eyes to see through the mist and rain, she noticed the brooding figure of Liza in the distance. Her hood was off, probably blown back by the winds; her cold-blooded eyes were pointed straight at them – waiting, watching, ready. Despite the virulent force of the winds circling the edge of the vortex at which she waited, she was perfectly still, unmoved by the chaos around her.

Zoldon slowed to a halt directly opposite.

Justina sat up and straightened, peering into the vortex. She could almost make out Earth's scattered dots. Sensing a pivotal moment, the voices grew louder, urging her to put an end to what would surely be a monumental catastrophe. "Now, Justina", "You can't let this happen.", "You can stop them, we're with you." The louder they shouted, the more she felt connected to them, their voices becoming hers, as though they were one.

"It's time, Liza. Do it, now!" shouted Zoldon. She leaned forwards to whisper in Elias' right ear. His eyes widened as he stretched his wings, turning slowly to the right and commencing their flight.

"Seven times," shouted Zoldon. He did not expect a reply.

Lightning and thunder began to sound their disapproval as Elias completed the first circuit. One time, two times, three times. An acute stirring occurred in Justina's chest, ripping through her like a raging electric current. Her body vibrated as thousands of dead souls coursed through her veins.

Four times…

Five times...

Justina's mouth opened, and she screamed.

"Noooooooooooooooooooooo!"

Fuelled by the force and angst of thousands of lost souls, an immense volcanic surge was unleashed, propelling an angry explosion of fire that smashed into everything around them. In an instant, Liza was thrown off the back of Elias, and both were sent crashing through the mass of clouds and sky beneath them, falling at breakneck speeds as Justina looked on, breathless from the thousands of spirits that had just surged through her body. Instinctively, Zoldon lunged towards them, chasing as fast as he could in a desperate attempt to save his greatest weapon. Justina shuddered as she watched her former accomplice descend in a violent ball of flames. Despite their differences and whatever Liza had become, Justina cared for her.

"Faster!" shouted Justina as Liza began to fall out of view. "You need to go faster, Zoldon, before they…"

To their astonishment, Liza was no longer falling. She had somehow defied gravity, standing perfectly still in mid-air, eyes shut and arms outstretched, as though summoning the firmaments around her. Her lips were moving, uttering a babble of unknown – and nigh unheard – words. Zoldon slowed to a halt, relieved that Liza was alive, once again marvelling at her giftings, powers he never thought possible. But before he could say anything, Elias resurfaced, bursting from a mass of dark clouds as he glided towards Liza. Still with her arms outstretched and eyes shut, she drew him to her with frightening and unspoken authority. Only when Elias was inches from her did her eyes open, burning with rage, piercing his own fear-filled gaze. She grinned before climbing back onto his spell-struck body.

"Go," Liza told him.

Like a tormented soul, Elias began hurtling towards Justina and Zoldon with ferocious speed and visible terror, swatting the air with knife-like wings before grinding to a halt a few metres in front of them.

"Are you okay, Liza?" enquired Zoldon, slightly shaken by what he had just witnessed. Liza did not answer. A veneer of calm had over-taken her dark red eyes, numbing her senses and emotions. She remained perfectly still for some seconds, glaring at Justina and Zoldon. They were one and the same to her; shadows of a past that she now found repulsive. Unnerved by her silence, Zoldon peered into her eyes, hoping to connect with whatever was left of the young lady he had chosen to be his right hand.

"It's no use, Zoldon," Justina pleaded, "whatever that is, it isn't her. We need to leave this place before..."

Without warning, Liza raised her left arm, pointing it towards the two figures in front of her as her eyes closed again, surrendering to the sinis-ter forces that had seized her. Her closed eyes illu-mined in blood red, which began to spread across the entirety of her body, enabling a legion of hungry, whispery flames to garland the surface of her skin. Elias winced at the pain of her fiery body against his back but remained otherwise silent.

"Zoldon, we need to…" Justina once again began to plead.

"Quiet, Justina; I know she's in there somewhere."

Zoldon peered deeper, conscious of the ease with which Elias would catch them should they attempt to get away. Finding a way to unearth the Liza they knew was the only way to prevent Zoldon's once impenetrable house of cards from being desecrated. "Liza… Liza, listen to me; I know you can hear me."

As Zoldon spoke, a wave of energy surged through the flames lapping at Liza's body, rapidly running its course down her arm and towards her outstretched palm. "No, Liza," Zoldon begged, suddenly aware of the reality that there was nothing he could say to prevent what came next. "This is not the way… Liza, no…"

It was too late. At one with the evil that had seized her, Liza released a voluminous torrent of flames. Immediately, Justina raised her right arm, releasing a powerful wave of energy in response. Justina was able to shield herself and Zoldon from the flames, but it did not take long for Liza's sheer, raw power to burst through the barrier Justina had created.

"Zoldon, do something!" shouted Justina. "I can't hold her on my own. You need to do something!"

Zoldon tilted his head back a little to catch a glimpse of Justina, then glanced at the thunderous clash of flames and energy in front of him. All he had to do was breathe his fire, and it would all be over; a combination of Justina's force and his flames would be too much even for Liza – he knew that. Once more, he tilted his head to see his erstwhile apprentice, the girl he had, in many ways, fathered since she was young.

"Liza, I know you can hear me. You must stop this now!" he shouted, once more fixing his eyes on the demon-like figure before of him. "Stop this now, Liza." But rather than recede, Liza's flames grew more violent and angry, bursting through Justina's shield of energy with venomous rage. Zoldon sighed, broken by what he was about to do. A lone, lost tear had found itself on the ridge of his nose as he closed his eyes and breathed in, summoning the fires inside to do his already remorseful bidding. He breathed out again, sending forth rapturous flames in Liza's direction. But no sooner had he done so did Liza's outburst increase in intensity, pushing his own flames back with such ferocious brutality that he was soon ensconced in a whirl of heat and light, causing him to lose balance and tumble through the clouds below. Shaken and scorched by the burst of flames, Justina lost her balance and in an instant was separated from Zoldon, causing her to spiral downwards towards her death. She felt somehow liberated as images of those she loved flashed through her mind – her brother – Tom – her Mum and Dad... Zoldon... Alex. She knew she would miss Alex the most, but it was for the best – better for him to be with someone more... normal. There would be less baggage that way. At least she would soon be with her family, and free at last from her life of torture. As she shut her eyes in anticipation of her end, something grabbed her, flipping her into the air like a weightless pancake before she landed on its back. Somewhat confused, she leaned to her left to get a better view. The torso was neither burnt nor remotely singed. Surely, Zoldon could not have recovered so quickly.

"I take it you're okay."

Justina recognised the voice – it was the one from the forest. "Ra... Raphael! How did you..."

"Let's just say I was watching from afar. Anyway, there is no time for small talk; we need to make haste. We have not seen the last of your friend." Though conscious of the unlikelihood of outpacing Elias, Raphael surged forward, gathering speed with each flap of his outstretched wings. On and on they soared, darting across the pale skies in frantic hope and desperation. After several minutes, Raphael began to slow down a little, scanning the air around them both, daring to believe that Liza had left them to their own devices. With his heart pounding faster and harder than he could remember, he eased into a gentle glide, using the opportunity to gather his breath – it had been long since he exerted himself with such ferocity.

"Do you think we've lost her?" asked Justina, glancing in all directions for signs of their predator.

"Let us hope she is searching for Zoldon; at least that gives us a little time to consider what to do next." Deep down, he sensed his brother was most likely dead. Raphael had seen him fall from the distance, engulfed in a ball of fire that was surely too fierce to abate. For a split second, he had considered trying to save Zoldon but thought better of it; placing his hopes in the possibility of Zoldon's change of heart was a notion he had surrendered long ago.

"Wait, what's that?" said Justina. Her heart quickened as the silhouette of a lone hooded figure and two outstretched wings appeared in the far distance. "What? Where?" said Raphael, terrified by the possibility of what could unfold – safety had long since ceased being a reality, no matter how far or hard he flew.

"Over there, right in front of us," replied Justina. The silhouette had morphed into the sight of Liza and Elias, gliding towards them with unerring certainty. "What do we do? We can't make a run for it; he's too fast."

Unable to respond, Raphael looked around, taking a deep breath and stretching out his wings. Again, he scanned his surroundings. He wanted to at least try, for Justina's sake, if not his.

"You of all people know how fast your friend is, Raphael. Why delay the inevitable?" Liza muttered. She was now just a few feet away from them, the dark veins on her temples and bloody red eyes confirming what both Raphael and Justina already suspected – there was no reaching her. It was their end, and they knew it... Liza knew it.

"Elias! Elias, can you hear me? I know you're in there. Try to resist her, Elias. I know you can hear me. Resist her, Elias!" shouted Raphael. Finding a way to reach his old friend was their only chance of survival. He had witnessed Liza's powers earlier; she was too strong for the both of them. Elias' glazed eyes flickered a little but quickly resumed their numb haze. He could hear Raphael but was powerless to do anything other than obey Liza's will.

"Liza, there's no need for this. Think about your mum... your dad... Destroying the world will destroy them too!" shouted Justina.

The sides of Liza's lips curled as she raised her right arm towards her enemies, summoning the furnace inside her. As tongues of flames encircled her body, she thrust her left arm forward, sending a flurry of fiery darts in their direction. Immediately raising both arms, Justina did the only thing she could: send a force of energy to thwart Liza's flames, creating a mighty collision of torrents and fire, and for a time preventing the seemingly inevitable; but the more she willed her power, the greater her energy sapped.

"Raphael, do something," Justina implored him. "I... I can't take much more!" She was groaning now, unable to withstand the force of Liza's power. "Raphael, please... I can't..."

Raphael glanced at Justina, still clinging to his hope of reaching Elias but deep down knowing his efforts were futile. He glanced at Liza, searching for a sign that the girl he once knew was still inside, but all he could see was a bitter rage that yearned for destruction. Sadness and remorse gripped his heart as he accepted the only available course of action.

"Raphael, please... you have to..." Unable to complete her plea for help, Justina's arms were now at a right angle, forced back by the searing force of Liza's flames. Finally at peace with the decision he had been trying to resist, Raphael breathed in, gathering all the strength and power within him, and with a deafening roar, unleashed a torrent of tempestuous flames, piercing through the streams of energy Justina and Liza were launching at each other, consuming both Liza and Elias. In an instant, both bodies were sent tumbling through the clouds in a bright orange blaze. Gasping for breath, Justina looked on as her former accomplice descended in a ball of fire, relieved to have been saved but saddened by her wretched ending.

*

Raphael and Justina scoured the terrain from the skies for over an hour, Raphael desperately searching for his friend, each passing second reducing the chances of finding him alive. In time, Raphael's strength began to wane as his worst fears began to manifest. No longer able to cut through the skies at will, the tension in his wings loosened, reducing their flight to a tired crawl. Justina gently caressed the side of his head, feeling the sweat on his reptilian skin as it moistened her hand. He shirked, refusing to soften, but the furious beating of his heart had reduced to gentle taps on her knee. He did not want her kindness – a part of him blamed her for Elias' fate. He certainly had not forgiven her for turning his apprentice, even though he now realised that Liza was always destined to become the person she became. But his conviction was weak, and so he slowly descended towards the west corner of the great forest, once again feeling empty, guilty... lost.

They landed in silent contemplation and remained stationary for a while, bereft of comfort – Raphael staring into the distance and Justina's head drooped and heavy. She could hear fallen leaves rustling in the forest as the now gentle breeze glided over them. The leaves seemed to be rustling every few seconds in response to the wind's charms. Thick clumps of her still wet hair dangled over her face like upside down statues in perfect symmetry. Suddenly, it occurred to her that her hair was not only still sodden with rainwater, but also not responding to mother nature. She lifted her head and glanced towards the area the rustling was coming from, tapping Raphael's neck to alert him, but he did not respond. She tapped him a little harder.

"Raphael!" she aggressively whispered. He stirred, wondering what she wanted. "Raphael, listen."

He did his best to cooperate, but the mist in his head remained too thick and foggy. Justina jumped off his back and walked towards the forest, breaking into a run after a few steps. Only when she disappeared from view did Raphael's senses begin to awaken. Worried for her safety, he sat up.

"Raphael! Raphael, come quickly!" came her voice. Immediately, he made his way towards the forest, his pulse racing once more as an unkind mix of anxiety, hope and worry bedraggled his mind. Seconds later, he saw Justina, crouched beside Elias' body with her head on his chest. Raphael noticed the redness in Justina's eyes as she stroked Elias's nigh motionless torso. "I think… he's still breathing!" she exclaimed.

Raphael hurried to them, leaned his head down and placed his face next to Elias's lips. He could feel the faintest of breaths, laboured and weak. Upon opening his dying eyes one last time to see Raphael by his side, Elias was filled with a warm glow of pride and joy, comforted by his friend's presence – the gentle touch of Justina's hand on his side, tense with concern but careful not to cause harm, was added proof that it had all been worthwhile. Elias closed his eyes in the knowledge that she had made it... *they* had made it. Strangely at peace with the air of sorrow that had enveloped her heart, Justina placed her head on his chest, hoping to hear his faint heart one final time. It was love's pain and grief, as well as the throes of joy and elation, that gave life meaning.

*

Raphael and Justina remained by Elias' side long after his gentle spirit departed, struggling to come to terms with their bittersweet victory. They had managed to save the world from an unspeakable tragedy, but at what cost? Justina blamed herself for the many grievous events that had taken place over the years; the sadistic slaughter of thousands of innocent lives – mothers, fathers, children; leading a grieving young girl down a path of darkness she was never able to turn back from – all because Justina wanted to protect herself from heartache. There was nothing anyone could say to convince her otherwise, not even the voices in her head. The voices were a part of her now; forever connected by her terrible deeds and her redemptive action. They had kept their promise, and she had heeded their plea – she would forever have them with her. Only when evening turned to night did they get up to bury Elias, digging in silence as sadness caroused them. Once done, they stood by his grave and mourned him some more, reluctant to allow their lives to continue. Eventually, they began to look for Liza's body. Not once was her name uttered as they searched the surrounding area. They both searched for many hours, combing through bushes, fields, tops of trees, but found nothing. Deep down, they both suspected she was dead – for surely not even someone with her abilities could survive such a fall. Nonetheless, they kept their thoughts to themselves; experience had taught them both that wishful thinking and false hope were pathways to disappointment and pain. Either way, neither wanted to bring more misery to the other by sharing their thoughts – so they searched half-heartedly, hoping they would find a body, some confirmation that it was all over.

As their search petered out, Justina felt the need to say something that had been troubling her heart since they buried Elias. "We should bury your brother, Raphael," she said, hoping her choice of words would soften his angry heart. She was finally in no doubt that Zoldon had taken advantage of her grief and used her for his own sinister agenda, yet he had been the closest thing she had to a father for much of her life. Without him, she may never have survived. And so, despite the risk of aggravating the emotions of an already angry and emotional Raphael, she felt the need to say it. "We have to, Raphael; he was your brother... and my friend."

"As you wish," replied Raphael with an irritated grunt. The thought of burying the brother he had killed filled him with sadness and dread.

*

It did not take long for them to retrace their steps, finding Zoldon's burnt body as they had left it the day before. They dug another grave and buried him in a solemn, serious manner; no sooner was his body buried deep beneath the earth had Raphael walked away. Justina waited by the grave for some minutes, recollecting the day she first met Zoldon. He had given her a reason to live, helped her to overcome her grief. No matter how things unfolded during the final days, she knew that deep down Zoldon had loved her too, perhaps as a daughter.

"So, what do you plan to do now?" asked Raphael. He was standing several meters away, having severed himself of memories of his brother.

There was only one thing she wanted to do, but she feared it might be too late. "I... I don't really know. My life has always been about one thing, and now that... It is over, isn't it? I mean, there's nothing more we have to do, right?"

"I believe so. The death of Zoldon and... Let's just say that there is little else we need to worry about. Their plan was thwarted, and I very much doubt that there was a plan B. Especially with those two gone..."

Neither had had much of an experience of a life without the scheming and strategizing of wars and objectives. This unfamiliar circumstance brought with it a vacuum of emptiness that neither knew how to approach.

"I'll focus on getting my college degree, I guess," Justina thought aloud.

"Yes, that is a good and sensible plan."

An uncomfortable silence descended, both unsure how to address their short acquaintance.

"Well... I suppose I will be seeing you, Justina... or perhaps not," Raphael eventually said. "You know where to find me, should you need to; there is no doubt you are more than capable of travelling between our two worlds."

He took a few steps towards her, wanting to allow his heart to speak, but it remained unable to express itself; there was too much bad blood between them. With her heart finally open, she crossed the ocean between them and stretched out her hand, placing it gently on his cheek. The warmth and sincerity of her smile overwhelmed him. He could never have imagined such a beautiful soul existed all those years ago.

"Thank you, Raphael," she whispered. Her eyes stayed on his for a while as a small smile fought its way across the corner of Raphael's mouth. Perhaps this was destiny showing its mysterious hand once again.

"You are welcome."

*

The Prime Minister's motorcade had been crawling at a snail's pace for over an hour and had finally ground to a halt. A mass protest was taking place to demonstrate the nation's disapproval of Britain's involvement in yet another unnecessary war. The angst over her decision to side with an overly aggressive American foreign policy was widespread and further exacerbated by a suspicion that oil was at the root of the agenda. Her chief of staff had suggested they take another route that morning, but she had insisted on traversing through the busier one, explaining that she wanted to sample the public mood with her own eyes.

It was as she expected: anger, fury, dismay, disgust. The problem with the western world was that people felt a need to voice their opinion all too often. It irritated her. What did they know about what was really going on? Why should she have to explain everything to them? If she told them the truth, they would hide in their houses and never open their doors. And besides, is that not what they voted her in for? To make decisions for their protection and well-being?

She watched them through her dark tinted windows, shouting and chanting, waving placards and their hoisted-up banners, standing, marching, jumping up and down en masse. She was glad they could not see her. She had taken to using tinted windows ever since a crazed individual attacked her car in broad daylight. The woman had been waiting for the traffic light to go red when she spotted the Prime Minister in her vehicle. Without hesitation, she ran to the rear window and started banging and screaming. It gave her quite a shock – not the fact that it happened, but that it happened so easily. Ever against bulldozing her way through traffic with sirens blaring, she opted for dark tinted windows, despite the uncomfortable similarity with the mindless and chaotic motorcades of third-world leaders.

A week had passed since the failed attempt to reset the world. Things could have been so different, better... peaceful. She could not help thinking that half the protesters had taken to the streets more out of a frustration with their own lives, as against a vehement ideal. And yet, she would show her understanding, convey an empathy that would defuse their anger – it is what she always did, what she was good at.

She watched for signs of those without emotion. It was something she had subconsciously started doing ever since the botched attempt to destroy hope and love. Somewhere inside her was a belief that something must have happened, even if to just a handful of people. She had spent some days trying to reach her friend, the secret-keeper, but her friend did not answer her phone. Sarah wondered why, where she was, whether she was alright.

She had heard nothing from Zoldon or his two girls, and for a time she felt alone and abandoned. She still did, to some extent, as the people she had been colluding so closely with for a number of years had suddenly vanished out of sight. It was four days later that Abaddon gave her the grave news of Zoldon's death. She struggled to believe it at first; despite the reality of one day having to somehow end him, she had always seen him through a lens of invincibility, a kind of a demi-god. Surely it was too early in the race for such a prominent player to die? And the girl, the brunette – she could never remember her name. Dead as well? In that moment, she realised their plan was dead. All that mattered to her after that was the whereabouts of her friend. If only she would answer her phone.

The motorcade inched along the road like a sick tortoise until finally they came to the turning of their road, enabling their cars to stretch their legs once again. The office building stood firm in the distance, drawing them into its sprawling arms like a monstrous magnet. She was glad to see it; the countless meetings and never-ending documents to dissect and analyse rendered it the one place wherein she felt truly at ease. She checked her watch and breathed a heavy sigh, irritated by the consequences of her delayed journey. She picked up her phone to call her friend again. Still no answer. She started to worry that something had happened to her too. Surely, she was not involved in any way? She had cut herself off from the mission a long time ago, preferring to watch from the sidelines. She was never against their plan but also did not support it. It was the one thing she found a little unnerving about her. What made her tick? The only thing she seemed to care about was her daughter, who for all intents and purposes remained a permanent mystery, never mentioning her name or where she was.

It suddenly occurred to her that she did not even know where she lived. And yet, at university, they knew everything about each other – at least she had thought they did. Not once did she bring up or divulge her secret, rescuing her from attempting to take her own life. Mara had called that night to check on her beloved friend and housemate, as she was away for the weekend, only to find Sarah in a dangerous state of mind, having had her heart broken by her long-time boyfriend.

After promising her the world, he had proceeded to sever their relationship without thought or care, telling her he had fallen for someone else.

"I know this must be difficult for you, Sarah. Please believe me when I say that it is for me too. I didn't plan for this, it just happened, and now I realise I love her and not you."

Her world came crashing down that night, and she had no desire to keep going. It was as though he had sadistically cut out her heart and tossed it into the dustbin, walking away without so much as a glance in her direction. She pleaded with him to have a face to face, but he refused, telling her there was no point. She kept asking why until he blurted out the words that inevitably pushed her over the edge:

"Because I don't love you, Sarah. It's her I love, not you."

Thirty minutes later, Sarah was holding a bottle of pills in her hands; staring, accepting her sad fate. Then the phone rang. For years, she wondered what made her answer it. What was the point? Maybe deep down she wanted to hear her friend's voice one last time, to say goodbye.

"Hello?" she said, holding back her tears.

"Sandie, are you okay?"

"Yeah, sure... why?"

"Because I know you're not. I can hear it in your voice. Have you been crying?"

"No... no, I... He broke up with me. Said he is in love with someone else. Mara, I don't think I can get through this." The shaky dam had burst. An explosion of tears flooded her eyes as her body began to tremble.

"Sandie…! Sandie…! Sandie, are you there?"

"Hmm..."

"Right, what are you doing right now? Where are you?"

"In my bedroom... staring at a bottle of pills."

"Don't you dare! I'm coming now!"

"I can't take it anymore, Mara. I just can't; it hurts too much."

"Hey, you're gonna be fine. Just hold on, I'm coming now."

"But you're in—"

"I'm coming now, Sandie, just don't do anything stupid. I'll never forgive you if you do."

Mara drove the hundred and fifty miles from her parent's house, relieved to find her friend sitting on her bed with an unopened bottle of pills in her hand. She held her throughout the night, drawing her away from death's door.

A few weeks later, Sarah's ex-boyfriend fell from a tall building and died on the spot. Some said he took his own life as a result of a painful breakup. But according to the girl he abandoned Sarah for, there never was a breakup. Sarah always suspected Mara had something to do with it, especially after finding out about her powers; but it made no difference to her love for her.

Lost in her thoughts, she was unaware of her vehicle coming to a stop in front of her office.

"We're here, ma'am," said the driver, addressing her through his rear-view mirror.

"Oh, thank you, Al… thank you. I'll probably be working late tonight, so you should probably warn Eileen. How is she by the way? And the kids?" She was out of the car and approaching the entrance before he could answer.

The office building seemed quieter than usual. The usually busy corridors of chatter and scheming were still and soulless. As always, she stopped a couple times to chat with senior personnel before getting to the lift, forever greasing her wheel for the difficult days that periodically turned up in their shady clusters. When the doors of the lift opened upon reaching her floor, she was met by Michael.

How does he do that? she wondered, aghast by his ability to know exactly when she would arrive.

"Good morning, Prime Minister. I hear you took the scenic route this morning."

"It's too early for your sarcasm, Michael."

"Apologies, ma'am; too tempting to refuse."

"Have you rescheduled my meetings?"

"Yes, ma'am, everything pushed back two hours. Looks like you're in for a long day."

He opened her door and let her in, then closed it again and headed back to his desk.

She made her way to her table and eyed the in-tray – a foreign office dossier on the Syrian government lay on the top of an imposing pile of documents. She picked it up and scanned through the first couple of pages, suddenly putting it down as she sensed a presence above her. She turned to the gallery and gasped, warmed by the sight she had been wanting to see for the past week, but shaken by her ability to appear from nowhere.

"What... what are you doing here? I've been trying to reach you for over a week. You had me worried. And how do you do that?"

"What happened the other day? I sense things didn't go to plan," said Mara.

There was a lack of warmth about her – something Sarah had noticed more and more during the preceding weeks and months. Despite their closeness and history, there seemed to be some kind of a barrier between them, an intimidating authority that made Sarah nervous.

"You don't know?"

"I was away during that period. Wasn't sure I wanted to witness it." She started to make her way down the staircase. Her long, hooded gown flowed behind her like that of a mighty ruler.

"Mara, you really don't know?"

"Know what?" she asked as they came face to face.

"It all went horribly wrong, Mara. Zoldon, he's—"

"He's what, Sandie?" said Mara, growing visibly irritated.

"Dead, Mara – Zoldon's dead. Something went wrong somewhere. I think it was the girl."

"Which one?"

"The blonde one. Apparently, she changed sides. Never knew she had such... I mean, I knew

336

she had powers, but not to such an extent." Mara closed her flickering eyes, pursed her lips and slowly breathed in and out, putting both arms behind her back. After some seconds, her eyes opened again, and she moved slowly to the window.

"And the other one?"

"The other?"

"The other girl, Sarah." Her tone was quiet but forceful, threatening almost.

"I'm afraid she died, too – a terrible tragedy." Mara's eyes floated into the vastness of space on the other side of the windowpane, searching for somewhere to rest. She clasped her hands tighter, resisting the surge of fury that was erupting inside her.

Sarah stayed put where she was, unsure of what to say or do. Something seemed off; why ask about the other girl? A long, uncomfortable silence widened the chasm between them, crushing all sentiment in its path.

"Are you okay?" asked Sarah, finally summoning up the courage to speak.

"She's not dead," replied Mara.

"But she's—"

"She's not dead," said Mara even more forcefully as she turned to Sarah.

"How... how can you be so sure? They told me the other two were—"

"Because she's my daughter!" shouted Mara, causing the entire office to quake and rumble, ornaments and chandeliers on the verge of imploding beneath the surge of her voice.

Sarah Clark placed her hand over her mouth, her knees buckled as she tried in vain to restrain the vile mix of shock, horror and guilt that had taken root in the pit of her stomach.

"Oh Mara, I... I'm so—"

"I said, she's not dead." Her voice was a whisper again, contradicting the blaze of detest in her glare.

"So, what are you going to do? Are you sure?"

"Find her, of course. I would know if my own daughter was dead." She did not wait for a reply, disappearing before Sarah could respond. So that was how she did it. Sarah staggered to her chair and slumped onto it, horrified by the revelation of Liza's true identity. Her mind raced – the constant hiding, shielding, watching, questions. Despite the trauma of it all, it started to make sense.

*

A crumpled, white linen duvet clung to the edge of the bottom of the bed, having been intermittently kicked away during the night. The standing fan next to it churned its fabricated air, spinning and weaving as it had done for much of the night. Elongated rays of sunlight stretched across the bed, uncaring of their disturbance.

Justina was still asleep, curled up like a foetus in a baggy pair of sky-blue boxer shorts and a loose T-shirt. She had only drifted off a couple of hours earlier, having spent most of the night harangued by thoughts and memories of Alex. Four weeks had passed since she seized her opportunity to break up with him, and yet the pain was worsening.

She had wanted to go to him and apologise, explain why she did what she did and plead forgiveness, but had struggled with the heavy notion of 'how'. How could he possibly trust her again, allow himself to open up to her, after being so coldly discarded? After all, their relationship had been coasting along smoothly, their love for each other growing and attaining unassailable heights of joy and delirium. The agonising sadness on his face haunted her, often bringing tears to her eyes.

She hated herself for causing him so much anguish and did not feel she deserved forgiveness, nor a second chance. She would just have to deal with the sorrowful consequences and plough on, hoping each day would lessen her misery that little bit more. She often wandered around Christ Church Meadows, reliving memories of their happy walks. Sometimes she could feel him next to her, holding her hand, whispering his funny nonsense in his fading accent.

On one occasion, he was teasing her, causing her to tilt her head a little as she told him to "stop it" whilst laughing. A couple strolling towards her veered slightly to the left and pretended not to have seen her.

On the few occasions she did see him, walking or running in the distance, she was unable to summon the courage to call out his name. One time, upon seeing him some one hundred yards away, walking towards the main road, she started to run towards him, unsure of what she would do if she caught up with him. She knew she would not be able to catch up, but just wanted to lay eyes on him again. By the time she reached the main road, he had long turned right. Just seeing the back of his head, bobbing in and out amongst the fray of pedestrians walking down the street, filled her heart with a joy that only he could muster.

As weeks unfolded, she ventured there less often, telling herself to toughen up and move on. For some time, she really did feel like she was moving on, but by the fourth week, everything suddenly changed. Feelings that had merely taken a brief intermission came roaring back, even stronger than before, plaguing her with 'what ifs' and 'if onlys', dragging her vulnerable heart from side to side as her mind sank under a weight of fond memories.

He was all she could think about.

She tried meditating more, focused her mind and energy on her studies, made new friends and ventured out a couple of times, but nothing changed. Consciously or unconsciously, she longed for him every day, barely able to pass a minute without thinking of him. She hated herself for it – it made her feel weak and pathetic.

In that fourth week, she resorted to seeking help from the only person she felt would understand.

"Hello, Aunt Silv... Can you hear me, Aunt Silv?"

Nothing came back, so she called her name again.

"Aunt Silv... Aunty, can you hear me?"

A few more seconds passed before she finally heard the faint and weakened voice of her dear aunt. She was being looked after in an old people's home, and although Justina regularly checked up on her, the guilt of not visiting her more regularly never strayed far. She had already made the decision to go and see her during the summer holidays. She knew her aunt would barely be able to respond, let alone advise or counsel her, but she needed to open up to someone, tell her how she was feeling and the things incessantly dancing a jig in her mind.

"Jus... Is that you, Jus?"

"Yes, Aunt Silv, it's me. How are you? Are they looking after you okay?"

"Oh, Jus... I'm all the better for hearing your sweet voice. Are you okay? When will I see you?"

"Soon, Aunt Silv. Very soon. I'll be coming during the summer holiday; July, in fact. Can't wait to see you."

She meant every word; she had missed her dearly. A few days after she had thwarted Zoldon and Liza, she had felt as though thousands of scales had been removed from her eyes as she began to realise the things that mattered most – Aunty Silv, fond memories of her family, Alex... love... hope.

"Oh, I'll be the happiest person in the world when I see your beautiful face, my sweet angel."

"And me when I see yours, Aunt Silv." Her eyes began to well-up; she had a feeling summer would be their last time together.

"Aunt Silv... I need your help."

She broke down in tears, sniffing and crying as she relayed her sad predicament. She told her aunty how she met Alex, the things they did together, the fun they had, the love they shared, his love of cooking her dinner, the way he would nervously feel the outside of her hand with his before holding it, the first time he told her he loved her, how constantly happy he made her feel; she even mimicked his accent.

And she told how she broke up with him, tossing him aside like he was worth nothing. She could not tell her why, but apart from that, she revealed all else. The phone breathed in silence for many seconds once she had finished. She waited for her aunty to respond but grew impatient. "Aunt Silv, are you there?"

"I'm here, dear, I'm here," she said. She slowly reached for her oxygen mask and placed it over her face, inhaling and exhaling twice before putting it down again. "So, now he's all you think about, and you're miserable without him. I understand, my love."

"What should I do? I don't think I can take it anymore."

"There's only one thing you can do, Jus."

"What's that?"

"Go to him and say you're sorry. You made a terrible mistake. Tell him how miserable you are without him. Ask him to forgive you, and tell him how much you love him, like you just told me. Don't let pride or fear get in the way, dear. Open up to him."

"But, what if he doesn't—"

"Then at least you would have tried. And if he doesn't take you back, then maybe he didn't love you as much as you thought he did. I know that may not be an easy thing to take, but love cannot be switched on and off like a tap. Real love is always willing and able to forgive and try again. Only when you have tried and know for sure will you be able to move on with your life. Until then, you'll just be in limbo."

"Yeah, I think you're right." A torrent of nervous excitement began to run through her as she thought about finally speaking with him again. She feared the worst but knew it was something she had to do, regardless of the outcome.

"What are you doing now, Jus?"

"You mean like, right now, today?"

"Yes, right this minute."

"Nothing. No plans, really, just—"

"Then go and see him now."

"What, right now?"

"Yes, right now! No time like the present. Humble yourself; nothing wrong with making yourself vulnerable. Go now and call me to let me know how it went. And remember, if it is meant to be, then everything will work out. And if not, then it means there's an even better person waiting for you. Don't be afraid of making yourself vulnerable."

Justina checked her watch – quarter to five. *He should definitely be there*, she thought. She took a deep breath and closed her eyes, accepting the probability that she would be rejected. 'Don't be afraid of making yourself vulnerable?' It was what she feared more than anything. She opened her eyes again and wondered what to wear. 'Humble yourself'. Better to dress appropriately. She put on a pair of jeans and a T-shirt, and slipped on her trainers, rejecting the advances of the lipstick on her table. She had an idea: she would borrow from the Love Actually film and write the words

'I'm sorry' in big bold letters on a white placard. Maybe it would make him laugh and soften his defences. She feared the worst; there was no way he could forgive her. She had not only unfairly judged him but broken his trust in her. But it was better to know once and for all, rather than continuously wishing and wandering what if – whatever happened, it would provide some closure.

Muttering to herself like a mad person, the short walk to the café provided an opportunity to prepare her plea.

"I know I really hurt you, but I... No, Jus; that won't fly."

"I never judged you. I think I was just looking for a way out... No, that won't work, why were you looking for a way out? Tell him about the other stuff and he'll run a mile."

In a daze, she hot-footed her way down the road to the café, heart pumping as her moment of reckoning approached. She wanted to slow down, gather herself together and breathe, but doing so would allow her fears to build an insurmountable barricade, and so she kept going at a pace, ignoring the negative thoughts, still unsure of what she would say, placard aside.

She paused a few doors from the café to observe her reflection, raising both corners of her lips, then letting them down again. Not too impressed with the dishevelled nature of her hair, she reached into her handbag and pulled out her hairbrush, but after looking at her reflection again, she shrugged her shoulders and put it back in the bag.

"Get a grip, Jus, just be yourself," she muttered.

She turned to complete her mission, only to return to the window again, placing the placard in front of her chest to ensure it read properly. Still not satisfied, and now approaching a state of mild insanity, she drew the placard closer to her chest and corked her head to the left to assess the words with naked eyes. 'I'm sorry' – correct spelling. Good to go. She inhaled slowly and released the tension that had built up inside her, proceeded to the entrance of the café and opened it without a moment's hesitation.

Two sets of expensive-looking brown leather corner sofas and cream mahogany coffee tables had given the place a fresh and airy living room-feel. The dull-looking counter was also gone, replaced by thick frosted glass and shiny metallic silver rims. The mood was lighter, happier, modern – a completely different ambience to the slightly gothic one of before, but she liked it. It lifted her spirits somewhat, which is precisely what she needed at that point in time. Alex was sitting on a sofa, showing a middle-aged looking woman the pictures in an album. She had seen it before – old black and white photos of the city of Oxford. She remembered being freaked out by how so many buildings still looked the same, and yet, there seemed to be something purer and more genuine about those years. She wished she could go back in time and plonk herself in another age.

Her hair was jet black, its full and alluring body flowing effortlessly over her slender shoulders. She wondered whether Alex had an older sister he had not told her about. Better to be his sister than someone else... or something else. A red silk scarf was delicately draped over her shoulders, matching her bright red plimsolls, rounding off an aesthetically appealing chicness. Both were gleefully immersed in the pictures, ooing and ahhing like proud parents watching their kid in a school play.

"Oh my God, is that what I think it is?" Even her voice was chic.

"Aye, Worcester College. Hasn't changed a bit, has it?"

"I can't believe it. I used to visit friends there. Incredible! How come a Scotsman knows so much about Oxford?"

"Ahh, now that's a long story, and one I'm sure you don't have the time to listen to. But the short version is that I somehow got admitted to Oxford and found myself developing a passion for history."

Sensing someone at the door, she looked up, smiled and cleared her throat, alerting Alex to the presence of a new customer. His heart jumped when he saw Justina, not knowing whether to leap for joy or recoil and hide. He had just started to believe he might heal, recover from the brokenness of the past few weeks, only for her to walk back into his life. He tried to clear the tickly dryness at the back of his throat, searching for something to say, but his mouth was as numb as the rest of him.

Justina's right hand had fastened onto the left one, her right index finger tapping the back of her left hand. She had arrived without a plan – if only she had paused to work on some kind of a speech. Then she remembered the placard lodged under her right armpit and placed her hands on either side, checking to ensure it was the right way up. She held it out, smiling nervously, expecting nothing in return. She would swallow the awkward silence, walk out, and never return. Her heart melted as his smile embraced the spark in his eyes.

"Please, excuse me," he said, getting to his feet. He walked over to her, put his hands on either side of the placard and placed it on the floor, then just stood there, gazing into her eyes, elated and relieved that she was back in his life.

"Alex, I—"

"Shhhh... I know you didn't mean what you said. Maybe one day you'll tell me what was really going on. What matters, all that really matters, is that you're here now."

She leaned in and kissed him, grateful for her aunt's advice.

"Here, have a seat. Tea, coffee?"

"A wee dram, if you please, kind sir," she teased.

"Tea it is, then."

They giggled. They always made each other giggle. Justina made her way to the sofa and sat down, sending a happy smile in the direction of the woman sitting opposite her.

"Hope you don't mind me saying so, but that there was love, if I ever saw it. Never seen him so gaga."

"I'm just relieved he'll have me back." All her nerves and fears floated into the past, and she was breathing freely once more.

"Well, my advice to you is that when something good comes into your life, hold onto it with everything you've got. My name's Imara, by the way, but my friends call me Mara."

"I'm Justina, pleasure to meet you."

Printed in Great Britain
by Amazon